Three Times Tempted

A Scandal in Mayfair Book 3

ANNA CAMPBELL

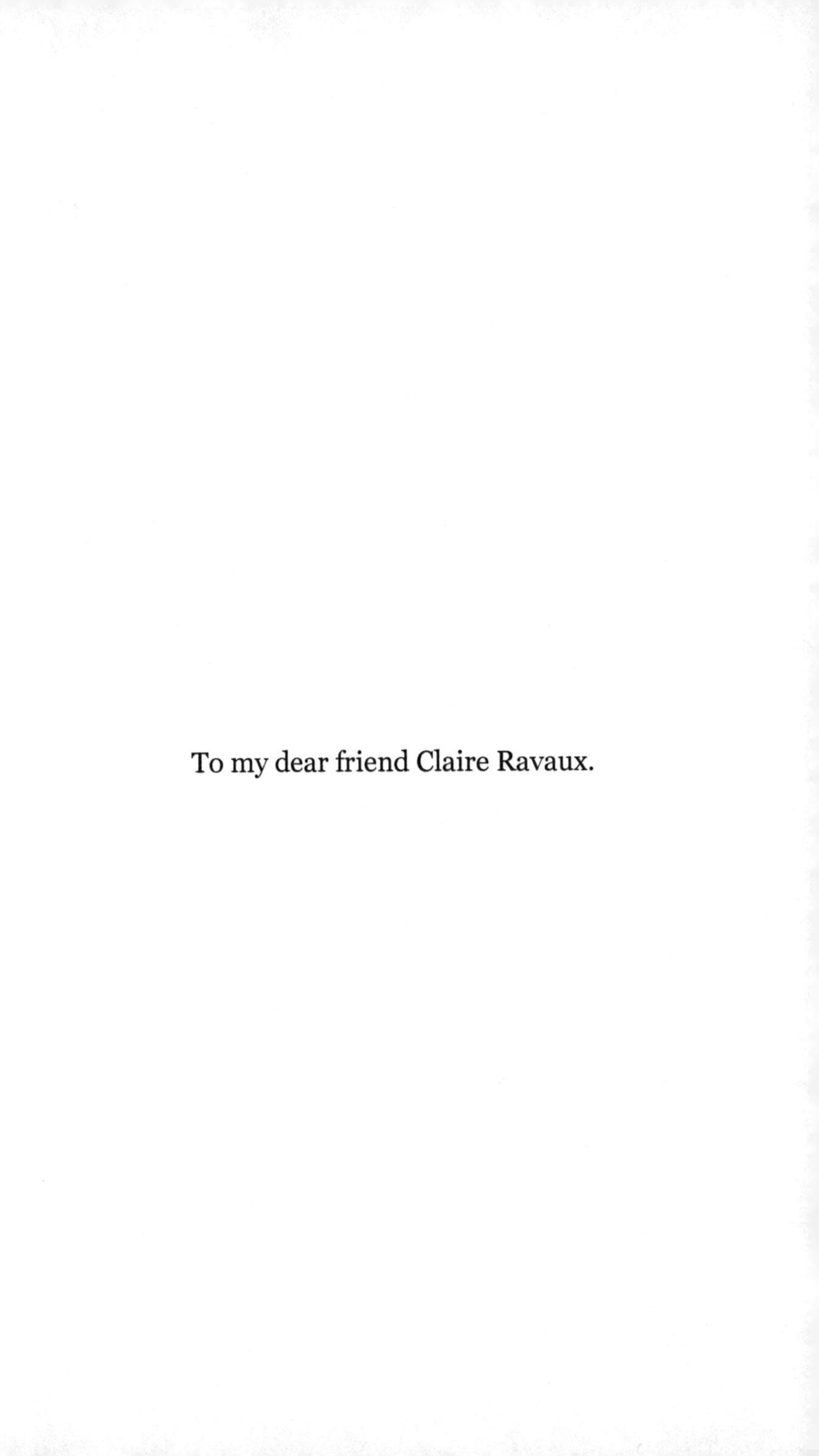

To my dear friend Claire Ravaux.

PROLOGUE

Prestwick Place, Buckinghamshire, June 1816

A furious hammering at the main door downstairs woke Stella Maddox, Countess of Halston, from deep sleep. Beside her, her husband was stirring, too, and his arm tightened around her shoulders in a way that she couldn't help but read as protective.

"What the devil is all that blasted row?" Gray asked sleepily.

"It sounds like an emergency."

He dropped a kiss on her lips and rolled out of bed. Stella heard a rustle and a couple of scrapes before light bloomed from the candle on the nightstand. She pushed up against the pillows and couldn't help stealing a second to admire how magnificent her husband looked without a stitch to cover him. By heaven, she was a lucky girl.

As he met her eyes, a smile curled his expressive mouth. "If you keep looking at me like that, whoever is downstairs breaching the peace will have to wait."

With a low laugh, she stretched out against the sheets, even as the knocking persisted. She was no closer to dressed than Gray was, and a month of marriage had confirmed her confidence in her power to arouse him. Behind his ruffled dark head, the gold clock on the mantel read a quarter to three.

"Perhaps you should go and find out what's going on, then you can come back to me. Who needs sleep?"

That wolfish smile broadened, as green eyes conducted a swift but comprehensive survey of her naked body. "Certainly not me."

The racket came to an abrupt end, which must mean that Philpott the butler had risen to answer the door. "Don't be long."

Once Gray had gone, Stella tugged a nightdress over her head and wrapped a royal blue silk robe around herself. But when she appeared on the landing above the hall, all thoughts of dalliance with her new husband vanished like smoke in a stiff breeze.

Below her, Gray faced down her odious uncle, the Earl of Deerforth. The uncle who had disowned her in unforgivable terms. She'd never expected him to speak to her again – much to her relief. Ten years of servitude in his household had taught her to loathe Charles Ridley.

Whatever crisis brought him here must be dire indeed. One thing hadn't changed since their last meeting. He was still spitting with anger and puffed up with arrogant bluster. He was shouting at Gray about something, as Philpott and a couple of footmen moved around lighting candles.

She came down a couple of stairs. "Gray, what's happened?"

Her uncle's face turned red with rage as he watched her descent. "Where is she, you traitorous bitch?"

"Philpott, Lord Deerforth is leaving," Gray snapped, as Stella descended the last few stairs to stand beside him. "Now!"

"My lord, if you'll come this way," Philpott said in his stoic manner.

Deerforth ignored the butler and glared at Gray and Stella. The hatred in his eyes was nothing new either. "What have you done with her? I'll tear this house apart before I let you keep her from me."

As fear set cold claws into her soul, Stella frowned. "Has something happened to Imogen?"

A paroxysm of fury distorted Deerforth's features, and he loomed toward her in unmistakable threat. "As if you don't know."

Stella shrank back behind Gray, who stepped between her and her uncle. "I've asked you to leave," he said in the voice of command. "You can do it on your own two feet, or the servants will throw you out. Your choice."

When Stella placed a hand on her husband's arm, she felt his vibrating rage. "Gray, wait." She made herself meet her uncle's eyes. There was anger there. There was always anger there. But she saw other things, too. Worry. Desperation. Fear. "Stop carrying on like a mad bull, Uncle, and tell us what has happened."

Her uncle sucked in a breath and managed a halfway sensible response at last. "Is she here?"

"No."

His eyes narrowed, and his hands clenched at his sides as if he battled the urge to shake the truth out of her. "She'd run to you if she ran anywhere."

"That might be true, but I haven't seen Imogen since you tossed me out of your house and told me never to darken your door again. Did something happen at Hamble Park?" Imogen, Deerforth's daughter and Stella's cousin, had lived at the family estate in Gloucestershire for the last few weeks. Ever since the scandal surrounding Stella's marriage to Halston had curtailed her first London season.

"No. She's always been happy there."

It was true. Imogen fancied herself as a gardener, and she filled her days ordering the outdoor staff around.

"Perhaps she went for a walk and got lost," Stella suggested, desperate to come up for an innocent reason for her cousin's disappearance.

That idea made Deerforth snarl. For once, Stella couldn't blame him. Gloucestershire wasn't the South American jungles. And Imogen was familiar with her immediate surroundings and all the neighbors.

"Some of her clothes are missing, and her maid says she's taken things like her hairbrush."

Stella frowned, seriously worried now. She shared a concerned glance with her husband. This sounded very much like Imogen had left on purpose.

"When did you last see her?" Gray asked.

The footmen bowed and left them alone. At a nod from Gray, Philpott remained.

"A month ago." As his rage ebbed, her uncle sounded lost and bewildered. "I arrived home yesterday from London to discover the household in an uproar. She hadn't slept in her bed. There's a note." With shaking hands, Deerforth tugged a crumpled paper from his pocket and shoved it at Stella.

Well, that put paid to any notion of Imogen's disappearance being accidental. Stella smoothed the letter out so she could read it.

Dear Papa,

By the time you get this, I'll be far away. Don't worry – I'm safe and happy.

Your affectionate daughter,
Imogen.

"But that says nothing," Stella said, increasingly concerned as she passed the paper across to Gray.

Deerforth released a heavy sigh. "She's missed you. So it seemed to make sense that..."

"You have my word that she's not here," Gray said. He looked at Stella. "This smacks of an elopement to me. Had she set her heart on a young man?"

It smacked of an elopement to Stella, too. "I sometimes thought—"

Deerforth lurched toward Stella again. "If you're involved—"

Gray pushed him back. "You will not touch my wife. Do you imagine if Stella knew anything, she wouldn't tell you? Can't you see she's worried sick?"

"It's terrible timing," her uncle said. "I've invited Lord Chippenham down to pursue his courtship. He's due next week."

Stella's certainty that her cousin had run off with some mysterious lover hardened. Lord Chippenham was a middle-aged widower with a grown family. Deerforth favored the match because he wanted the man's support in parliament.

Imogen had never been interested in her unappealing suitor. Even more telling, Imogen had just turned twenty-one, so now she was legally able to marry without her father's permission.

"She doesn't want to marry Chippenham," Stella said, wishing with futile regret that she'd pushed Imogen to confide in her. But during those few weeks in London, she'd been so engrossed with falling in love with Gray that she'd taken her eye off her cousin.

"Who did she talk about instead?" Hope sparked in Deerforth's beady eyes. "If she fancied some fellow, she must have said something."

"No, she never mentioned anyone." Stella took Gray's hand. Like her, he must know that if Imogen had set her heart on an eligible gentleman, she wouldn't have had to run away. That meant the gentleman she'd eloped with wasn't eligible.

Deerforth groaned and sagged, looking older than his sixty years. "God damn it, she's fallen into some fortune hunter's hands. I know it."

Gray turned to Stella. "We need to go to Hamble Park and see what we can find out."

"Yes, you're right." Stella looked across at Deerforth. "Have you spoken to Harriet Comerford? If Imogen confided in anyone, it would be Harriet." Harriet was Lord and Lady Lumsden's daughter, and she and Imogen had always been inseparable.

"Harriet's still in London, enjoying her season." Resentment edged Deerforth's words, although he bore most of the blame for the scandal that had brought Imogen's stay in London to a premature end.

"I doubt if she'll talk to you," Stella said. "I need to go up to Town. But someone should still go to Hamble Park. Someone who won't terrify the servants into silence."

"I won't have you—" Deerforth began.

"I'm offering my help. Take it or leave it." Gray regarded him with weary dislike. "Otherwise I'll go to London with Stella and see what we can learn there."

"I've talked to everyone in the household." Bullied more like, Stella couldn't help thinking. Lord Deerforth was an incorrigible tyrant. "Nobody knows anything. I haven't asked the neighbors yet, because I want to save my girl from scandal."

"It's too late for that," Gray snapped. "We need to make sure she's safe."

Deerforth's anger gained ground again. "This is all bloody Eliot's fault. If he'd watched out for his sister, instead of chasing notorious strumpets, none of this would have happened. He should be here now, not in Paris enjoying himself."

Eliot, Imogen's brother, had recently married and was currently in France on his honeymoon. Despite Stella's overriding concern for Imogen, she couldn't help thinking that her uncle had had a bad few weeks. He'd lost his unpaid dogsbody of a niece; scandal had enveloped the family; he'd disowned his son; now his daughter had run away.

It was almost a pity that she was too worried right now to appreciate Deerforth's well-deserved comeuppance. "We need to go now, Gray. If Imogen has fallen into some rake's clutches, the sooner we rescue her, the better."

"I agree." Gray regarded her uncle down his haughty nose. "Are you willing to let me come to Hamble Park and interview the servants? I realize that Stella would find out more because the staff know her, but Harriet Comerford is our best hope of discovering where Imogen's gone. I doubt if she'll break Imogen's confidence to me, whereas she might to Stella."

By rights, Deerforth should be grateful. But clearly the words "thank you" stuck in his craw. He merely nodded to Gray, unable to hide his loathing, even now. "My coach is outside."

Stella read Gray's barely hidden horror at the prospect of remaining cooped up with her boorish guardian all the way to Gloucestershire. "I'll ride," he said. "It will be faster."

"And I'll set out for London as soon as I've dressed." Despite everything, she couldn't stifle a twinge of pity for Deerforth. Pity that he'd despise, she knew. "I'll place a bedroom at your disposal, Uncle, and have some refreshments and hot water brought up. The Chinese room, I think, Philpott."

"Very good, my lady." Philpott bowed and left to make arrangements.

Stella's mind buzzed with possibilities, none of them good. What on earth was Imogen playing at? She'd tried a ploy like this in London. In fact, her scheming had inadvertently brought Gray and Stella together. But this current situation seemed altogether more serious. And out of character for the person that Imogen had become.

During her weeks in Town, Imogen had seemed to mature from the spoiled, impulsive girl that she'd once been. But this escapade hinted that she was as harum–scarum as ever. If it turned out that her disappearance was another childish prank, Stella would box the little minx's delicate ears.

Although a prank might offer the best outcome. If Imogen was wandering the kingdom with her seducer, the scandal would eclipse the gossip that had recently engulfed the Ridley family. Not to mention that Stella loved her cousin and hated the idea of her making an unwise marriage. Or worse, being ruined and abandoned.

"She could be back at Hamble Park, waiting for you," she said to Deerforth.

"Do you think she's up to some game?" Gray asked.

"It wouldn't be the first time." Although something about that terse note told Stella that this time, Imogen wasn't pretending to elope.

"If it turns out that this is some trick, I'll join you in London."

Gray wouldn't want to stay under Deerforth's roof any longer than necessary. He'd never liked the man, but Lord Deerforth's violent reaction to his niece's marriage had tipped dislike over into detestation.

"Stop yapping and get ready to go," Deerforth growled.

Stella watched Gray's jaw shift, as he ground his teeth against ordering the man to mind his manners. Especially when he was in someone else's house. Not to mention that at this moment, Deerforth needed help from that someone else.

She admired his control. So much was at stake. Gray liked Imogen. More than that, he understood how much the girl meant to Stella. Over their month of marriage, she'd come to realize that in loving her, this marvelous man made an unconditional commitment to her causes.

If Imogen was missing, Gray would do everything in his power to find her. He'd even put up with her oaf of an uncle to follow the girl's trail.

Stella squeezed his hand. "Thank you, my darling."

His quick smile spoke volumes of love. "Anything for you, my love."

It sounded like meaningless flattery, but Stella knew that he meant it. She drew a deep breath and felt her churning fear settle. At least a little.

Another thing she'd discovered about Gray was that he was a supremely competent man. And nobody knew Imogen better than she did. Between the two of them, they'd track down her runaway cousin.

As she turned to face her uncle, some small, selfish part of her couldn't help but regret that this brouhaha shattered her blissful idyll here at Prestwick Place. After so many unhappy years, she'd started to find a home for herself. Even the thought of parting from her husband while she went to London weighted her heart.

"I wish..." she said in a low voice.

Gray's grip on her hand tightened. "I know."

She sighed and stepped away. "Uncle, let me show you to your room. We'll go as soon as we can. With any luck, this is all a storm in a teacup."

Her uncle didn't look reassured. Nor did Stella have great confidence in her optimistic predictions.

Imogen, what on earth have you done? And where on earth are you?

CHAPTER ONE

*Comerford House, Lorimer Square, Mayfair,
London, Two Months Earlier*

Lord and Lady Lumsden's garden in London was unusually large for the capital and on a cold spring night, dark enough to feel a little eerie. The music from the crowded ballroom jangled in the sinister atmosphere, as Lady Imogen Ridley penetrated deeper into the thick shrubbery.

In such freezing weather, nobody ventured outside to catch a breath of fresh air or to find privacy for a naughty assignation.

Except her.

Her shiver wasn't completely a response to the chill, although her blue silk ballgown wasn't designed for wintry temperatures. This had all seemed such a lark when she'd come up with her plan to tryst with a dark and dangerous rake in an isolated gazebo.

But that had been when she was warm and safe in her luxurious bedroom on the other side of Lorimer Square. Right now, she felt vulnerable and alone, and she was too aware that her cousin Stella would ring a peal over her head because of her recklessness.

Not to mention the way her volatile father would stamp and shout and in general act like a bear with a sore head.

There were a few lanterns along the path. But the sparse lighting only made it more obvious that she was heading into the shadows to meet a stranger with a bad reputation. She hoped to heaven that Stella, her companion and governess, had found the note announcing her scandalous intentions. She'd left it out in open view, after all.

What if Stella had respected her privacy? What if Imogen was on her own in the dark? On her own, apart from a notorious rake.

That was if the notorious rake had accepted her brazen invitation to meet her.

Only the pretty Chinese-style wooden gazebo looming out of the blackness ahead stopped her from fleeing back to the ballroom. Where that ageing bore – and boor – Lord Chippenham waited to dance with her. Her father favored a match between Imogen and the stout, balding baron who controlled a powerful parliamentary faction.

She was so close, she refused to succumb to an attack of the collywobbles. Even if right now, courage smacked of criminal carelessness with her reputation. She prayed that her reputation was the only thing she risked.

Soft light spilled from the building ahead, although nobody else braved the weather to take advantage of it. Or at least, that was Imogen's hope.

She'd assumed that Lord Halston wouldn't leap on her and have his wicked way, the second he caught sight of her. She'd assumed that Stella would scurry to her rescue before any great harm was done.

As she steeled herself to climb the short flight of steps to the doorway, she couldn't help recognizing that the success of her plan relied on a lot of assumptions. The mouthful of cold air she gulped didn't ease the frantic race of her heart as she stepped inside.

"Good evening," a man said from where he stood warming his hands over the glowing brazier of coals in the center of the tiled floor. "I wasn't expecting company."

Imogen backed away and pressed a hand to where her pulse jumped at the base of her throat. The man was tall and lean with dark hair. He wasn't wearing evening dress. Instead, he was in a brown coat and buff breeches and boots. He wouldn't look out of place wandering across a field.

"You're not Lord Halston," she said in a shaky voice, as every instinct screamed to run, run now. Her fingers curled around the string of pearls encircling her neck. They were worth stealing, as were the pearl earbobs and the delicate gold and pearl bracelet on her wrist.

There was enough light for her to see his faint smile. "No, that I'm not. Are you here for a rendezvous? I can go away if you'd prefer."

That was remarkably cooperative. Nor had he made any sudden moves. Perhaps he didn't mean to knock her on the head and make off with her jewelry.

"I'm..." she began, wondering how to explain the Machiavellian scheme that brought her here. Wondering why she even considered explaining.

"Why don't you come and stand by the brazier? You must be turning into an icicle over there."

The marble beneath her thin dancing slippers was freezing. It was clear that her plot had failed. Lord Halston hadn't come to meet her. Stella hadn't appeared to rescue her, although Imogen had been very specific about her assignation at ten in the Lumsden gazebo.

But something kept her here. Perhaps the fact that this was the closest she'd come to freedom since leaving Hamble Park two weeks ago.

Fearing that she'd gone completely mad, she ventured closer to the stranger. The brazier contained scented pastilles as well as hot coals. The faint sweetness of incense tickled her nose.

"I should go," she said, making no attempt to follow through with her statement.

"To meet this Lord Heston? He's a lucky fellow."

There were a couple of small lamps set around the gazebo, and her eyes had adjusted to the darkness while she made her way along the path. She could see her companion quite well. Wondering why she wasn't frightened, she took a moment to study him. She'd be frightened if she was alone with Lord Halston.

Perhaps she wasn't frightened because there was nothing daunting about this man's manner. The dim light and the isolation should lend him a devilish air, but somehow they didn't. He had a thin face and a long nose, and the amiable curiosity in his expression put her at ease.

Perhaps she was a fool. The benign demeanor could be part of his game to lure her into his clutches. On the other hand, she'd worked with men for years on the gardens at Hamble Park. The male of the species wasn't a complete mystery. This one didn't seem too menacing. Even his compliment had been delivered in such a casual tone that it hadn't raised her hackles.

Imogen sucked in another deep breath and relaxed. She found herself smothering a wry laugh.

"Halston, not Heston." The fact that this man didn't know Lord Halston indicated that he wasn't part of high society. Although he was far from a beggar. That coat mightn't be made for a ballroom, but it fit those broad shoulders to an inch. It reeked of bespoke tailoring. "And no, I'm not so eager to see him."

The shameful truth was that she was so curious about this stranger, she had no wish to go anywhere else. Although if someone caught them together, her reputation would fare no better than it would if she was discovered with Halston.

The interest in the man's regard matched hers. "Then why in tarnation are you out here freezing in the dark?" He frowned. "And I do beg your pardon for my lack of manners. My only excuse is that you took me by surprise when you turned up out of the night like a fairy."

She watched him shrug out of his coat. "I'm a little too practical to be a fairy."

"I've always imagined that fairies need to keep their minds on earthy reality. Otherwise think of all the mischief that magic might create."

Imogen gave another short laugh. "Fairies like mischief."

"If you're out here unchaperoned, I have a feeling you might like mischief, too." He held up the coat. "May I?"

"You'll get cold."

"In New York State, we call this a balmy summer's night."

Astonishment gripped her, although she'd already noticed his accent. He didn't sound uncultured. He just sounded different. Something about the way that he pronounced his R's. "You're American?"

"I am." He stepped around the brazier and draped the coat over her shoulders.

It was the most daring thing that anyone had ever done to her. Sharing a man's clothes hinted at a sensual intimacy unprecedented in her sheltered life. When she'd ordered the workmen around in Gloucestershire, her rank and her father's famous temper always protected her from unsuitable approaches.

Imogen should give the man his coat back. Not just because it was improper to wear it, but because despite his lighthearted response, it really was too cold for him to go around in shirtsleeves. But the immediate warmth that enveloped her was so delicious. Even more shocking – even more delicious – an exotic and very pleasant scent teased her nostrils and mixed with the cinnamon and cloves of the incense. Something clean and fresh, with an intriguing hint of man.

"How..."

When he moved back to the other side of the brazier, his intense scrutiny made her shift from one foot to another. She still wasn't frightened, but something between them had changed.

"How does an American find himself in a dark London garden, talking to a pretty girl, while a ball takes place a few yards away?" he finished for her.

That wasn't her only question, but it would do for a beginning.

The strange thing – one of the many strange things – was that when this fellow called her pretty, it made her knees wobble in a way that no compliment from a wellborn young gentleman ever had.

She should go back to the ballroom. Stella clearly wasn't coming to her rescue, and Lord

Halston must have decided that debutantes weren't for him. Which was no surprise.

But this was the most interesting thing that had happened to her since she'd come to London, a place she didn't much like. While it was fun to be made a fuss of, Mayfair had nothing to do with her real life back in Gloucestershire. "Are you a burglar?"

He burst out laughing and something tight and unhappy inside her chest loosened. She'd felt out of sorts since she'd left home. She didn't feel like that now.

"Good Lord, no. I'm very respectable."

"Then why aren't you at the ball?"

One elegant hand made a dismissive gesture. "Oh, I'm respectable, but not eligible, at least in this company. I'm trade."

Imogen despised the snobberies that she'd grown up with. Some of the finest people she knew didn't have a drop of aristocratic blood in their veins, whereas she knew some absolute blackguards who held the highest rank. "I'm glad you're not a burglar."

When he smiled, that odd, wobbly feeling in her legs intensified. It wasn't nerves, although being in a stranger's company should make her nervous. Or perhaps it was the sort of nerves that one felt standing on the edge of a precipice.

The feeling, whatever it was, was very nice. Her heart was skipping, too, and every so often, her breath caught in her throat. The closest she came to describing the sensation was the way she felt galloping along on her horse Merlin and approaching a high fence that she wasn't sure she'd clear.

"So am I."

"Then what are you doing here?"

When his eyes settled on her, the butterflies fluttering in her stomach started diving and crashing together. "I feel we need to be introduced before I share the shocking secrets of my life."

It was her turn to laugh, a breathy little giggle that didn't sound at all like her. "I like the sound of shocking secrets."

"Enough to tell me your name?"

It was stupid to blush. But she was blushing. And those butterflies still flung themselves around inside her tummy in a most disconcerting fashion. "My name is Imogen Ridley."

He bowed. "I'm delighted to make your acquaintance, Miss Ridley. I'm Caleb Black of Saratoga in New York State."

She dropped into a curtsy. "What brings you to England, Mr. Black?"

The focus that he leveled on her made her heart race, although a young miss on the London marriage market faced inspection day after day and the eyes weren't always kind. Perhaps this felt different because she liked the way that Mr. Black looked at her, as if he'd never seen anything so wonderful in his life.

Imogen tried to tell herself that her giddy reaction resulted from the night and the romantic lighting and the fact that she broke every rule. But as she'd told Mr. Black, at heart she was a practical creature. Beneath all the enjoyable turmoil, she recognized a kindred spirit.

"That's simple enough. Lord Tierney is rebuilding his gardens at Sander Hall. My family runs a landscaping business, and we're hoping to set up a branch in England. I'm here to tout for the contract. And to see if I can pick up some more clients. In the meantime, I'm staying with the Tierneys. Tonight I fancied seeing what high society looks like when it's out and about. So when the gate wasn't locked and nobody turned up to stop me, I thought I'd try some harmless trespassing."

Imogen had hardly listened since he'd said the word "garden." Wide-eyed, she stared at him, having trouble believing what she heard. It seemed too outlandish, too lucky, to be true. A kindred spirit indeed. "Gardens?"

"Yes. Lord Tierney's cousin was touring America and saw some of our work in the Hudson Valley. He thought we might produce something out of the ordinary over here. If his lordship chooses Black & Sons, it's the perfect entrée into the English market. I have ambitions, you see."

So had her father. For his daughter to marry a man of wealth and influence and to promote the family's fortunes and prestige. Or more specifically to promote Charles Ridley's fortunes and prestige. He'd be livid if he knew that Imogen was out here with a colonial. He'd be livid to think that she was out here with any man.

She edged from one slippered foot to the other and told herself that she should go back to the ballroom, but a force more powerful than fear of repercussions kept her here. "You're returning to America soon?"

She cursed the wistful note in her inquiry. This was a fleeting encounter. An accidental meeting. And it wasn't done for a lady to express overt attraction to a gentleman.

Although in London terms, Caleb Black wasn't a gentleman. Even if his manners were as nice as any she'd ever seen.

He didn't seem to mind her question, thank goodness. "No, I'm here for a couple of months. Once I've sorted out our business, I'm hoping to tour

Europe and make notes on the gardens there, too. Now the war is over, that's possible."

"How lucky you are." This time, she didn't try to hide her longing. "I've dreamed of seeing the gardens in France and Italy."

"Have you?" He looked startled, and the already intense concentration became even more marked. "So have I."

For a moment, they stared at each other through the gloom. Imogen couldn't help feeling that some question was asked and answered in the affirmative. Even if she had difficulty putting that question into precise words.

Mr. Black stepped toward her, then stopped. "Don't you have to go and find Lord Halston?"

She shook her head, as she viewed the ruin of her rash scheme without regret. The angels must have been watching over her. What had happened instead was so much better. "He didn't come."

Mr. Black's marked dark eyebrows creased in puzzlement. "By Harry, if a girl as pretty as you invited me to a rendezvous, I wouldn't stand her up. The man is clearly a knave."

Again he called her pretty. Again the word made something soft and female inside her melt with pleasure. "I think he's being un-knavish, actually."

"Oh?"

She sighed. "I don't like London. I want to go home. So I put together a scheme where my chaperone would catch me alone with a rake and tell my father. He'd send me back to Gloucestershire in disgrace." She paused. "It all sounds a bit silly now."

Imogen waited for Mr. Black to tell her how foolish she'd been. Her plan had relied on the usually canny Stella turning up before any harm was done. She couldn't repress a shiver, as she wondered how this prank might have played out, if she'd encountered Lord Halston instead of this charming American. She could have been in real trouble. It might be lucky that Halston had ignored her presumptuous note, inviting him to meet a total stranger.

"I'd be very sad if you went back to Gloucestershire." Something in the low rumble of Mr. Black's voice warmed her skin, despite the cold night.

She couldn't look away. "You would?"

"In London, there's a small chance that you and I might meet again. I'd like that."

So would she. However unacceptable that thought was.

"Elizabeth Tierney and I usually attend the same balls." Elizabeth was a friend and another debutante.

He dipped his head in acknowledgment. "Then perhaps we'll speak again."

"Tomorrow night, I'm going to the Delacorte ball." It would be difficult to slip outside, but not impossible. Her cousin kept an eye on her, but didn't hover. Stella trusted Imogen – a thought which should make her feel guilty but didn't.

"I'll see if I can be there." Mr. Black looked up toward the ballroom. "You must go. Even I know young ladies shouldn't be out of sight for too long, if they wish to remain in society's good graces, instead of retiring back to Gloucestershire under a cloud."

He was right. Stella might have missed the letter agreeing to meet Lord Halston that Imogen had left on her dressing table – which astonished her, because she'd put it in an obvious place. But her cousin would worry if she couldn't find Imogen inside.

She'd just met this man, yet already she'd rather remain with him than go back to the ballroom. "I'd like to stay in London now," she said softly.

Even such short acquaintance had revealed that Mr. Black was clever. He knew what she was saying. The genuine delight in his smile made her heart dance. "I'm pleased to hear it, Miss Ridley."

Still she didn't go, although she really must. "I need to give you your coat back."

"If you appear in the ballroom like that, you might set a new fashion."

A spluttering laugh escaped. She still felt odd and giddy and giggly. "Or I might set every tongue wagging."

"Well, we can't have that."

When he moved behind her, her heart swooped like a swallow in flight. She'd never felt like this before, although she had an inkling of what was happening. When her friends developed a penchant for a gentleman, they'd described this dizzy, breathless response to the chosen man's presence.

Imogen had always thought it sounded rather uncomfortable. But then, so far in her life, no male had caught her interest. Now that one did, she had to agree that this excitement might be disconcerting, but it wasn't disagreeable. Not disagreeable at all.

When he placed his hands lightly on her shoulders, Imogen's heart performed acrobatics worthy of Astley's Amphitheatre. To her regret, he didn't linger as he lifted the coat away. As soon as it was gone, she missed its warmth and that heady scent.

She hadn't expected attraction to be quite so physical. Or so immediate. But this felt like a new life starting. There was Imogen Ridley before she met Caleb Black and Imogen Ridley after.

She turned to watch, as he tugged the coat over his shoulders. He was very tall. Her father and brother were both tall men. Mr. Black was taller.

Her hands curled at her sides, as she resisted the urge to trace that impressive form. She'd never before hungered to put her hands on a man. The strength of that need was another surprise.

With every second, the idea of leaving this fascinating stranger in the darkness and returning to a social whirl that had always seemed trivial, and seemed less important now, became more unappealing. She wanted to stay out here and learn all about Caleb Black. She wanted to stay out here, basking in an admiration that surely she didn't mistake.

It couldn't be mere wishful thinking that he liked her. She'd attended assemblies at home and house parties, not to mention a slew of events in London. She knew what it meant when a man devoted that intense attention to a girl.

"Miss Ridley, you really must go. Your good name will suffer if anyone finds us alone together."

She even found it in herself to like the way he looked after her. Although she'd like it much better if she could stay.

"Good night, then." Regret darkened her tone.

"Good night. It's been a delightful encounter. The villainous Lord Halston's loss is my gain."

Imogen stared at him, imprinting every shadowy detail on her mind. She already knew that she'd dream of him tonight.

Then she turned and darted along the path back to the ballroom.

CHAPTER TWO

aleb watched the lovely girl in the pale blue dress disappear into the darkness and he cursed hidebound English mores. In America, no social barriers would separate him from this lady. As the second son of successful entrepreneurs, he was considered a great catch in New York. In his democratic homeland, he was welcome in any ballroom. He could ask the lady to dance and take his time noting the details of a beauty that the gazebo's uncertain light only hinted at.

But here in London, because he had no noble ancestry and even worse, he worked for his living, he wasn't considered fit to associate with wellborn young ladies.

During his few days with the Tierneys, that hadn't been a source of regret. In fact, convinced that equality was the way of the future, Caleb had even found the strict social divisions amusing.

He wasn't amused now. Tonight something astonishing had happened, something unprecedented.

At twenty-five, he'd had his share of flirtations. He liked girls. He liked holding all that perfumed softness in his arms. But he also liked talking to girls and looking at girls. But his response to this surprising meeting extended a thousand miles past mere entertainment.

After a few minutes with Miss Imogen Ridley, it seemed wrong that she left him alone in the gazebo to return to the house. Where, no doubt, blue-blooded young men lined up to dance with her and pay her compliments and plan marriage proposals.

Caleb wanted to be the only man with the right to claim the lady.

He'd never felt like this before. He hadn't realized that he could feel like this.

Until now, his life had been easy and comfortable. His family was happy and loving. He was good at his work, and he was one of those fortunate beings whose occupation was also his vocation. If he wanted something, most of the time he got it. On the rare occasion that he didn't get it, he shrugged his shoulders and fixed his attention on something else.

As Miss Ridley disappeared from sight, he'd never felt less like shrugging his shoulders in his life.

He shivered. Despite every instinct urging him to follow Miss Ridley, he edged closer to the brazier. He'd been cold in his shirtsleeves and was grateful for the return of his coat. Although she'd looked much better in it than he did.

Was that faint drift of floral scent only in his imagination? He drew a deep breath to take in more of that elusive fragrance.

What an exquisite girl. Curvy and graceful, with a weight of dark hair and huge eyes that he guessed were blue. He wondered if they'd ever meet in daylight so he discovered the exact color of her eyes and skin and hair. The precise pink of her lips. The shadows hadn't hidden the pillowy softness of those, oh, so kissable lips.

By God, when he'd placed his coat around her shoulders, he'd been tempted to whirl her around and kiss her. For a charged moment, he'd considered actually doing it.

But he'd held back. Miss Ridley hadn't been frightened of him, although perhaps she should have been. After all, she didn't know him from Adam.

Would caution counsel her against slipping out to meet him in the Delacortes' garden tomorrow? Something told him that she'd found him almost as interesting as he found her. She'd been in no rush to go, and when she left at last, he'd read reluctance in her face and voice.

He extended his hands over the coals, as his mind dwelled on the encounter. He'd been in England a fortnight, long enough to get a feeling for the place. Imogen wasn't like any of the other young misses that he'd met here. She was more forthright, more like an American girl. But still with that lovely English air, with her cut-glass vowels and rather old-fashioned sweetness.

He'd enjoyed his travels, and he was looking forward to seeing more of the Old World before he returned to America. But tonight, enjoyment had transformed into enchantment, thanks to a pretty girl's smile. He felt like he'd swallowed a sky full of fireworks.

Tomorrow night seemed an eon away.

Imogen didn't have to wait until the Delacorte ball to see Mr. Black. Which was a relief. Since that short conversation in the gazebo, she'd been in a fever to meet him again.

It mightn't have been a complete accident that the next morning, she called on the Tierneys. She'd only met Elizabeth Tierney two weeks ago, but she and the pretty blonde had become great friends. They'd attended a lot of the same parties and had enjoyed several outings to London's attractions.

When Imogen asked her cousin if she could visit the Tierney town house, Stella showed no sign of suspecting an ulterior motive. Because it was an informal gathering and just across Lorimer Square from the house that Lord Deerforth had rented for the season, Imogen was allowed to go with only her maid to accompany her.

After last night's antics, Stella remained out of charity with Imogen. In the carriage on the way home from the Lumsden ball, she'd scolded her charge about her risky plot to engineer a return to Hamble Park.

It turned out that Stella had seen Imogen's strategically placed letter and had indeed set off into the cold to save her cousin from ruin at wicked Lord Halston's hands. But neither Stella nor Imogen had counted on there being two gazebos in the Lumsdens' garden. While Imogen had met the intriguing Mr. Black in one, her cousin had discovered Lord Halston waiting at the other. His lordship had accepted Imogen's brazen invitation, after all.

Imogen couldn't help but be grateful that she'd gone to the wrong gazebo. It would have been so easy never to have met Mr. Black, and that would be a crying shame. Especially if a scandal had eventuated, and her father packed her off to Gloucestershire.

Stella would have put the infamous earl in his place. Her cousin, who was nearly ten years older than she was, could be quite formidable when she wished. No rake, however naughty, would gain the advantage over that redoubtable lady.

Luck remained on Imogen's side at the Tierneys'. As she took tea with Elizabeth, she didn't even have to broach the subject of interesting guests staying in the house. Elizabeth did it for her.

"You must meet our American," Elizabeth said with her usual enthusiasm. Unlike Imogen, she'd adored every moment of her London season.

"Your American?" Harriet Comerford asked from where she sat beside Imogen on a pretty pink chaise longue.

Harriet was Imogen's best friend. The families were neighbors in the country, and she and Lord and Lady Lumsden's daughter had grown up together. Until now, she and Harriet had shared everything. Odd to realize that she felt no urge to confide in Harriet about her encounter with Mr. Black.

"Goodness me, is it safe?" In her chair near the blazing fire, Lily Bilson curled a slender white hand against her generous bosom and regarded her friends in dismay. "Mamma says that the former colonies are overrun by wild savages and desperate criminals."

Lily was another popular debutante. Her father was a rich landowner from Derbyshire, and she was counted quite a catch, not just because of her plump prettiness, but because she was worth twenty thousand pounds a year.

Elizabeth's laugh held a scoffing edge. "Mamma confiscated his tomahawk when he came to the door, and I think moccasins look charming with evening dress."

"Elizabeth, don't tease her," Harriet said. "It's not kind."

"But is he dangerous?" Lily asked.

"Goodness me, no. He's perfectly respectable. Papa has invited him to my ball."

Imogen's overexercised heart took another giddy leap. Mr. Black would be at the Tierney ball in a couple of weeks? More reason than ever to stay in London. Perhaps he might ask her to dance. The idea stirred more of those strange, tremulous flickers of excitement in her stomach.

Lily didn't look convinced. "I'm sure it would be unwise to dance with him. He might scalp me."

Harriet and Imogen shared a surreptitious roll of the eyes at Lily's foolishness. Harriet might have a generous heart, but she was awake to life's absurdities. She and Imogen had spent many a tea party mocking their neighbors' pretensions, and London society had only given them a wider canvas.

"All the more dances for me, then," Elizabeth said. "He's very charming and rather handsome. It's a pity that he's in trade and not at all eligible."

Imogen wanted to agree with her friend, at least about the handsome and charming part. Although her father would have a fit if he knew that she thought so favorably of a man who worked for his living. Not to mention a foreigner with no pedigree.

But she kept silent. If anyone discovered that she'd escaped last night's ball to flirt with a man in the darkness, she'd cause a scandal. Yesterday, scandal had seemed the solution to all her problems. Today, the thought of leaving Town made her heart howl in protest.

"We'll keep you safe, Lily," Harriet said with theatrical fervor. "Your scalp shall remain in place, or my name isn't Harriet Comerford."

Lily regarded Harriet uncertainly. She was just eighteen, and she'd led a more sheltered existence than the older girls. On occasions like this, the difference in age and experience became obvious. "I don't think Mamma would like me to meet such a man."

Elizabeth shrugged. "Then stay here. I've got the new *Belle Assemblée* and *Ackermann's Repository* over there on the side table. They should keep you amused."

Lily clearly didn't want to be left behind. "But—"

"I've never met an American," Harriet said. "Imogen?"

Imogen hoped her friends wouldn't notice the faint heat in her cheeks. Or if they did, they'd blame the stuffy room with its roaring fire.

"I'm always up for an adventure," she said, guiltily aware that the statement held more truth than her friends realized. If they learned of last night's escapade, they'd be utterly horrified.

Elizabeth clapped her hands in satisfaction. "That's grand. Mr. Black is here to help Papa redesign the grounds at Sander Hall. They're hopelessly old-fashioned."

Harriet sent Imogen a meaningful glance. "He's a gardener?"

"A most urbane one," Elizabeth said. "Quite socially acceptable."

Imogen, who considered most of the gardeners she knew a cut above the flibbertigibbets and idlers she'd encountered in society, smiled. "I look forward to meeting him, then."

More than her friends could imagine.

"He might have some ideas you can use at Hamble Park," Harriet said.

It was Elizabeth's turn to roll her eyes. "If I introduce you girls to a good-looking man, I hope we'll have better things to talk about than water features and terracing. When he and Papa are at dinner, I vow it's like being on a construction site."

"I'd like that," Imogen said.

"You're a strange creature, Imogen," Elizabeth said. "But don't you dare monopolize the conversation."

"I won't." Right now, her tremulous anticipation threatened to silence her altogether. She'd never felt this nervous about seeing a gentleman again. Or at all. She'd been perfectly calm meeting the men who graced the beau monde, because she didn't give a fig for any of them.

Even after one short meeting, she had the inescapable feeling that she gave more than a fig for Mr. Black and his good opinion.

Stop it, Imogen. When you see him, you'll probably realize that he's not nearly as exceptional as you remember. You met him in the dark when you were in a state about whether your scheme would succeed. In the light of day, away from the glamour of a forbidden meeting and deceptive lamplight, he'll turn into just another man.

But when she and her three friends trouped into the morning room where Mr. Black had set up an office – Lily had in the end decided that company would repel any attack – it turned out that Mr. Black was even more appealing in daylight.

He stood at a high drawing table in front of the French windows that poured gray light over the sheet of paper he was working on. Last night's cold weather had resulted in a bleak morning with a hint of snow in the air.

The sight of Mr. Black's long, lean frame silhouetted against the stark light jammed the breath in Imogen's lungs. Those fluttery feelings that turned her knees to jelly were back. With a vengeance. As her friends traipsed in ahead of her, she flattened a shaking hand on the doorframe.

"Mr. Black, we all want to see what you're doing. I told my friends about your plans for Sander Hall. They're agog to hear more."

Mr. Black turned as Elizabeth spoke and put down his pencil, before he performed a creditable bow. He was dressed as he had been when he'd lurked in the Lumsdens' garden. Imogen had thought him dashing then. She thought him dashing now. Little wonder Elizabeth was in such a dither, no matter what sort of marriage prospect he was.

Mr. Black's gaze drifted across the intruders before dwelling for a sizzling moment on Imogen. The blush that she'd tried to hide in the drawing room must now make her look like a tomato. In general, she wasn't a vain girl, but something deeply feminine inside her didn't want her flustered and red-faced when Mr. Black saw her. She wanted to look like a rose, not a tomato.

"Good morning, Miss Elizabeth." His voice was just as deep as she remembered, with that attractive drawl.

Elizabeth stepped aside and gestured to Mr. Black. "Harriet, Lily, and Imogen, may I present Mr. Caleb Black of Black & Sons Landscaping in New York State? Mr. Black, I thought you might like to meet some of my friends before you come to my ball in a few weeks. This is Lady Harriet Comerford. Her parents are Lord and Lady Lumsden, whose ball I attended last night. This is Miss Lily Bilson of Gadsden in Derbyshire." Elizabeth glanced up, looking for Imogen who hovered in the doorway. "And Lady Imogen Ridley of Hamble Park in Gloucestershire."

Mr. Black bowed again with more of that breathtaking elegance that set Imogen's heart somersaulting. "Lady Harriet, Miss Bilson." He paused so infinitesimally that Imogen was sure that only she noticed. "Lady Imogen."

Last night, she hadn't mentioned her title. Only now did it occur to her that Mr. Black might think she'd presented herself under false pretenses.

Their eyes met, and the world stopped. She caught her breath with an audible gasp. There was that immediate charge in the air that she'd felt in the gazebo. Stronger.

Now that she could see him properly, he was even more engaging. His thick hair was a rich mahogany brown, and one lock showed a beguiling tendency to tumble down over his high forehead. His eyes were deep chestnut, and she hadn't imagined their warmth. Nor the warmth in his smile, which set appealing creases around his eyes and on his cheeks.

He wasn't classically handsome like her brother or Lord Halston, to whom she'd finally been introduced last night. But it was an interesting face – and to Imogen that was much more pleasing than mere good looks.

She shifted in discomfort as three pairs of curious eyes settled on her. It wasn't like her to be retiring, nor to lose herself in bashfulness. She realized that Lily and Harriet must have already responded to Mr. Black's greeting. While she stood like a moonstruck ninny, gaping at Mr. Black as if she'd never seen a man before.

She gulped for air as she stepped into the room and performed a hurried curtsy. "Mr. Black, I hope you're enjoying your visit to London."

In her ears, her voice sounded thready and artificial. She hoped to goodness that nobody else noticed. Harriet cast her a sharp look. But then, Harriet and she had been toddlers together. She'd guess that something outside the ordinary was going on.

Did Mr. Black's smile warm a few degrees when his gaze fell on Imogen? "How could I fail to enjoy my visit? Lord and Lady Tierney have been wonderful hosts, and there's so much to do in the capital."

"What have you seen so far, Mr. Black?" Harriet asked, to Imogen's relief diverting his attention.

Imogen was more than happy for Mr. Black to stare at her, but right now she was too afraid of betraying an unseemly interest in the attractive American to her audience. It had been easier to enjoy his company in the gazebo. At least the shadows had hidden her blushes.

While Mr. Black delivered an amusing account of his activities in London, Imogen had time to conduct a surreptitious inspection. He was appealing when his face was still. When he was involved in conversation, the animation in his expression made him irresistible.

Last night, she'd gained an impression of humor and cleverness and kindness. Now she observed all these qualities and more. Perhaps most unexpected was a social assurance remarkable in a man of such inferior rank. Here he was, talking to four highborn young ladies, without the slightest trace of obsequiousness.

She realized that one of the things that had made her trust him last night was that he was a man with nothing to prove. He knew who he was and counted himself equal to anyone he met. That confidence was infernally attractive. She had the oddest sensation that if she put her faith in Mr. Black, he'd never let her down.

Which seemed both premature and irrelevant, when all that could exist between them was a brief, secret flirtation. Heaven help her, there shouldn't even be as much as that.

Her father had spent a fortune to bring her to London in search of a suitable match. In fact, in her father's mind, he'd already chosen a perfect husband in Lord Chippenham. He might forsake his plans for Chippenham if she attracted an even more eligible suitor. He'd be appalled to think that she'd set her heart on a commoner like Caleb Black.

Shock had her blocking that thought, the instant it entered her mind. Set her heart? How could their brief conversation spark such an idea?

But years of working with the outside staff at Hamble Park had taught Imogen to sum people up swiftly and accurately. Aside from her storm of feminine reaction to Mr. Black, her practical streak had immediately recognized that he was honest and trustworthy and nice. If she hadn't thought that, she'd never have lingered in the gazebo.

As she watched now, she saw nothing to change that original assessment. He even had that nervous nitwit Lily blushing and giggling at his stories of the animals' antics at the Royal Menagerie. Elizabeth positively glowed in his presence. At least Imogen had the comfort of knowing that she wasn't alone in finding the Tierneys' American visitor engaging.

"Black, will you come into the study? I want to get your thoughts on a new folio of Italian garden designs that just arrived."

Imogen had been so busy staring at Mr. Black that she hadn't noticed Lord Tierney at the other door. The glance that he gave Elizabeth and her friends was indulgent rather than disapproving. "That is if you can tear yourself away from your admirers for a few minutes." He bowed to the curtsying girls. "Lady Imogen. Lady Harriet. Miss Bilson. Your servant."

"At once, my lord." Mr. Black bestowed a charmingly rueful smile on his audience. "You'll excuse me, my ladies?"

"Elizabeth, I've told you before that Mr. Black is here to work, not for your entertainment."

"Yes, Papa," Elizabeth said, uncrushed by the gentle reprimand.

Mr. Black's manner with the earl held no hint of toadying. Imogen liked his self-confidence in this elevated company. It reminded her of one of her favorite people, her father's head gardener. Blaine might have been born one of twelve children in a hovel on the estate, but he judged himself as good as any person living, and better than most. Having worked beside him since she was thirteen, Imogen would agree.

There was something so inviting about Mr. Black's ease with himself. Especially in London, where everyone scrabbled for just a little more prestige, a shred of advantage, a favor from someone further up the pecking order.

Mr. Black bowed again and turned to follow Lord Tierney out of the room. Did his glance linger a moment longer on Imogen than on her friends? Or was she falling victim to wishful thinking? He hadn't paid her any special attention. Perhaps because Imogen had been absurdly tongue-tied in his presence, in stark contrast to her volubility last night.

Harriet lingered behind Lily and Elizabeth as they returned to the drawing room. "You didn't have much to say for yourself in there. Are you feeling all right?"

For pity's sake, Imogen hoped she wasn't blushing again. "Perfectly."

"I thought you'd want to badger Mr. Black about gardens. We usually can't shut you up when there's someone around with an interest in landscaping."

"Elizabeth told me not to monopolize the conversation."

"Since when do you listen to Elizabeth?" Harriet's glance was unimpressed. "You never listen to anyone. Goodness me, your father terrifies everyone, and I don't think you even listen to him."

Hurt, Imogen stopped as Elizabeth and Lily progressed further along the corridor. "You make me sound frightfully selfish."

Harriet stopped, too. "I don't think you're selfish. Or no more than most people."

Not exactly a ringing endorsement. This was her supposed best friend speaking. Perhaps Harriet was right to call her self-willed. But that didn't make Imogen any happier to hear the criticism. "Thanks very much," she said with some sarcasm.

Harriet shook her head, her light blue eyes serious. "You like to go your own way."

"Doesn't everyone?"

"Except you achieve it more than any girl I know. I'm surprised you haven't worked out a way to get back to Hamble Park."

Another of those horrid flushes heated Imogen's face. She hadn't confided in Harriet about her plans to be sent home in disgrace, although her friend knew that she was interested in neither a quick marriage nor a London season.

Or at least she hadn't been, until she met Mr. Black.

Harriet was in general cautious and obedient. She wouldn't approve of Imogen taking matters into her own hands.

"I've decided to stay in London," she mumbled.

Harriet rolled her eyes. "That's just like you. You complain your head off about something, then change your mind on a sixpence."

"Why are you being so mean?"

Harriet's delicate jaw set. She was a pretty girl, and she and Imogen had been the belles of the Gloucester assemblies since they'd come out to local society four years ago. "I'm not being mean."

"Yes, you are."

"Harriet, Imogen, what are you two squabbling about back there?" Elizabeth asked from the drawing room doorway.

"Nothing," Imogen said, feeling awkward. "I'm at home to callers this afternoon. I'd better go, or Stella will come looking for me." As if to confirm what she said, the clock in the drawing room chimed twelve.

"Are you coming to the Delacorte ball tonight?" Elizabeth asked.

"Yes. Are you?"

"I'll see you there." A footman passed with a note on a tray, probably for Lord Tierney.

Lord Tierney was closeted away with the man who was the reason behind Imogen's changed attitude to her London season. Perhaps she might once have tried to get Harriet alone, so she could tell her about last night's rendezvous. But right now, she was out of charity with Harriet, the way that Stella was out of charity with her. Disharmony ruled in Lorimer Square today.

"Frederick, when you go back downstairs, can you please summon Lady Imogen's maid?" Elizabeth said to the servant. "Her ladyship is just going."

Imogen said goodbye to Elizabeth and Lily, and even managed a smile for Harriet, although that didn't stop her friend from looking disgruntled.

Imogen's thoughts drifted away from Harriet to what was coming up. She had an afternoon of polite conversation to get through, followed by dinner. Then she'd be at the Delacorte ball, looking for a chance to slip out to meet Mr. Black.

The thought sparked a ripple of excitement. She was about to break every rule laid down for well-bred young ladies. Again.

Last night had started her on the path to scandal. Perhaps Harriet's criticism might hold just an atom of truth. Although that didn't give her the right to say those hurtful things.

It never occurred to Imogen to miss her appointment with Mr. Black. Instead, anticipation made her feel as if she'd swallowed a bottle of champagne. Her very blood fizzed.

The hours before she escaped into the Delacorte garden would hang heavy indeed.

CHAPTER THREE

When Caleb heard light, rapid footsteps approaching along the path, he reached out through the greenery to catch Lady Imogen's arm. "Be careful," he whispered, tugging her into the thicket. "The Delacortes have a watchman on duty."

"And Papa is here tonight, watching me like a hawk." She was quick enough to reply in an immediate whisper.

She stared up at him. It was too dark for her face to be anything but a pale blur, but he now knew that her wide eyes were the deep blue of delphiniums and that her wealth of black hair had the glossy sheen of a raven's wing. He also knew that those soft lips were the delicate pink of the amaryllis lily in his Redouté book at home in Saratoga.

In the Lumsdens' gazebo, he'd seen that she was beautiful. But today at the Tierney house, her loveliness had stolen his breath away.

Caleb was afraid that she might be in danger of stealing his heart away, too. As he'd watched her struggle to hide how flustered she was to meet him in public, he'd wanted to carry her away and kiss her until she was dizzy.

He'd wanted to kiss her last night, too. He wanted to kiss her now. He feared wanting to kiss her might turn into a lifelong affliction. "I had to climb the wall. The back gate was locked."

"What a pest."

"Exactly. You'd think they were worried about intruders."

Caleb heard a muffled giggle, which reminded him that he still clasped her slender arm. He should let her go. His hand didn't hear his mind's half-hearted command.

She was wearing something pale and floaty. Completely unsuitable for hanging about in the cold. But the smooth skin beneath his fingers was enticingly warm and standing close to her like this, he sensed the heat radiating from her body.

"I've never encountered a watchman at a ball before," she said. "In most cases, the hosts encourage their guests to stroll in the gardens."

"It's too chilly for strolling."

"It was too chilly last night."

"I'm glad you braved the weather."

"So am I."

For a long moment, they studied each other, although it was too dark for him to see her expression. He was overjoyed that she was here, until something she'd said earlier niggled at him. "Why?"

"Why what?" She kept her attention on his face and didn't move away.

"Why is your father watching you like a hawk? Did someone see us together last night?"

"No, I don't think so." Her sigh expressed frustration. "But Lord Halston sent flowers and called at the house this afternoon. His sudden interest has Papa in alt. He's very keen on the idea of Halston offering for me."

Caleb didn't like the sound of that. He didn't like it at all. "But the fellow's a rake."

He'd managed to find out a little about the man Lady Imogen had so rashly invited to meet her last night. It hadn't been difficult. Gossip raged about the disreputable earl. The latest *on-dit* was that his mistress had shot him in the arm after he served the woman with her marching orders.

Given Caleb didn't know the man, he probably shouldn't wish that the mistress had better aim. Anything to stop Halston from ruining Lady Imogen's life. She deserved better than a man with such a besmirched reputation.

Caleb was thinking purely altruistically of course.

The hell he was.

"He's also rich and influential, and so far he's proven elusive when it comes to choosing a wife."

"And I've heard that he's handsome."

"Very."

"Damn it..."

"You sound...jealous."

He felt her studying him through the darkness. His hand still wasn't obeying his mind, because it edged her a fraction closer. Since last night, her delicate floral scent had tormented his memory. Now with every breath, he caught an alluring drift of sweetness. He fought the urge to sweep her into his arms and bury his face in her soft white skin until he drowned in that haunting fragrance.

"I only met you last night."

"I know."

He exhaled in surrender. "But I am jealous. I don't want handsome, rich, eligible gentlemen courting you. Feel free to tell me I'm an idiot."

"You're not an idiot."

Shock as powerful as a blow from a prizefighter crashed through him. "Lady Imogen—"

A boot scuffed on the gravel path, and the faint glow of a lantern penetrated the leaves. Caleb drew her deeper into the shadows. Somehow that meant pulling her against his body. Her warmth seeped into him, and his arm found its way around those lush female curves.

She was shaking. With cold? With fear of discovery? Hell, never let it be because she was afraid of him.

He didn't think so. She wasn't trying to escape. When she twined her arms around his waist, pressing closer, his heart skipped a beat.

No, she wasn't afraid of him, thank the Lord.

Knowing that he asked for trouble, he rested his cheek against the silky cushion of her hair. He shouldn't touch her. She shouldn't rest so willingly in his embrace. But by Jericho, he loved that she did.

The watchman came to a halt outside the shrubbery. Did he suspect that someone was concealed there?

Caleb's hold firmed around Lady Imogen, although if they were discovered, that wouldn't help them at all. It wouldn't be too bad for him. He'd lose the Tierney contract and any chance of further commissions in England. But he could survive that.

Lady Imogen would suffer a scandal and the loss of her good name. He was well aware what was at stake for her. American girls might have more freedom than their English counterparts, but women who were reckless with their reputations paid the price in the New World, the same way that they did in the Old.

Caleb heard a few scrapes, before the pungent smell of tobacco tinged the cold air. He lifted his face from Lady Imogen's hair and heaved a silent sigh of relief. The man paused to light his pipe from the flame inside the lantern.

When Lady Imogen inched closer, Caleb's embrace tightened. Just to keep her from the night air, he told himself, although he didn't believe it.

After a minute, the watchman ambled off and the scent of cheap tobacco faded with him. For a little longer, Caleb and Lady Imogen remained entangled, then to his great regret, she shifted.

"I can't stay." Her voice was unsteady. He hoped that was because she found the experience of touching him as powerful as he found the experience of touching her. Although she was an innocent, so perhaps the strangeness of a man's embrace ruffled her. "I'm supposed to dance a waltz with Lord Halston before supper."

"Will I see you tomorrow?"

"It's the Wetherby musicale. I won't be able to sneak out." She went on in a hurry. "But I need to tell you something before I go."

"That this is all too dangerous?" Caleb was grimly aware that she took an awful risk, meeting him like this. He mightn't approve of strict divisions of rank, but this was the world that this delightful girl inhabited and she was subject to its rules. "If I had any honor, I'd finish this now."

"I wouldn't like that."

For an English girl, she was very plainspoken. He liked that. He liked it even better that she wanted to see him again. "Neither would I."

To his surprise, she reached out to touch his arm. "I want..."

He burned to hear what she said next, but she shook her head and lifted her hand away. He retained just enough sense not to seize it back. "What? What do you want?"

"I must go." He heard her muffle a sigh. "But before I do, I must tell you that Lord Halston has invited me to his house in the country for a few days from Saturday, and Papa wants me to go."

"I'm developing a great dislike for Lord Halston." And for the father who used this girl to further his ambitions.

"He's very charming," Lady Imogen said, with a hint of the teasing humor that he always found so disarming.

Halston must be charming. From what the Tierneys' servants said, he'd seduced half the females in the kingdom.

"Damn him, I'm sure he is." Then the significance of what she'd said sank in. "You're leaving London?"

"Only for a little while."

How could that sound like an unbearable punishment? He'd known this girl little more than twenty-four hours. It shouldn't matter that he wouldn't see her tomorrow night, or that she'd move out of reach for a couple of days after that.

But it did matter. It mattered more than anything else he could remember. What in blazes was happening to him? "Where?"

"Prestwick Place. It's in Buckinghamshire. That's not far from London."

Was she hinting that she'd like him to follow? He didn't care if she was. He wasn't letting her out of his sight, especially in the company of that devil with the ladies, Lord Halston.

Through Caleb's fit of unreasonable jealousy, something sparked at the back of his mind. "Prestwick Place, did you say?"

"Yes. Do you think—"

He caught her hand and lifted it to his lips for a quick kiss that affected him more than the brush of lips over satin-covered fingers should. He heard her breath catch. Shock or pleasure? "Leave it with me."

"You want to see me again?"

His laugh held a mocking edge. "What do you think?"

For a breathtaking second, her fingers curled around his, and he cursed that she couldn't stay. "I'm glad."

"Let me check that it's safe to go." In any rightly run world, she wouldn't have to go at all.

Caleb inched out onto the path and confirmed that the watchman wasn't in sight. Lilting music drifted from the house. Through the French windows, he saw people dancing. Soon that crowd would include Imogen, twirling around in Lord Halston's arms. By Harry, that stung.

"You should be fine to go," he whispered, as Imogen emerged from the thicket.

"I wish we had longer."

That same aching regret he felt rang in her low voice. She spoke with the perfect upper-crust accent that always sounded absurd and artificial to him, as if London high society consisted of painted dolls or actors playing a part in a silly play. But something about Lady Imogen's voice pleased his ears. He could listen to her all day.

As if he'd ever have the chance to do that.

"So do I. But if I follow you to the country, it should be easier for us to meet."

His vision had adjusted to the darkness enough for him to see the way her gaze focused on him. "Can you do that?"

"I think so. I'll try and get a message to you."

Even in the gloom, he knew that she smiled. "It would be lovely if you could come to Buckinghamshire."

Caleb smiled back, enchanted. "Wouldn't it?"

"I must go."

"Wait." He caught her arm as she turned. During these last forbidden minutes, he'd touched her often. Certainly more than a gentleman should. Yet he couldn't regret it. In fact, he was greedy for more. Perhaps if he arranged things as he hoped, in the country they could escape observation. "You've got a leaf in your hair."

As he carefully picked away the offending greenery, trying not to muss her hair, he heard another of those muffled laughs that always made him want to smile. She was such a game girl. No shrinking violet would dare society's disapproval by sneaking out to a secret assignation with an ineligible suitor.

A suitor? Was that what he was?

The thought crashed through him and settled in his mind, even while his more practical side told him that he was being an idiot. Worse, he invited an ocean of trouble. He had a grim premonition that if he persisted in pursuing Imogen, things would get very messy indeed. And not just for him.

Lady Imogen Ridley had been brought up to marry a man of fortune and breeding. Not a brash American, who might be doing very well for himself on his own terms, but couldn't vie with the aristocratic men who courted her. Not in wealth and not in lineage, and certainly not in prestige.

Caleb was a proud man, and he was proud of his family and the work they did. But he knew that the beau monde placed him only a step above the folk who sold them their food or cleaned their houses.

The beau monde, apart from Imogen herself. She looked him in the eye and spoke to him as an equal. That was enough to make her extraordinary, even without factoring in her beauty and intelligence.

He'd met her three times. The encounters had been brief. It turned out that they were long enough for him to set his heart on her.

God help him.

"Good night, Mr. Black," she whispered.

Warmth flowed up his arm from where he held her. Every time he touched her, satisfaction settled in his gut. Satisfaction, and a burgeoning hunger to touch her often and for much longer.

Who knew? Perhaps he'd get the chance at Prestwick Place.

"Good night, Lady Imogen." It still felt wrong to let her go, whereas surely what was wrong was keeping her out here with him.

For a second, she lingered. He felt her gaze on him like sunlight, despite the cold night. Then she turned and with the airy grace that made his heart sing, ran back toward her glittering world.

"Dream of me," Caleb murmured after her.

Imogen's heart fluttered, as she let herself in by the French doors leading to the morning room. She'd checked from the empty terrace that none of the guests had sought refuge there. It was lit with candles and a fire burned in the hearth, just in case anyone wanted a moment of quiet or privacy. She paused in front of the hearth to defrost. Her champagne silk ballgown wasn't much defense against a freezing April night.

In Mr. Black's presence, excitement kept her blood flowing, however icy the air. Now she feared that she was likely to arrive blue with cold when she returned to the ballroom as she must, much as she'd rather have stayed with Mr. Black.

Could he follow her to Lord Halston's estate? He'd sounded confident that he could. The promise of seeing more of him than these fraught, snatched meetings allowed made her stomach churn with anticipation. Perhaps if they met in the country, he'd kiss her.

It had been terrifying when the watchman had nearly caught them in the bushes. But so thrilling, too, with Mr. Black clasping her tight against his powerful body.

Imogen hadn't been cold then. The precise opposite, in fact. She'd curled her arms around him and wished in a most improper fashion that she could stay like this forever.

She'd crushed her face into his chest and breathed deep of rich, masculine scent, familiar from when he'd lent her his coat. But stronger and better now that she crammed her nose so close to his skin. Spice and sandalwood soap and something tangy and unforgettable that she suspected might be just him. Mere air couldn't compete with that alluring mixture.

"Imogen, there you are. I've been looking everywhere. Where on earth have you been? Are you unwell?"

Imogen turned from the hearth to see her cousin Stella standing in the doorway, cross with her, as she'd been cross with her since discovering her deception about eloping with Lord Halston. How very cross Stella would be if she knew what Imogen had just been up to in the garden.

Over the crackle of the fire, she hadn't heard the door open. Not to mention the distraction of wicked thoughts about kissing handsome Americans.

"I needed the retiring room." Imogen couldn't blame Stella for looking annoyed. She loved her cousin and she knew that lately, she'd been a major trial to her.

"That was half an hour ago." Stella stepped into the room.

She wore a made-up castoff of Imogen's that did nothing for her tawny beauty. Her cousin had scraped her hair back in a severe and unbecoming bun that made Imogen's head ache with sympathy when she looked at it.

Stella had done her best to disappear into the wallpaper since they'd come to London. That was at her father's insistence, but Imogen hated it. Her cousin was a poor relation, forced to seek a home with Lord Deerforth, who treated her little better than a skivvy. For the last ten years, she'd been Imogen's governess and companion. Imogen felt guilty as she realized that she'd always accepted that service as her due. Until last night, when she'd started to question how Stella might feel about her lowly status.

After all, while Stella's father had been a poor artist, her mother had been an earl's daughter, as highborn as Imogen herself. If Stella's mother hadn't eloped to Naples with her handsome drawing master, she would have made a glittering marriage.

Did her cousin have dreams and hopes that went beyond looking after Imogen?

Imogen took a moment to study her displeased governess and realized that in many ways, Stella was a mystery. This morning, Harriet had accused Imogen of being self-centered. Did that criticism hold a kernel of truth?

She sighed. Life was getting more complicated by the minute. "Then I took a moment..." Quite a few moments, actually. "...to catch my breath. The ballroom is so stuffy, and some of the people in there should wash more often."

Despite her exasperation, Stella struggled to hide a smile at Imogen's assessment of society's standards of hygiene. "Many of them prefer the lavish application of strong perfume to the regular use of soap and water. But you still shouldn't disappear like that. I wondered if perhaps you schemed to cause a scandal again, except that you told me that you're happy to continue with your season."

It was an unspoken question. "I promise that I wasn't arranging to elope with Lord Halston."

Stella's smile faded. She must still resent the necessity of having to deal with his disreputable lordship last night. "It's nearly time for your dance with him. Your father will hit the roof if you don't do the pretty."

Her father's unreliable temper ruled the household. Everyone from the kitchen maid to Imogen herself lived in dread of it. Most often, he took his bad moods out on Stella, which Imogen had long felt was unfair. Her cousin was powerless to retaliate.

Imogen strolled toward the door. "I'm ready."

A waltz with the notorious Lord Halston awaited. She couldn't be less enthused at the prospect, although tonight, for the first time in weeks, her father hadn't mentioned Chippenham. Or scolded her for not paying sufficient attention to her portly suitor. Lord Chippenham might be rich and influential, but Halston's influence and wealth eclipsed Chippenham's, the way the sun eclipsed a candle.

At least Halston's unexpected interest meant that at last she'd see the famous gardens at Prestwick Place. She'd dreamed of visiting the grounds there since she was twelve and she'd found a folio of etchings of the estate in Hamble Park's library.

Now Mr. Black might be able to follow her to Buckinghamshire. That would be like having her cake and eating it, too.

Imogen loved cake.

It was time to return to playing the debutante. Given that his arm was in a sling, she wondered how Lord Halston would manage a waltz. Probably with the aplomb that he demonstrated in everything else.

She tried not to store up trouble ahead by worrying what she'd do if his lordship expressed a serious interest. He was handsome and charming, but far too old and experienced for her. She didn't want a man who treated her as a sweet little amusement. She wanted a husband who regarded her as an equal.

If she said that to her father, he wouldn't understand. But she had an inkling that Mr. Black would approve.

CHAPTER FOUR

From the first, the Wetherby musicale had promised to be a great bore. Imogen would always rather be out amongst growing green things than indoors listening to someone caterwauling in a language that she didn't understand or thumping their way through a Haydn piano sonata.

With her father sitting beside her, and with no possibility, even without his supervision, of slipping out to meet Mr. Black, the evening turned into sheer torture.

Lord Chippenham wasn't present, but Lord Halston sat toward the back of the crowded room. When she cast a quick glance in his direction, he seemed to be looking across at her, where she sat between her father and Stella, who was dressed in her usual drab style.

Oh, no. Could the notorious rake have fixed his interest on her, as her father hoped? She couldn't imagine why. They had nothing in common. But then, she'd been in society long enough, both at home and in London, to know that her pristine reputation, acceptable looks, distinguished lineage, and large fortune made her a catch. Most men considered those more than adequate qualifications in a bride. The idea of sharing a genuine relationship with the woman they married didn't enter their calculations at all.

Imogen couldn't, however, help feeling a slight pang of disappointment in his lordship. He must be irredeemably shallow to think that they might suit, whereas she was convinced that they didn't, in any sense apart from the worldliest. When they'd met, she'd been surprised at how sensible he seemed. If he'd waited until his mid-thirties to choose a wife, why not choose one he loved and who loved him back?

She was well aware that almost everyone in the ton, including her fond father, would scoff at that thought's naivety. But if one pledged one's life to another person, some touch of genuine affection and respect might come in handy.

She also knew that everyone in the ton would look on a proposal from Lord Halston as a great triumph for any girl. If Imogen had the temerity to refuse to become the Countess of Halston, society would be aghast.

Worse, her father would be as mad as a hornet if she said no. She desperately hoped that Lord Halston soon turned his attention elsewhere, so the crisis never arose. He'd danced with Elizabeth and Lily and Harriet as often as he'd danced with her. While her friends were also too inexperienced to take on the licentious earl, she'd much rather that he directed his marital sights toward one of them.

She frowned. There she went again, sounding self-centered. Could Harriet be right? A hint of coldness lingered between her and her best friend. She hadn't yet confided in Harriet about her secret meetings with the Tierneys' American guest. Something shrank from trying to explain to anyone, even someone who knew her as well as Harriet did, why she took such dreadful risks with her reputation. And purely for the sake of a few stolen minutes with a young man who her father would never accept as a suitor. With a young man who, in any case, hadn't expressed honorable intentions. Perhaps he viewed these meetings with Imogen as an amusing way to pass the time during his London stay.

She didn't think so, even if neither of them had yet spoken about the future. While she was new to flirtation, Imogen's every instinct insisted that Mr. Black was serious about following this attraction where it led.

"Stop wriggling," Stella hissed from beside her, as a famous violinist sawed his way through an endless series of variations on a Scottish air. Imogen wished the blockhead would move to Scotland. Or Timbuctoo. Or, even better, the moon. "Plague take you, you're like a trout on a line."

"This has gone for hours," Imogen whispered back.

"Twenty minutes. And you've got another hour before supper. Then the concert continues for at least another hour after that."

"Oh, no."

"Oh, yes. And if you don't sit still, I swear I'll get a footman to tie you to your chair."

"Shh!" said Lady Pollock from behind them.

"I'm sorry, my lady," Imogen muttered and tried to pretend that she appreciated all this noise. What a pity that Mr. Black hadn't kissed her last night. If he had, she'd have something much nicer to think about.

Imogen's artistic woes continued the next night when she shared a box at the opera with Lord and Lady Lumsden. Why did one's season have to be so infernally musical? Why couldn't everyone go on a nice long walk instead?

Among the many things that she didn't like about London was how ladies were hedged in. A short stroll in the manicured surrounds of Lorimer Square's central garden or through Hyde Park counted as vigorous outdoor exercise. Although she supposed that if a debutante was in demand, she got plenty of exercise dancing the night away.

That was all very well, but while Imogen loved to dance, she got very tired of spending every night in a crowded room.

She couldn't wait until she and Stella left for Prestwick Place the day after tomorrow. The prospect of hours in the famous gardens felt like the promise of water to a man dying of thirst.

So far, Mr. Black hadn't contacted her. By heaven, she hoped that he did. She had a feeling that no amount of ferneries and greenhouses would make up for his absence.

How could she miss someone with whom she'd spent so little actual time? Yet she did. She also blushed to remember how she'd dreamed about his kisses. She wished that she had something real to compare with those fantasies.

Harriet leaned over the front of the box to observe the audience. "Isn't that Mr. Black down there in the pit?"

With a start, Imogen stirred from her doze. The opera was very loud, but she'd had a string of late nights in a row. The dim lighting gave her a chance to close her eyes and drift off.

"Who's Mr. Black?" Lady Lumsden asked idly.

"He's Elizabeth's tame American. He's over here to design a garden for Lord Tierney. She introduced us to him when we were there the other morning, didn't he, Imogen?"

"Yes, she did," Imogen said, her cheeks heating. The dim lighting came in handy for more than a short snooze, it turned out.

"Lily was such a henwit. She's afraid he's going to murder all the Tierneys in their beds."

"Harriet Comerford, that's not kind. Lily hasn't seen much of the world."

Her mother's gentle scolding made no impression on Harriet. "Lily hasn't got any brains, rather. She expected to find a half-naked Indian brave in the Tierneys' library."

The image of Mr. Black running around wearing only a loincloth jolted Imogen's heart in a most disconcerting manner.

"I can't see the Tierneys inviting someone like that to stay," Lord Lumsden, who was unusual enough to attend the opera to listen to the music, said with a smile.

"Mr. Black had rather elegant manners, don't you think, Imogen?" Harriet turned back to her friend. "And he's quite handsome. Elizabeth certainly thinks so. She was very silly and giggly when she introduced him to us."

Imogen struggled not to sound too silly and giggly herself. "The Tierneys have invited him to their ball."

"Then he must be a very superior sort of tradesman," Lord Lumsden said. "Now, do you think perhaps we could take advantage of these excellent seats and enjoy the opera?"

Imogen struggled to hide a wince at Lord Lumsden's unthinking snobbery. Even more galling, he would think that he paid Mr. Black a compliment.

As Imogen slid her chair forward, Harriet went back to surveying the auditorium.

"Where is he?" With luck, the shrieking soprano on stage masked the excitement throbbing in her question.

Harriet pointed to a familiar dark brown head below them. Imogen had never seen him in formal wear. The stark black and white evening dress suited him, setting off that fine bone structure.

Imogen's unreliable heart performed a somersault. The two days since they'd last met felt like a month.

"There he is." Harriet kept her voice down, so that her father didn't ask her to be quiet again.

As if he felt their gaze, Mr. Black glanced up and performed a bow in their direction. Harriet bent her head in acknowledgment.

How Imogen wished that she was down there with him. Or even better, that they were alone somewhere, with a chance to talk properly. Or perhaps – how wicked she was – improperly.

The temptation was to linger at the edge of the box and feast her eyes on him. But if she did that, she feared what her expression might betray. Especially when the Lumsdens knew her so well. Against every inclination, she returned her chair to its former position.

After the opera, the foyer was packed. Imogen stuck close to the Comerfords, even as she surreptitiously sought Mr. Black. He'd stayed until the end, but she'd lost sight of him afterward.

When someone bumped her from behind, she turned and found herself staring into glittering brown eyes. "Mr. Black."

"I beg your pardon, Lady Imogen."

When she extended her hand, he took it and bowed. Through her thin lace gloves, she felt the scratch of paper. Automatically she curled her fingers around the note and lowered her hand to hide it in her skirts.

Harriet turned and smiled. "Mr. Black, good evening. Did you like the opera? Wasn't Signorelli marvelous?"

"Good evening, Lady Harriet. Yes, I did enjoy the opera, but I'm no connoisseur."

Lord and Lady Lumsden checked back to see what delayed the girls.

"Harriet?" her mother asked with a hint of disapproval. It wasn't good form for a well-bred young lady to converse with strange young men.

"Mamma, may I present Mr. Caleb Black of Saratoga in New York State? He's working on Lord Tierney's new garden at Sander Hall."

"Mr. Black," Lady Lumsden said with no great warmth. If a middle-class man addressed her daughter in public, he committed a major breach of manners.

Imogen was very fond of Lady Lumsden, who had offered her a mother's guidance after the early death of her own. But right now, she wanted to give that worthy woman a lecture on innate worth versus society's shallow judgments.

To hide her annoyance, she dipped her head. The note crackled in her hand. However desperate she was to read it, she had to wait until she was alone.

"My lady." Caleb bowed and stepped back.

"Come along, Caroline," Lord Lumsden said from ahead. "Our carriage will be outside."

"Lady Imogen, Lady Harriet, your servant," Mr. Black said with another bow, before he disappeared into the crowd.

Lady Lumsden took Harriet's arm. "I thought you said that young man had excellent manners. He clearly didn't know better than to speak to you."

"I spoke to him, Mamma," Harriet protested. "He could hardly ignore me. That would be rude, too."

Imogen hung back to slip the minutely folded note into her reticule. Did it say that Mr. Black was following her to the country? She dearly hoped so.

"She has a point," Lord Lumsden said. "Anyway, he's a colonial. You can't expect him to understand the nuances of polite behavior. I thought his manners were very pleasant."

"Well, I hope he learns a little more about society's ways before he turns up at the Tierney ball," Lady Lumsden said. "Imogen, don't dawdle back there. I want to get out of this crush before my grocer decides to invite me to tea."

More unthinking snobbery. Imogen struggled to smile, as she wondered why she was such a misfit in this world that she inhabited.

Why shouldn't people of different ranks speak to one another? They might learn something. Lady Lumsden's grocer might be a man of wit and culture. He might even be cultured enough to appreciate something as complicated as opera. Whereas Imogen, whose noble ancestry extended back to the Garden of Eden, couldn't make head nor tail of it.

As she hurried to catch up with the Lumsdens, she couldn't help but resent the way that they'd dismissed Mr. Black as beneath their notice without pausing to assess him as an individual. Hadn't there

been a revolution in France that put paid to all these old prejudices?

Imogen didn't have a chance to read Mr. Black's note until she was settled in bed. Stella had sat up for her, and she had to make a show of describing an interesting night, when the most interesting part of her evening was something that she couldn't share with a governess. Then she had to endure all the fuss of Nancy, her maid, helping her to change out of her finery ready for bed.

With shaking hands, she retrieved her reticule from the nightstand drawer. Maybe the note didn't arrange a meeting in Buckinghamshire, but instead said that further contact was too risky, both for Imogen's reputation and Mr. Black's business ambitions.

She fished out the scrap of paper and held it close to the candle as she unfolded it. She'd never received a clandestine message from a young man before.

For a moment, her attention lingered on the slashing handwriting. Mr. Black had struck her as a purposeful individual. The script in his note bristled with that same energy and determination. Then she read the words, and joy made her want to sing.

Lady Imogen, I've arranged to visit Prestwick Place to inspect the gardens there. I'll be staying with George Perrett, the head gardener. I've seen a plan of the grounds and there appears to be a walled garden to the rear of the house. I'll meet you there at dawn the first morning of your visit. With my deepest regard, Caleb Black.

Imogen's heart thundered as if she'd just run a mile. The note wasn't particularly loverlike, apart from the sheer fact of its existence and its promise of a future rendezvous. And while "with my deepest regard" was a warmer than usual way to sign off a letter, it was far from a declaration of undying love.

But the most important thing was that she and Mr. Black would soon be together. Knowing she behaved like a besotted ninny, she lifted the note to her lips before she slid it under her pillow.

CHAPTER FIVE

Caleb waited for Lady Imogen in the small walled garden behind the sprawling Jacobean house. The sun hadn't come up yet, although the air was alive with birdsong. Spring was finally underway, after a very slow start.

Growing up in Saratoga, he'd heard so much about the glories of the British landscape, but his experience so far had been cold, mud, gray skies, and bare trees. His mother, a devotee of the English poets, would be most disappointed.

It was so early that the kitchen staff hadn't started work yet. Odd that he was so certain Lady Imogen would risk joining him.

Lord Halston's guests had arrived yesterday, and Caleb couldn't imagine that the aristocratic crowd gathered for the house party had gone to bed early. Despite the presence of his patron, Lord Tierney, Caleb wasn't treated as a guest. Or not at the big house, which was a charming old stone manor that suited this pretty valley.

Against his will – by all reports, Lord Halston had his eye on the girl who he wanted for himself – the unpretentious beauty of the house and estate impressed him. He'd imagined some showy mansion with much to overawe and little in the way of human-scale comforts.

The grounds lived up to their reputation as the finest man-made landscape in England. At least they were the finest he'd ever seen. He explored their glories with the assistance of Mr. Perrett, Lord Halston's head gardener, who reminded him of his father. That same appealing blend of personal humility and absolute confidence in his skills, mixed with a crusty manner that hid unexpected sensitivity.

He was staying with Mr. Perrett and his family in a fine brick house in a pleasant enclave just behind the stables. For his purposes, this was more convenient than being a guest in the manor house. Nobody checked his movements. In fact, people would say that he wasted his visit, if he wasn't out inspecting the expansive grounds at all times of the day. Lord Tierney fancied creating a garden to rival Prestwick Place. He expected Caleb to return from Buckinghamshire, inspired to achieve that goal.

Caleb glanced around the walled space and yet again found himself commending Lord Halston's taste. However reluctantly. The charming setting was outmoded, with high walls in mellow brown, rose, and cream brick. Its survival despite changes in fashion was a credit to its owner's discernment.

In this sheltered nook, daffodils and narcissi perfumed the air. Fragrant blossom covered espaliered pears and apples lining the walls. A lichen-covered stone cherub presided over a dry fountain in the center.

"Oh, this is lovely."

At the sound of Lady Imogen's voice, Caleb glanced up. She was poised in the arch leading into this enclosed patch of paradise.

He'd only ever seen her in her London finery. Silks and jewels and elaborate hairstyles. Even when she'd called on the Tierneys, she'd been dressed to the nines. But this morning, she was dressed much more simply in a plain yellow merino dress, and her hair was confined in a thick plait. Because of the cold, she'd wrapped a cashmere shawl around her shoulders. The rich rust and blue colours made her skin appear even whiter. To him, she'd never looked more beautiful.

He reached out to flatten one hand against the cool bricks, as he told himself that he didn't yet have the right to cross the short distance between them and seize her in his arms. Every other time that they'd met, he'd been unable to forget the social gulf separating them. But at this moment, she just looked like a pretty girl who made him ache with desire.

"Mr. Black?" she asked, when he didn't speak straightaway. "Is something wrong?"

To his regret, far too much was wrong. Including the fact that he couldn't court this lady in the open as he wanted to. He wasn't accustomed to secrecy and deceit.

On the other hand, this promised to be a beautiful day, he had nowhere else that he had to be, and the loveliest girl in England had abandoned a nice warm bed to seek his company.

"By Harry, you came," he said and cursed his clumsiness. At home, he was accounted a charmer, but Lady Imogen put him off-kilter in a way that he'd never experienced. The scale of his hopes seemed so impossible compared to what was feasible in the world that they inhabited.

"I told you I would." She didn't seem to mind his lack of address. A happy smile curled her lips. Such full, pink lips.

With dawn's approach, the light strengthened. Caleb had only seen Lady Imogen in daylight once before, when his patron's daughter had brought her friends in to meet him, the way that she might show them some exotic, caged animal.

Then he'd been painfully aware that he couldn't pay too much attention to Imogen, although he'd burned to feast his eyes on her. In the end, he'd dared only a few stolen glances. But this morning, he could linger to take in that shining black hair; the brightness of her dark blue eyes; the creamy whiteness of her skin.

"I'm glad." He couldn't help smiling back. "Good morning."

"Good morning, Mr. Black."

His smile intensified. He was far from convinced that his serious interest in this girl, his first serious interest in a girl, would end in anything other than disaster. But right now, the privilege of her company outweighed the threat of future heartache.

"Given we're breaking a million rules by meeting, I hope we can dispense with formalities. My name is Caleb."

He stepped forward to narrow the gap between them. In his opinion, any gap between them was too large. That intriguing smile broadened. It hinted at spice to accompany her alluring sweetness.

Of course there was spice. Wasn't this the girl who had made a secret rendezvous with a rake, then tarried to enchant a lonely American instead?

"Perhaps not a million...Caleb."

The sound of his name on her lips had him advancing another step. The sun just appeared over the treetops surrounding this walled garden. The gold light lit Lady Imogen to fire. "I like hearing you say that."

"So do I."

By Jericho, he had to kiss her or he'd go mad. He spoke in a sudden rush and extended his hand. "We're too close to the house. The servants will soon be about. Will you come with me…Imogen?"

Her wide eyes became impossibly wider. They were an extraordinary color. A rim of black around the iris deepened the shade almost to violet. Heaven help him, she was lovely. No wonder suitors crowded about her, clamoring for her attention.

But right now, he didn't have to share her with anyone else. What a lucky devil he was.

Caleb waited for a demurral. After all, he hadn't yet told her that his intentions were honorable, however questionable his methods of pursuing them. But after a second's hesitation, she accepted his hand. At the contact, her gasp of shock mirrored the sharp leap of his heart.

He'd touched her hand several times, which was scandalous enough, given that he was a lowborn foreigner and she was a noble lady. On those occasions, she'd worn gloves. This was the first time that skin had encountered skin.

Her hand was cool, just as the air was cool. But warm life pulsed under those chilled fingers.

As her spectacular eyes darkened to indigo, her smile faltered. The porcelain skin heated to pink, and her lips parted on a tremulous breath.

"Caleb…" she began, as he firmed his hold and drew her across the dewy grass to the arch on the other side of the garden.

"Not yet. There's a summerhouse near the lakes that should give us some privacy."

The three lakes at Prestwick Place were famous. He wondered how Lord Tierney would react if he knew that his landscape architect hadn't spent his first day in the country scoping out ideas for the new gardens. Instead, he'd been looking for places where he could get Imogen Ridley to himself.

This time, Imogen's soft gasp expressed anticipation instead of shock. She didn't resist the pull of his hand. "Another gazebo?"

"I've become mighty fond of gazebos. Very useful buildings. The Tierneys may find themselves with a forest of gazebos. At least a dozen."

A choked gurgle of laughter greeted his whimsy. "An excellent plan."

He hurried her across a small patch of open lawn behind the walled garden and into a coppice. "You're trembling. Are you frightened?"

"No." She paused. "Or perhaps a little. Papa would have a fit, if he knew what I was up to."

The prospect of a furious Lord Deerforth pursuing his daughter and wrecking Caleb's plans was daunting. "Is he here?"

When the Tierneys dined at home, Caleb joined them and kept his ears open for mention of Imogen or her family. He now knew that she had a straitlaced older brother, who sounded like a bit of a bore, and a father notorious for his irascible temper and vaunting ambition. The vaunting ambition didn't come as news, given his plans for an advantageous match for Imogen. The irascible temper reminded Caleb to be careful in his dealings with this girl. She took far more serious risks than he did.

Every time he saw her, being careful became more difficult. He wanted to make her his and tell all those eligible suitors to jump into Lord Halston's famous lakes.

"No, Papa had political business in London. He's entrusted me to the Lumsdens, our neighbors in Gloucestershire. And as usual, Stella is here to chaperone me."

"Stella is your cousin?" The Tierneys disapproved of Lord Deerforth's behavior toward his niece. Apparently he treated her like a servant. Worse than a servant. At least he paid his servants.

"Yes, she's a darling – mostly."

They followed a wooded path that skirted the edge of the wildest of the lakes. A rising slope hid Caleb and Imogen from the house. The setting had been designed with theatrical intent. Cunningly placed paths offered a glimpse of a view, then the surprise of a wide vista when one least expected it. "Will she miss you this morning?"

"She won't check on me. She trusts me. Even if she does wonder where I am, she won't be surprised to hear I couldn't resist exploring the grounds. I'd rather be outdoors than inside."

"So would I." They shared a smile at finding something in common.

He wasn't surprised that she led an active life. Most London ladies minced around, but Imogen walked as though she was going somewhere and intended to reach her destination as soon as she could.

Anticipation buzzed in his blood, once the summerhouse's black-tiled roof appeared over the bare tops of the trees. He led Imogen onto a point that came out at a small bay. A graceful white stone building was tucked into the woods on the other side.

"The Temple of Diana," Imogen said.

Surprised, Caleb glanced at her. "You've been here before?"

When she stepped up beside him, the warmth of her body whispered an invitation to close the mere inch between them. "No, Papa had a folio of etchings of the estate. This was one of the loveliest pictures in the book. It's even lovelier in real life."

She was interested in gardens? He turned to ask her, but she already forged ahead, keeping her hand in his. All thoughts of landscape abandoned him, despite garden design being his constant obsession.

"Let's take a closer look." She glanced back, eagerness sparkling in her eyes. Was Imogen just as frantic to explore this attraction burning between them as he was?

He hurried to catch her and took the lead. Somehow they both ended up running, hampered by their linked hands but neither willing to relinquish the physical connection.

By the time Caleb dashed up the stone stairs to the pillared doorway, he was breathless. More with excitement than exertion. He burst into the rotunda and stopped in the middle of a black and white floor tiled in radiating triangles.

Releasing his hand, Imogen stopped a foot away and stared at him. With trembling fingers, he reached out to smooth the stray tendrils of hair that escaped to frame her glowing face. Tenderly he brushed back the errant strands, before he cupped the back of her head. She stood unmoving, as he bent his head and brushed his lips across hers.

The contact was over in an instant, but an impression of warmth and sweetness lingered.

"Caleb?" she murmured, slowly opening the eyes that she'd closed when he kissed her.

His hand tightened in her hair, which turned out to be even silkier than it looked. He slid his other hand around her waist. Under his palm, she was as supple as a willow wand.

"Again?" he whispered, although their only witness was the stone statue of Diana in the niche behind Imogen.

She tilted forward in silent encouragement. "Yes, please."

He smiled. Something about her politeness made him want to hug her.

Caleb angled her face higher. This time, he paused to let his senses bask in the cushiony softness of her lips and the enticing scent of her skin. The first time they were together, he'd noticed that she smelled of flowers. She still smelled like flowers, as if she was part of the spring burgeoning around them.

She curled her arms around him and clung closer. Her wordless encouragement sent reaction crashing through him. The next time he kissed her, her lips moved under his in the beginnings of response. He drew her closer and deepened the kiss.

When she made a muffled sound, he raised his head. In her flushed face, her eyes were vivid blue. And dazed with surprise and awakening sensual awareness.

He kept his hands loosely linked around her waist. "Am I frightening you?"

She was no longer pressed against him, which was probably a good thing. When she was too close, he started imagining all sorts of eventualities sure to shock a gently bred young lady.

She bit a bottom lip that was swollen and glistening after those chaste kisses. The sight of her small white teeth teasing rosy flesh made him stifle a groan. He needed to control himself, or he might do something unforgivable.

After a pause that threatened to burn him to ash, she shook her head. "No." To his relief, she smiled. "That was rather nice."

This time, he groaned aloud and rolled his eyes. "Just nice?"

"I haven't got anything to compare it to."

Her confession didn't shock him. Despite her forthrightness, she'd always struck him as an innocent. "You've never kissed anyone before?"

"No. I'm glad my first kiss was from you." More of that disarming candor.

"So am I. But we need to lift the standard from merely nice."

"*Very* nice, then."

He laughed. How she charmed him. He'd been lost from the first. "Still not good enough."

"Perhaps if we tried again?"

Caleb released her waist and cradled her face between his palms. "That's an excellent suggestion."

The eyes that met his held an uncharacteristic hint of shyness. "Perhaps if you tell me what to do, things will progress faster."

He stared into that lovely face, enchanted anew, even as a wry smile twisted his lips. "I'm not sure progressing faster is wise."

"I stopped being wise the day I met you," she admitted.

"So did I." He leaned forward and kissed a line from her temple to the corner of her mouth. Then he dropped kisses on her chin and her forehead, and on that proud little nose and her fluttering eyelids with their thick fringes of black lashes.

With a faint protest, she edged closer. "You're teasing me."

"Yes. And myself."

"Then stop." With an abrupt movement, she turned her face until her half-open mouth met his.

An incoherent sound emerged from deep in Caleb's throat. Despite knowing that he took things too far too fast, he wrapped his arms around Imogen and lashed her to his body.

CHAPTER SIX

Imogen gasped as Caleb's mouth opened against hers. The intimacy of the act was astonishing. She shared her breath with him. He shared his breath with her. It was as if they joined together to create a single living entity.

Dizzy, she clung to his shoulders. A volley of sensual impressions pelted through her. His complex, salty taste. The heat of his lips. The way every subtle change in pressure set off a new earthquake inside her.

Nice? This went way beyond that lukewarm description. As Caleb's mouth moved with such devastating effect on hers, "nice" was incinerated in the flames of "extraordinary," "glorious," "life-altering."

Her pulse thundered in her ears, and her knees threatened to collapse. Then the world flared into lightning, as his tongue swept along her lips and dipped inside.

Even more intimate. Even more shocking. Even more wonderful. A moan escaped her, and her grip on his shoulders tightened as the world reeled around her.

When he drew away, disappointment almost as sharp as the unprecedented pleasure made her stagger. Only then did she realize that she was in no danger of falling because his hands curved around her waist.

"Why...why did you stop?" She didn't recognize that quivery murmur as hers.

"I didn't want to frighten you." The glitter in his dark eyes made her pulses rush.

He looked different, more alive, more...male in a way that she couldn't quite describe. A flush marked his spectacular cheekbones, and his chiseled features seemed harder and sharper as he stared at her. While his mouth – that clever mouth that turned her into a version of herself she didn't know – was fuller and softer.

Before she thought to question her actions, she raised one hand to touch his lips. When he pursed those lips to kiss the tips of her fingers, physical awareness jolted her. She was still innocent, but she wasn't quite as innocent as she'd been mere minutes ago.

"I'm not frightened. That was lovely." She lowered her hand to rest it over his chest, where his heart pounded hard and fast. More intimacy. Each new detail that she discovered felt like a prize.

She'd feared that she might be getting in over her head with this flirtation. Right now, she was drowning, and she'd never been so happy in her entire life.

Imogen had spent the last few nights dreaming of Caleb Black taking her into his arms and kissing her. When she danced with a dull partner, she'd daydreamed about Mr. Black deciding he couldn't survive another moment without tasting her lips.

It turned out that she'd had no idea what she was asking for. Brief, worshipful pecks on the lips had occupied her imaginings. They didn't begin to compare to the overwhelming effect when a man one...fancied surrendered to the force of attraction.

She shivered with excitement, as she recalled those tumultuous moments when his tongue had slipped inside her mouth. If anyone had told her kissing involved something so bizarre, she'd have scoffed. Perhaps even been repulsed.

When Caleb's tongue had flickered between her lips, she'd felt no urge to scoff. She certainly hadn't been repulsed. The shameful truth was that she was eager for him to do it again.

"Lovely is better than nice." The smile that made her silly heart caper like an overexcited puppy lifted the corners of his lips.

As his breathing settled, he sounded more like the man she knew. The heartbeat beneath her palm eased back from its hectic gallop.

"It is." Even when he'd been a shadowy silhouette in the Lumsdens' gazebo, Imogen had been more conscious of Caleb as a physical entity than she'd ever been of anyone else. Now that she'd kissed him, that physical awareness felt like a solid, earthy presence.

His smile faded, and his expression turned serious. "I don't want to do anything that scares or disgusts you."

"I'm neither scared nor disgusted." She paused. "I don't want you to think I'm too forward either."

Her silly heart melted when tenderness lit his gaze. "I'd never think that."

"I'm not acting like a proper English miss."

As she was guiltily aware, she hadn't behaved like a proper English miss since she'd met him. Her behavior would horrify Stella. If her father found out, he'd lock her up and throw away the key. Or perhaps keep hold of it and only let her out to marry

Lord Halston. Or even worse, the dreary Lord Chippenham.

"Thank the Lord for that. I want to kiss a real girl, not a pretty little poppet without an opinion to her name. By Jericho, imagine if I'd kissed your decorative friend Lily Bilson. She'd faint away in my arms. Or die of shock. Every time I said a word the other day, she eyed me like a chicken eyes a fox."

Imogen couldn't help giggling. "She's such a goose."

"Not a chicken?"

"That, too."

His grip on her waist firmed. "Imogen, I need to kiss you again."

Need not want? More excitement tumbled through her. He sounded desperate. She'd guessed – hoped – he was, but she was too new to the tempestuous world of sexual attraction to be sure. At times, she feared that most of this affair took place inside her foolish head.

She studied his face. He looked on edge and hungry. He looked as though his very existence pivoted on this moment. She felt the same. Her yen for Caleb felt like life and death.

"I'd like that," she said in a shaky voice. Logic might insist that she didn't know this man. But something inside her shouted down the counsel of prudence.

From the first, her heart had recognized Caleb Black as her other half. Now her heart refused to heed any doubts. Her heart made her lean into Caleb's body and tilt her chin in silent invitation. When he pulled her against him for another kiss, her heart gave a great cheer.

This kiss was different, a closer reflection of the depth of craving that she saw in his eyes. His mouth was more demanding, his exploration less tentative.

What they'd done before was thrilling, but this turned her blood to roaring flame.

His tongue flicked against her closed lips. Instinct made her open. An unknown world of pleasure exploded inside her, as he took his time discovering the interior of her mouth.

When she dared to move her tongue against his, his growl of approval made her toes curl in her practical half boots. She did it again, and the kiss caught fire. Heat rushed through her body and threatened to immolate her.

Her hands drifted along his strong shoulders before rising to clasp his head. Her fingers tangled in the thick silk of his hair, as she brought him nearer. For a long interval, they teased and tasted one another. Imogen learned the rapture that lips and teeth and tongue could create.

When he kissed her neck, she almost collapsed with sheer delight. Her breasts swelled against her bodice. It was wicked, but she burned to feel his hands on her. Heat settled between her thighs, as her hips tilted in instinctive yearning.

He groaned against the sensitive place where her neck curved into her shoulder. She wriggled closer, only to stop when a hard ridge of flesh pressed into her stomach.

She knew what that meant. In the country, girls soon became aware of the basics of reproduction. She and Caleb were two healthy young animals in a lather to mate with each other. But she was also a well-brought-up young lady. She couldn't let a handsome stranger tumble her on the grass like a wanton milkmaid.

Disbelief slammed through her. Was she thinking of giving herself to Caleb? Her imaginings hadn't ventured past chaste kisses. Yet one meeting in the dawn light flung those pallid fantasies to the devil.

Which was where Imogen feared that she might end up, if she wasn't careful.

"Caleb..." The haze of mindless surrender faded, and she grabbed his arms. "Caleb, stop."

She sounded breathless and frantic. It would be too easy to forget who she was and where she was and pursue these kisses to their sinful end. Easy? It would be heavenly, at least until she counted consequences.

"Caleb..."

He didn't seem to hear. Instead, he scraped his teeth along the nerve that ran up her neck. She struggled to resist another wave of intoxicating sensation and leaned back against the arms that he'd twined around her. "We can't. Not here. Not now."

With every second, her will to end this encounter faltered. She dug her fingers into his biceps, wondering what she'd do if he didn't stop.

"Caleb, that's enough!" she insisted, despite a wail of protest from her wanton soul.

Imogen felt him go still, and thank goodness, he stopped nibbling at her neck. She wasn't sure that she could stick to the straight and narrow if he kept that up.

Then so abruptly that she was left disoriented, he was standing several feet away and regarding her in horror. "Imogen...my lady, forgive me. I didn't mean to..."

It was a struggle to find her balance. She couldn't ask him to hold her up. At this pitch of arousal, if he touched her again, who knew where they'd end up? Most likely, with her sneaking back into Prestwick Place without her maidenhead.

"Call me Imogen. We've gone beyond the formalities." She tried to sound composed and amused, but her reedy tone betrayed her turmoil.

When she licked her lips, she tasted Caleb. Her first kiss had been marvelous, but she hadn't been prepared for how quickly sweet experiment could become overpowering desire.

"I didn't have any intention of..."

She'd come back to herself enough to give him a tremulous but genuine smile. "Neither did I." She paused, and her innate honesty made her add, "Well, I hoped you'd kiss me, but I pictured something much less..."

They both seemed to be having trouble finishing their sentences. "Less all-encompassing?"

"Yes."

"I'm sorry if I frightened you." He sounded less devastated. She'd hated to hear him so appalled and guilty and unhappy. Partly because if they'd done wrong, it wasn't his fault. Even in her innocence, she knew that without her excessive encouragement, he'd have remembered that he was a gentleman long before she had to stop him.

She shook her head. "It was wonderful."

At last, he smiled back with a hint of self-mockery. "Wasn't it just?"

She stepped forward then faltered, torn between the need to feel his arms around her and the demands of common sense. "Will you do it again?"

He groaned. "Imogen..."

"Or is that tempting trouble?" On the subject of trouble, she realized that the sun had risen long ago. She had no idea what time Lord Halston's gardeners started work, but if they were anything like the outdoor staff at Hamble Park, it was early.

Caleb made a sweeping gesture with one hand. "Do you trust me?"

Her wayward heart skipped a beat, as she studied him. Caleb mightn't be classically handsome, but by heaven, he was attractive. Especially now when excitement shone in his eyes and his thick hair was ruffled. Another forbidden thrill sizzled through her as she recalled plowing her fingers through that hair. Its beguiling untidiness was her fault.

"Yes," she answered without even thinking.

Pleasure broadened his smile. "Then I'll do my best to justify your faith in me. Will you chance another meeting?"

When she rolled her eyes, he laughed. "You know I will."

"Good. Will you meet me here tomorrow morning?"

"Yes," she said, again with no hesitation.

He took her hand and lifted it to his lips. A soft sigh escaped her. Because now she knew what those lips could do when they moved upon hers. From today, her dreams of Caleb's kisses were going to be much more precise – and much more incendiary.

"Now you should go."

She tightened her grip on his hand. "I'd rather stay with you."

"I'd rather you stayed, too." The expression in Caleb's eyes stopped her breath and made the fine hairs rise on her skin.

"Will you kiss me again tomorrow?" By now, her forwardness didn't shock her.

"I won't be able to resist." He cupped her jaw then dropped his hand. "But we also have to talk."

"We haven't had much chance to do that, have we?"

Another of those disarming smiles that made her feel all melty and girlish. "I'd planned on talking this morning, but..."

"But we ended up kissing instead." Her cheeks heated, although it never occurred to her to censor her candor. From the first, she'd had the oddest idea that Caleb wanted the real Imogen, not the careful, polite young lady that society expected her to be. "I'm not sorry."

"Nor am I, but some conversation might keep me on the right side of self-control." He burst out laughing again. "Don't look so disappointed."

She couldn't help laughing, too, which somehow meant that she ended up in his arms with his lips on hers. Imogen sank into pleasure. This time, there wasn't as much delighted surprise, but there was even more enjoyment.

Pulling free required every ounce of willpower. "I have to go."

Caleb gave her a quick kiss. "I'll see you tomorrow. Damn it, Imogen, it feels like forever until then."

His desperation was gratifying. She wanted him to be desperate for her, because the sad truth was that she was desperate for him, too. This morning, they'd had longer together than ever before, but it still wasn't enough.

She bit back a grumble when he slid his arms free. "It's getting late."

"Yes," she said, still without moving. The voice of duty, until now shamefully silent, pointed out that if anyone found them together, the scandal wouldn't just engulf her. It would affect Caleb and her father and her brother and Stella. And the Tierneys as well.

The knowledge didn't make her consider putting an end to her meetings with Caleb. But it did remind her that she needed to be careful, even here in the country.

"Imogen..." His low growl expressed his frustration with the restrictions hemming them in.

For a fraught second, she almost returned to his arms. But that meant more kisses, and more kisses meant that she'd be even more reluctant to go. Caleb Black was the most interesting thing ever to happen to her, and his kisses were the most interesting part of knowing him. At least so far. She wanted to stamp her foot and rage against sneaking back into the house and making polite conversation and pretending that a dawn rendezvous hadn't transformed her world.

But if she didn't go back, she risked a scandal. A scandal would put a stop to any more kisses. She'd be sent back to Hamble Park in disgrace.

Nonetheless only with the most grudging acceptance did she turn to leave the summerhouse. "Tomorrow."

"Tomorrow."

Caleb had trouble concentrating on George's descriptions of how he and Lord Halston had restored the Elizabethan knot garden outside the south wing. Partly because his plans for the Tierneys didn't involve anything quite so formal, however charming the effect was here. Mostly, he couldn't focus on plantings and perspectives, because his mind buzzed with memories of kissing Imogen.

Their encounter hadn't gone as planned. He wasn't a saint – he'd hoped to kiss this girl who had become his obsession. But he hadn't expected his blood to ignite at the first touch of her lips. In the beginning, her inexperience had beguiled him, but it hadn't taken her long to pick up on the general idea. Then she'd changed his world forever.

God forgive him. However pure his intentions, for far too long he'd feasted on her like a starving man offered a sumptuous banquet.

Imogen had offered him a sumptuous banquet. The sweetness that had drawn him to her was even more delectable in her kisses. Sweetness, but also that hint of spice. Spice that soon flared into a sensual heat that beggared his experience.

He'd only just prevented himself from shaping his hands to her rump and taking the encounter far past kisses. Thank heaven Imogen had called a halt. He'd come close to dishonoring this girl who he honored above all others.

He might say thank heaven now, but at the time, every cell in his body had shrieked in protest. Damn him for an impetuous fool, he'd been on the verge of possessing her. Despite the fact that anyone could have wandered in. Not to mention that they hadn't spoken a word about what they expected from their forbidden attraction.

As Caleb pretended to listen to George talking about pruning privet hedges, he promised himself that tomorrow morning, he'd maintain his control. Tomorrow morning, he and Imogen would talk to each other, rather than yield to another storm of kissing.

He hoped to Jericho he stuck to his good intentions.

"I can show you the plans in his lordship's library, if you're interested," George said.

"Yes, I'd like that," Caleb said, feeling guilty that George made such sterling efforts to help him, while he acted like a complete moonling about a pretty girl.

On the other hand, the girl was exceptionally pretty, so perhaps George might understand. He and his dark-haired wife Mary had six rambunctious children, and Caleb hadn't missed the spark in their eyes when they looked at each other.

The easy affection within the Perrett family made him homesick. They were a rowdy, cheerful, curious lot, like the Blacks, and they'd accepted Caleb as a welcome addition to the household.

Caleb felt at home in Lord Halston's head gardener's house, in a way that he didn't with the Tierneys. The Tierneys mightn't be as starchy as most noble families, but rank still governed relations.

Rank affected his interactions with everyone who he met in England. Apart from his comely Imogen, who seemed to be a natural egalitarian.

"How old is the house at Sander Hall?" George asked. "Would it suit a formal garden?"

Caleb thought about the Tierneys' picturesque northern estate. The Cumbrian setting was much wilder than these gentle Buckinghamshire hills. "The house is about a hundred years old, and my feeling is that it needs something less structured. But everything depends on Lord Tierney. He'll make the final decision about what he wants."

"I've seen pictures of your family's work in America, lad. If he gives you your way with the design, he'll end up with a garden that's the talk of the nation."

For a few seconds, Caleb even forgot Imogen. He stared at George Perrett in astonishment. "That's a powerful compliment from the man who created the grounds at Prestwick Place."

George shrugged. "It's true, nonetheless. What I've seen since you arrived tells me that you've got the gift."

Pleasure flooded Caleb. Since he was a boy, George Perrett had been his hero. His father had owned a folio of etchings of the Prestwick Place gardens, probably the same folio that Imogen had seen.

The thought that George recognized his talent and supported his ideas was a welcome surprise. "Thank you. There's not a gardener in the world I admire more than you, and only one alive I admire as much."

"Your father?"

"Yes. You'd like him."

"I'm sure I would." George smiled, his weathered face full of intelligence and benevolence.

Caleb couldn't help thinking that a country that treated such a paragon as a servant went profoundly wrong somewhere. He liked Lord Tierney and appreciated his willingness to take a chance on an unknown American to build his new garden. But George Perrett was worth a hundred of his lordship.

"If we establish a business over here as we hope to, I'll bring him down to meet you."

"I'd like that." George gestured to the exquisite knot garden with its interlocking hedges and elaborate symbolism. "I can see this isn't what you've got in mind for the Tierney place. Come and see the rockery, which I hope might spark a few ideas."

Caleb slid his small leather-covered notebook into his pocket and turned to follow George, only to stop when a party of Lord Halston's guests strolled around the side of the house.

He saw the Tierneys and the Lumsdens and leading the way on her host's arm, the girl who had kissed him to heaven and back. Looking irritatingly happy, Imogen tripped along beside Lord Halston in Caleb's direction.

A storm of emotions assaulted Caleb. Pleasure in seeing her, that was for certain. Any glimpse of Imogen still felt like a gift. But there was also a vile, choking jealousy that shocked him and made him ashamed. He'd always mocked his friends if they succumbed to the green-eyed monster. Jealousy seemed such a useless, destructive emotion.

Jealousy still seemed pointless, but it turned out that Caleb had sneered without knowing what he was talking about. When he wanted a woman the way that he wanted Imogen, the sight of her laughing up at a handsome suitor made him feel like someone clouted him with a shovel. As he battled the urge to rush forward and rip Imogen away from Halston, his hands formed fists at his sides.

Every beat of his heart shouted, "You shall not have her. She's mine."

Despite the fact that society didn't consider him worthy of her. Despite the damage that he'd do if he made a public claim on her.

"My lord," George said from beside him and bowed.

A surreptitious kick to his booted foot penetrated the red mist descending over his vision. By Harry, he needed to be careful. He couldn't let his reckless masculine urges wreck everything.

Caleb sucked in a deep breath, uncurled his fists and performed a bow. He suspected that it wasn't as respectful as it should be, but it would have to do. Bowing didn't come naturally to him. "My lord," he muttered.

"Ah, Perrett, just the man I want to see." Halston smiled with what Caleb read as smug superiority. "Lady Imogen, this is my head gardener. Lady Imogen is an enthusiast of gardening design. I said you'll give her every assistance while she's a guest in my home."

Surprised, Caleb forgot his jealousy long enough to wonder if Imogen's interest in gardens was real, or if she just wanted an excuse to be outdoors and in Caleb's company.

Perrett bowed again. The Brits did a hell of a lot of bowing. Too much, in Caleb's resentful opinion. "I'd be honored, your lordship."

"Thank you, Mr. Perrett." Imogen's eyes drifted over Caleb in a way that he couldn't like, as if he was just another servant in a household full of servants. "I've always longed to see the famous gardens at Prestwick Place."

Caleb knew that she tried to be discreet. He recognized the necessity for pretending that he and she were strangers. But that didn't mean he had to enjoy it. And still she clung to that slimy bastard's arm, as if she couldn't stand on her own two feet.

Lord Tierney ambled up to join the conversation. "Halston, this is the young American landscaper I brought in to do my place near Kendal. I told you about him last night after dinner."

Caleb struggled to maintain a neutral expression, as a pair of sharp green eyes leveled on him. The intelligence in Lord Halston's sardonic gaze shouldn't surprise him. This man was responsible for commissioning this glorious landscape, and he was a clever player in the shark pools of society and politics. Since hearing about the earl's interest in Imogen, Caleb had kept his ears open to learn what he could about his rival. To his chagrin, his rival turned out to be too formidable for comfort.

He'd seen Halston at a distance before, but up close, the man was far too handsome for his own good as well. Tall and lean, and with the kind of masculine self-confidence that sent the female half of the population demented.

Was he sending Imogen demented? Caleb didn't trust himself to check. But he couldn't help thinking that this man offered serious competition, perhaps too serious. His lordship was rich as well as presentable, and he'd gained her father's favor in a way that a middle-class American who worked for his living never would.

What did Imogen want of Caleb? A few forbidden thrills before she settled for a society marriage? He hoped to the devil not. But if that was the case, he needed to find out before he got in too deep. A frank discussion was more than overdue.

Yet what on earth would he do if she was trifling with him? Continue with the flirtation as a bit of fun? Or end everything before she broke his heart?

"I recall you mentioning him. Welcome to England, Mr. Black. I'm sure Mr. Perrett is the perfect guide to this landscape." Halston's lazy drawl struck Caleb as insolent, although what remained of his common sense told him that the earl wouldn't waste any effort putting a menial in his place.

"Mr. Perrett has been very helpful, my lord," he said, only remembering to bow when he caught George's frown.

"Excellent."

"Thank you for allowing me to visit your magnificent estate." While Caleb appreciated Halston's hospitality, the man's interest in Imogen made his gratitude stick in his throat.

"I hope you find it inspirational. Tierney has high expectations for what you'll achieve in Cumbria."

"His lordship is too kind," Caleb said.

"Lady Imogen, let me show you my knot garden. It's our latest project at Prestwick." Halston smiled down at his pretty companion with an admiration that had Caleb grinding his teeth. Especially when Imogen responded with unconcealed delight.

"I'd like that. Thank you."

"We might continue our walk." Lady Lumsden didn't hide her amusement. "Once Imogen starts talking about garden beds, she doesn't stop."

It seemed Imogen really did care about gardens. Caleb remembered her mentioning her wish to see Prestwick Place. It seemed too good to be true that she shared his interest.

The fond indulgence in Halston's smile as he explained the intricacies of the design made Caleb bristle. He hadn't wanted to believe that the fellow fancied himself as Imogen's suitor. He must be at least a dozen years older than her. But now there was no question that Halston liked Imogen.

Did he like her enough to want to marry her?

Caleb would be a fool to imagine anything else. Hadn't the polecat invited Imogen to his home in the middle of the season?

"I'll consign you to Mr. Perrett's reliable hands then, Lady Imogen," Halston said after about ten minutes. "We keep country hours here, so dinner's at six. If you're not at the table, should I send a maid out with some refreshments?"

Imogen laughed at the gentle teasing. Gentle teasing that hinted at developing friendship – or more. "I wouldn't be so rude, my lord."

Halston tilted an eyebrow to express his doubt, and Imogen laughed again. "I'm sure Stella will come and get me long before dinner."

Lord Halston released her arm and stepped back with yet another blasted bow. "I'll continue with my duties as host, my lady."

She curtsied with notable elegance. In Caleb's disapproving opinion, she missed out on simpering. But not by much.

Caleb had never seen Imogen playing the aristocratic ingenue, although why wouldn't she? Girls spent their whole life preparing for their

London season and the hunt for a suitable husband. Much to his displeasure, Lord Halston was a catch.

He wished to Hades that he despised this new version of Imogen. But to his despair, she was just as charming now as she was when she escaped her obligations and came to meet him. The hint of artificiality lent her an exotic edge that he found fiendishly tempting.

"I'll sit over here and enjoy the view," Lady Tierney said, making her way to a bench against the wall of the house. "The rest of you go ahead. I'll see that Lady Imogen doesn't stay too long."

George bowed to Imogen, as the rest of the group wandered away. Caleb noticed that Elizabeth now clung to Halston's arm. Elizabeth was pretty and charming. Why the hell couldn't the amorous earl set his sights on her as his next countess?

"Lady Imogen, let me show you the plants that we chose for the beds inside the hedges. Spring has been slow to arrive this year, so unfortunately you won't see the full color scheme, but you'll get an idea."

As Caleb trailed behind George and Imogen, he recovered from his fit of ill temper enough to realize that it had been an understatement to say that Imogen was interested in gardens. She could converse about annuals and perennials with an expertise that rivaled his own.

George paused at the graceful unicorn fountain in the center of the formal plantings. The unicorn formed part of the Halston coat of arms. It made a sick sort of sense. Caleb could already tell that his lordship was a horny bastard. "Don't you agree, Caleb?"

Agree with what? For the first time, Caleb allowed himself to meet Imogen's sparkling blue eyes. Because she stood a little behind George, the older man wouldn't see her smile.

Sultry memories of this morning smashed through him. And an urge to gather her up and kiss her again. If he did, Lady Tierney, who drowsed in the late sun, would have a fit.

"Yes, I do."

Laughter lit Imogen's expression. She must guess that he hadn't paid a scrap of attention to the conversation.

"Mr. Black, all of this must be very different to what you're used to in America." Imogen spoke politely, as if he were a stranger, but her tone held no hint of condescension. She spoke to George as an equal, too.

"Not as different as you'd think," he said. "There's been so much trade in plants between the continents that I'm familiar with the common varieties here and at home. There are so many American native trees in Lord Halston's wild garden that I felt quite at home when I saw it. In Saratoga, we get colder winters, so that makes a difference."

"Cumbria is very cold in the winter."

"So Lord Tierney tells me. I believe that's one of the reasons that his lordship decided to take a chance on an American designer. He hoped I might have an insight into what will thrive."

"I hear the Lake District is very beautiful."

"With its mountains and lakes, it's a bit like New York State."

"Terracing is your friend, lad," George said. "I'll give you introductions to head gardeners at houses where they've cut into hills to make the most of the landscape."

"I'd appreciate that, George. My father corresponds with many of the most influential designers and plant breeders over here. A lot of them have ordered plants from our nursery. But nothing makes up for seeing the gardens themselves."

"What about Hamble Park, Lady Imogen?" George asked. "Would it be worthwhile for Caleb to call on your estate in Gloucestershire? You clearly know what you're about when it comes to plants."

Imogen's dismissive gesture was as natural as her manner with Halston hadn't been. "Hamble Park isn't worth the journey. Sadly, Papa won't fund my more elaborate plans. He indulges me, but only to a point. He sees my interest in gardens as something to keep me amused until I embark on a woman's real duties as a wife and mother."

The hint of bitterness in her voice made Caleb want to put his arms around her. She might enjoy all the benefits of rank and wealth, but freedom was a rare presence in her life.

Then an unpleasant thought struck him. If she wed Lord Halston, she'd be chatelaine not only of the spectacular Jacobean manor house behind him, but of these famous gardens.

He knew that she wasn't in love with Halston. If her heart belonged to the earl, she'd never have kissed Caleb the way that she had this morning.

But a month of associating with the British upper classes had taught him that love played little if no part in the nobility's marital arrangements. Property. Prestige. Power. Marriages were meant to extend those three things.

Was Imogen tempted to favor Lord Halston's courtship? Caleb might hate the notion, but how could he blame her if she did? Her father wanted her to marry Lord Halston. The earl was rich, clever, and much as Caleb hated admitting it, appealing to women.

Not only that, marriage to Halston would offer her scope for her landscaping ambitions. And Caleb now knew that her landscaping ambitions were grand indeed. Through his sulk, he'd vaguely heard her speaking about drainage and water features with a level of detail that astounded him.

What on earth could he offer in comparison? He wasn't an insecure man, and he was in general an optimist. But Prestwick Place's magnificence would deter any rival.

"I'd say your expertise extends well beyond a hobby, my lady," George said.

Imogen regarded George in shock. "That's...that's very kind of you, Mr. Perrett."

"It's not flattery. It's the truth. I'll be pleased to show you around more of the gardens tomorrow, if you can spare the time."

The older man's sincerity was palpable, and Caleb's heart melted as he watched pleasure brighten Imogen's face. The color in her cheeks turned her eyes ultramarine.

"Thank you," she stammered.

George's praise overwhelmed her. Caleb imagined that she received plenty of compliments on her beauty. But he suspected that nobody ever troubled to credit her skills as a gardener. "But I don't want to inconvenience you."

Caleb saw George's surprise at this response. Lord Halston respected his head gardener, but there was no question who gave the orders and who obeyed them. "His lordship asked me to put myself at your disposal, my lady."

The familiar wry smile flattened Imogen's lips. "We both know some things in the garden won't wait."

George smiled with approval. "True. But you won't scamper around, treading on seedlings and asking stupid questions. And I already have Mr. Black as my shadow. I doubt you'll cause any inconvenience. My daughter can accompany us, if you'd like a chaperone. She's nearly as garden mad as you are, my lady."

"She won't mind?"

"It means a break from her mother nagging her to help with the housework. She's not a lass made for indoors, our Polly."

Imogen's quick glance sent Caleb a message. He guessed that she'd come up with this plan so they could be together during the day. Thus far, it worked to his advantage that Imogen was a bit of a minx.

It would be torture to have to pretend that they were strangers, but at least she'd be away from Lord Halston. He loathed how jealousy still prickled.

Imogen returned her attention to George, who showed signs of becoming her obedient slave. Even through his emotional tumult, Caleb found that amusing.

"In that case, Mr. Perrett, I'd be grateful to learn from you."

"Capital. And lend an ear to young Mr. Black's thoughts, too. He's much more up-to-date than I am, as befits a young man from a young country."

Imogen didn't stifle the warmth of the smile that she bestowed upon Caleb. Her sparkling eyes made promises that set his heart surging. His hopes chimed very ill with common sense. "I look forward to lots of long talks with Mr. Black, too."

Yes, she was without question a minx. But as piquant anticipation flooded Caleb, he couldn't help thinking that she was *his* minx.

CHAPTER SEVEN

As Imogen approached the marble summerhouse through the dim predawn light, she couldn't help remembering the first time she'd encountered Caleb in the Lumsdens' London garden. Imagine if she'd gone to the right rendezvous and met Lord Halston. Her life would have followed a different path. She couldn't help but feel that fate had taken a hand.

Her heart raced when she climbed the small flight of shallow steps to the entrance. The birds chirping to greet the day were no less excited than she was.

The last time she and Caleb were alone, he'd kissed her. Would he kiss her again?

She very much hoped so. His kisses had been glorious. Far and away the nicest thing ever to happen to her. And she was well aware that her life had been full of undeserved pleasures.

Caleb was sitting on a bench beneath a window facing over the lake. He glanced up as she appeared. For one giddy moment, his welcoming smile stopped her heart. The warmth in his expression counteracted the chilly day, although it wasn't as cold as yesterday. Spring finally arrived. Or perhaps Imogen only felt like that because she was so overjoyed to see him again.

Still smiling, he rose. "Good morning, Imogen."

He was dressed in the neat, practical clothing that she was used to. A brown coat and black breeches and boots.

"Good morning, Caleb." She smiled back in pleasure. He struck her as just what she wanted to see in a man. Clever. Pragmatic. Useful.

In the privileged world that she inhabited, usefulness was an underrated quality.

Yesterday she'd loved the time that she'd spent with him touring the gardens. When she'd asked Halston to introduce her to his head gardener, she'd hoped that meant she'd see more of Caleb. But it had felt like an unexpected and wonderful gift when he was in the knot garden with Mr. Perrett.

The difficulty had been hiding her interest in the tall young American. She'd spent so many years longing to see Prestwick Place. Now that she was here, all she could think about was kisses.

Caleb held out his hand, and she stepped forward to take it. Immediate heat rushed through her. She thought that her heart already beat as fast as it could, but when his fingers twined around hers, it doubled its pace. His hand wasn't white and soft, like the hands of the men in her upper-class world. It was callused with hard work. She shivered at the wicked thought that one day, those hard, capable hands might touch her body.

He groaned and closed his eyes. "For pity's sake, don't look at me like that. It makes me want to kiss you again."

That elicited an incoherent murmur of disappointment. "I thought you would."

When he opened his eyes, the desire in his gaze made her shift from foot to foot. "We need to talk. If I kiss you, I won't manage one sensible word."

"I like kissing you." An understatement that would have amused her, if she hadn't been quite so overwrought.

Caleb's nearness made her feel all female and needy and conscious of the hot blood pumping through her. The restrictions that society placed around a lady's movements made sense to her now in a way that they never had before. The framework of polite courtships and dynastic marriages would shatter if girls were allowed to pursue their own inclinations.

As his smile widened, another forbidden thrill rippled through her. "I like kissing you, too. Too much."

She frowned as she recalled that frightening but also magnificent moment yesterday when he'd verged on losing control. "Does that mean you won't do it again?"

This time, wry humor laced his groan. "I couldn't bear that."

"Me either," she admitted.

"But we have things to clear up first." Still holding her hand, he drew her across to the bench. They sat with mere inches separating them, but to Imogen, the gap felt like a chasm.

Where did this hunger for physical contact come from? Every meeting only worsened her craving for his touch.

"You sound very serious."

"We haven't had much chance to talk." He set her hand on his knee and stared down at their interlaced fingers. "Yet with every meeting, we move deeper into intimacy."

Intimacy? A serious word to match his serious manner. A word to match her sense that she edged closer to Caleb Black, closer than she'd ever been to anyone else. With each day, Caleb became more important. More important than her father or Eliot or Stella or Harriet.

"Is that what you want?" She hated the quiver in her voice.

Instead of answering, Caleb turned his head and those perceptive brown eyes examined her features. Under that penetrating stare, she squirmed on the seat. She felt like he saw everything about her, the good and the bad. Did he like what he found?

"Is this just a game to you, Imogen?"

Horror slammed through her. How could he think such a thing? "No."

His expression didn't relax. "It's not a game for me either. I've never felt about a girl the way I feel about you."

"Nor me." She blushed. "I mean, I've never felt about a man the way I feel about you."

To her relief, his sternness faded. "We don't know much about each other."

It was her turn to subject him to a searching regard. His features pleased her, they always had. One of the oddest things about this altogether odd situation was that the first time she'd seen his face, it had felt familiar. Her response had been more "There you are at last," than "What a surprise to discover such a man."

She still felt like that.

"You don't feel like a stranger."

"Nor do you." At last, he smiled. "Your knowledge of gardening surprised me yesterday. You should have said something."

"I wasn't being deliberately mysterious. Our meetings have been so rushed that I never found the time to tell you. I suppose I just assumed that at some stage we'd get a chance to learn the day-to-day things about each other."

"Like now."

"Like now." She paused, as heat tinged her cheeks. It wasn't shame. The only shame would be denying herself the chance to kiss Caleb. "And yesterday—"

"Yesterday, I drove myself mad kissing you," he said with the self-deprecating humor that she so liked. Caleb was a modest man in a world dominated by larger-than-life characters like her father and Eliot and Lord Halston. Perhaps that was one of the reasons why she always felt so comfortable with him.

As a gardener, she liked subtle touches better than huge, grand effects. One of the marvelous things about Prestwick Place was that the landscape was on a human scale. It invited one to enjoy its beauties rather than overwhelmed one with its size and power.

"You drive me mad, too." Last night, she'd hardly slept, reliving those heady moments in his arms. She'd never imagined that she could feel like that. And since meeting Caleb, she'd done a lot of imagining. "When I discovered you loved gardens as much as I did, it felt significant. As if—"

"As if our meeting was meant to be."

"Yes." She exhaled in relief. "That was exactly how I felt."

He still stared at her face. "So you're not just toying with me before you go off and marry one of your noble suitors?"

"I'm not toying with you," she said. "But Papa is beside himself with excitement to think that I might marry Lord Halston."

"Has his lordship proposed?"

"No. And honestly, he hasn't shown me any special favor. He dances just as often with Harriet and Elizabeth and Lily."

"He seemed to enjoy your company yesterday." Caleb paused, then spoke with a hint of rancor. "You seemed to enjoy his."

Elation, however unworthy, filled Imogen. "You sound a little jealous."

"I'm not a little jealous." Self-mockery lengthened his lips. "I'm a lot jealous, my dear Lady Imogen."

Her heart performed one of its disconcerting flips. "You don't have to be, you know."

"Don't I?" Caleb's expressive sable eyebrows drew together. "He's handsome and rich, and he bears a great title."

"That's true," Imogen said, and dared to tease as she went on. "There's also the added attraction of Prestwick Place. While I have no special fondness for Lord Halston, his estate is a great temptation."

The brows lowered further. "Imogen..."

She laughed and leaned forward to kiss him quickly on the lips. "I don't mean it."

For a bristling second, she wondered if Caleb would kiss her back, but he caught her face in his hands and held her at a distance. Her attempt to lighten the brooding atmosphere hadn't succeeded. He still looked rather bleak.

"I can't offer you anything that compares. In America, I'm a successful man. But here, I'm a workman and a lackey. At least in the eyes of the society you move in. I'm hardly considered fit to eat in the servants' hall, let alone court a daughter of the aristocracy."

"C—court?" Imogen repeated, everything else that he'd said flying out of her mind. Astonishment thundered through her. And bone-deep gratification.

Caleb made an impatient sound deep in his throat. "Of course I'm courting you, my lovely goose. What on earth did you think I was up to?"

In the last few seconds, the world had changed. She'd moved through confusion and surprise and a burst of flaring happiness. Now, she recognized the gravity of the occasion. "I don't know. I know that from the moment we met, the bond between us has felt significant."

"It would have to be significant to justify the risks you run. If we're discovered, you'll be ruined."

"You'll lose your contract with the Tierneys."

He shrugged. "That would be a pity, but it's not the end of the world, however much my father supported my idea to expand our reach to England. He likes the idea of Americans showing the Old Country how it's done. If my plans don't come to fruition, we still have a prosperous business in Saratoga. But if people think you've compromised your honor, you'll be a pariah. Especially if you dallied with a man from a lower class."

Imogen summoned every last shred of courage. "So what are you saying, Caleb?"

He lowered his hands from her face, although his eyes still bored into hers. His gaze was somber, as if the destiny of nations depended on what he was about to say. "You're the most wonderful girl I've ever met, and I'd be honored if you'd consider a proposal of marriage."

Caleb saw Imogen's eyes widen in amazement, before joy turned her beauty incandescent. "You want to marry me?"

"I do." The words emerged with unshakeable certainty.

One slender hand sliced the air in a bewildered gesture. "But we hardly know each other."

"My lady, you shock me." His smile filled with tenderness. "You wouldn't kiss a stranger the way you kissed me yesterday."

"I'm so glad you understand." Another blush. One of the innumerable things he liked about Imogen was that she couldn't hide her true feelings. The rise of blood to her cheeks betrayed her every time. "I don't want you thinking that I run around kissing young men willy-nilly."

"You were caught up in the moment."

Her smile broadened. "It was magical." Emotion deepened her voice. "Every time I'm with you, it's magical."

Caleb regarded her in wonder. "It's the same for me. I saw you that first night and something inside me changed forever."

The pink in her cheeks deepened. "I felt like I'd known you all my life."

How on earth could he resist her? "My darling..." He caught her hand and lifted it to his lips for a quick kiss. "You're trembling. Are you cold?"

Unlike their first meeting where her silk ballgown hadn't provided much protection against the chill, she was covered neck to toe in a dark green wool pelisse this morning. The color suited her, made that porcelain skin look like milk. Fur edged the collar and cuffs. She looked ready to chase a polar bear across the snowy Arctic.

She shook her head. "No. I'm...overcome. This feels so momentous."

"It *is* momentous. The most momentous thing that can happen to two people." He leaned forward and kissed her with all the burgeoning longing in his heart. He'd told her that he wanted to talk rather than kiss, but that was a low-down lie. He always wanted to kiss her.

Caleb retreated before the kiss turned passionate. They had things to settle. One thing in particular. "So what do you say?"

"Say?" The kiss left her in a flap. Another thing he liked about Imogen was that she went at everything full tilt. If she'd been a mealymouthed coward, full of caution and prudence, they'd never have met.

Whatever the outcome of their forbidden flirtation, he could never regret meeting her.

He smiled, feeling rather overcome himself. "I believe I just proposed."

She frowned. Perhaps there was an element of caution, after all. "Caleb..."

He tightened his grip on her hands, wondering if his happiness was about to turn to dust. "Do you mean to refuse me?"

"I'd love to marry you. I'd love nothing more."

For a dazed moment, he stared at her. She spoke so easily of love. Was there a chance that she loved him? Despite good intentions, he couldn't resist gathering her up and kissing her properly.

Imogen responded with the same fervor that had kept him awake and needy all night. She parted her lips and joined in with gratifying enthusiasm when his tongue danced inside her mouth.

Caleb lifted his head, wishing he had the right to take this intoxicating pleasure to its proper end. He couldn't wait to wed this lovely girl and proclaim her as his to the entire world. "I'll go back to London and speak to your father."

To his surprise, Imogen struggled to her feet. Her face was rosy after his kisses, and her lips were soft and full. But her eyes flashed, and her hands clenched at her sides. "That's the absolute last thing you should do."

"I don't understand." He frowned in bafflement. "Didn't you just accept my proposal?"

"Yes, I did." When she sucked in a shaky breath, he read the genuine distress beneath her temper. "Of course I did."

"Then the next step is seeking your father's permission for the match. Or isn't that how it's done over here?"

She swept one hand through the air. "Yes, that's how it's done here. But if Papa picks up even a hint that I've been meeting you in secret, he'll bundle me out of reach and keep me there. At least until I agree to marry Lord Halston or Lord Chippenham or someone else of his choosing. Not only that, he'll set out to destroy you."

Caleb bared his teeth. "Let him try."

"You don't know him." Imogen's smile held no amusement. "He likes to get his own way. Woe betide anyone who tries to thwart him."

Caleb stared at her in dismay. He should have expected trouble, but he was so jubilant that Imogen had agreed to have him that he'd assumed every other obstacle would fall by the wayside. Although she'd dropped enough hints about her overbearing father. He should have paid more attention, damn it. "I'm not afraid."

"You should be." Her expression didn't lighten. "He's a powerful man, and he can't abide anyone opposing his will."

Caleb spread his hands. "But surely if he loves you, he wants you to be happy."

The cynicism in her short laugh startled him. "You must come from a happy family."

He frowned. "I do."

"I don't. Mamma died when I was eight, and by then, I think she was glad to go. Papa had exhausted her with his demands and his disappointment that she only managed to produce two children. Papa and my brother have always been at odds. He loathes my cousin Stella and does his best to humiliate her at every turn, because her mother ran off with a poor artist and caused a terrible scandal. He'll hit the roof, if he thinks I'm following my aunt's example and skipping out of an advantageous marriage."

"I'm not a poor man." Caleb tried to come to terms with what he heard. "I can offer my wife every comfort and a respected place in Saratoga society."

She shook her head. "But you're not a blue blood. Even worse than that, you're American. Papa thinks every American is a foul traitor."

"Even now?"

"Even now."

"So he doesn't love you enough to care about your wishes?"

"Oh, he loves me. I'm probably the only person he does love."

"Then surely—"

She interrupted him. "But he loves his own prestige and influence more. Anyway, in his mind, giving me to some lord or other proves his love. Papa has a bad habit of believing that what he wants is the best choice for everyone concerned."

"If I go to him and present my credentials—"

She made an impatient sound in her throat. "You're not listening to me. If he finds out about us, he'll send me so far away that we'll never see each other again. I couldn't bear that." Her voice started to shake. "Promise me that you won't go near Papa.

Promise me, Caleb, or all hope of us ever being together is lost."

For a long, fraught interval, he studied Imogen's face. He couldn't doubt that she meant it, and because he respected Imogen's intelligence, he had to accept that she knew what she was talking about.

With a sigh, he slumped back against the seat. When she'd told him that she'd marry him, he'd felt like he could conquer the world. He didn't feel like that anymore. "Then what in tarnation are we to do?"

Imogen sat beside him again. He couldn't resist curling his arm about her and cuddling her close. He found some comfort in the easy way that she rested her head on his shoulder.

"I turn twenty-one at the start of June. After that, I'm able to marry without parental consent. But if I go against Papa's wishes, it will still cause an almighty scandal. Especially if he carries on like an angry bear, which he will. I doubt you'll get much work in England, at least with the aristocracy, if you upset such a powerful man."

"That doesn't matter."

She regarded him with troubled eyes. "Yes, it does. You deserve to succeed. You're brilliant. Even Mr. Perrett says so, and I can tell he isn't generous with praise. You could achieve so much over here. You must know that yourself, or you wouldn't have come in the first place."

"Then let me put it this way – it doesn't matter as much as you do."

She searched his face. "Do you mean that?"

He didn't even hesitate. "More than I can say."

Her smile was misty. "Caleb, I'm so glad you feel that way."

"How can I help myself? But if your father disowns you, you'll be an outcast from everything you know and love. You'll lose your family." He paused. "I've seen enough of your world to know that you're sacrificing the chance to be a great lady, a leader of society. That's the role you were brought up to play. By God, if Halston proposes, you'll be chatelaine of Prestwick Place. That's no small thing."

Imogen touched his cheek with a tenderness that sweetened his blood to honey. "But I don't want to marry Halston, however glorious Prestwick Place is. I want to marry you."

"Sweetheart..." He gathered her up and kissed her again.

This time, the contact felt less urgent, more profound. As if recognizing their difficulties brought them closer. Even if they were no nearer to finding a satisfactory solution to their dilemma.

He lifted his head. "It seems we face complications."

She gave a choked little laugh. "Just one or two."

"It would be easier for you if you just forgot me." It had to be said. To his great regret, it was the truth.

"Who wants easy when they can have transcendent?" she asked, which made him kiss her.

"You're a tip-top girl," he said, when he finally made himself stop. Imogen's kisses were like a drug, and he was in danger of becoming addicted.

He could see that her natural courage surged anew. "I'm so glad you think so."

Caleb glanced around. The dawn had come and gone without him noticing. "You should go. It's getting late."

Her obvious disappointment quietened the foreboding in his heart. Surely if fate brought them together like this, fate couldn't mean to keep them apart.

She didn't shift. "Will you be with Mr. Perrett later?"

"Yes, although not much at Prestwick Place will suit Sander Hall."

Assuming that he ended up working on the Tierneys' property at all. If he and Imogen eloped, which seemed the likely outcome, he'd lose that commission. He felt a twinge of regret at the wasted opportunity, then dismissed it. Marrying a girl like Imogen was worth missing out on the chance to design a thousand spectacular gardens.

"I'll try and come out to see you. Nobody will question my interest."

"I'd like that." He brushed his lips across hers. "Except it's always such a strain not being able to kiss you."

"You can kiss me tomorrow morning." Laughter glittered in her eyes. "You can kiss me now."

What else could he do but accept that invitation? Even as the magnitude of the stumbling blocks ahead of them weighed down his heart.

CHAPTER EIGHT

Imogen rolled over in her comfortable bed in Lord Halston's opulent house and told herself for the hundredth time to go to sleep. It was late, well past midnight. So far, she'd survived the house party on nerves and sheer elation. But this was her fourth night at Prestwick Place, and she was running out of puff.

But how could she sleep, now that she and Caleb were engaged? She couldn't stop thinking about the lifetime of joy extending ahead. A lifetime with the man she loved.

Fear of the forces ranged against her betrothal tempered her happiness, but it was happiness nonetheless. When she'd visited the gardens this afternoon – to her chagrin, Lady Lumsden had demanded her company during the morning – she'd hardly dared to look at Caleb for fear that she'd give away her excitement. She wasn't used to keeping secrets. She suspected she wasn't very good at it.

This evening, Halston had held a small ball for his guests and neighbors, but it had started early and finished just after ten. Now that his bullet wound had healed and he'd abandoned his rather dashing sling, he'd led the dancing. He'd partnered Imogen but to her relief, he'd also partnered every other lady in the room, including her cousin Stella, which had made her like him better. Most people in society treated Stella like a servant, whereas on her mother's side at least, she came from very aristocratic stock indeed.

Imogen frowned into the darkness. She wasn't alone in looking a little ragged around the edges. Tonight Stella had seemed distracted, and her angular features were drawn with tiredness. Her cousin had mentioned that she, too, was having trouble sleeping.

Perhaps it would help if they suffered together.

Imogen slid out of bed and wrapped her cashmere shawl around her shoulders. Talking to Stella would settle her down for a few hours' sleep before she sneaked out to meet Caleb.

No matter how tired she was, she'd never miss that. Especially when she only had one more night at Prestwick Place. Once she returned to London, she wouldn't enjoy this degree of freedom.

The door connecting her room and Stella's was jammed. Imogen would have to brave the corridor outside and hope nobody saw her.

Despite its magnificence, Lord Halston's house had some maintenance problems. It wasn't only the jammed door. Late at night, when she lay awake alternatively fretting and hoping, she often heard rustling behind the wainscoting. She feared Lord Halston had rats.

Imogen opened Stella's door and marched in. Only to stop nonplussed in the center of the luxurious room. A room even more luxurious than hers, which had always struck her as odd, given that Stella was here as a chaperone rather than an official guest.

Nobody was there.

A faint click penetrated Imogen's troubled dreams. She rolled over and opened bleary eyes. She lay on Stella's bed, and candlelight lit the large room.

She pushed herself up against the pillows. "Stella?"

"Oh, my dear Lord!" her cousin gasped, her hand shaking so badly that the candle she held flickered and died. Now the banked fire provided the only light.

Imogen leaned over to the nightstand to fiddle with the tinderbox. What in heaven's name was going on? Was Stella all right?

"Please don't light a candle," Stella said in a strange voice, just as the wick caught and Imogen held up the chamber stick.

As she took in her cousin's appearance, her eyes widened. "Goodness me, Stella, where have you been?"

Her cousin looked...pleasured. Imogen now knew what that rumpled mass of tawny hair and those kiss-swollen lips meant. The sensual heaviness around Stella's eyes had nothing to do with sleep.

Imogen's proper, self-effacing, occasionally strict governess, had been with a lover.

Stella must know that there was no hiding the truth, too, because she cringed against the wood paneling.

Imogen's sense of unreality deepened as she took in what her cousin was – almost – wearing. "And where on earth did you get that nightdress?"

Stella always slept in sensible white flannel that covered her from neck to ankles. By day, she wore

Imogen's castoffs, made over to fit her, or chose from two or three plain gowns that she'd sewn from cheap material. That was the lot of a poor relation.

Guilt stabbed Imogen, as she realized that she'd never asked herself whether her cousin was content with the arrangement. Now she took a moment, woefully overdue, to imagine how she'd feel if everything she wore was old and shabby and unbecoming.

She wouldn't like it. She couldn't imagine that Stella did either.

There was nothing old, shabby or unbecoming about the courtesan's garment that her cousin sported tonight. The clinging slip of gold silk and lace adorning her cousin's long, lean body revealed more than it concealed.

The negligee must have cost some man a fortune. The way that it set off Stella's usually downplayed leonine beauty hinted that whoever had bought it had taken the trouble to choose the perfect color and fit.

"Imogen..." Stella began, and it was obvious that she struggled to come up with some face-saving lie.

But it was too late. Imogen slid across the bed to place her bare feet on the carpet. "I didn't hear the door and it squeaks, so I should have."

Yet another maintenance problem at Prestwick Place. Honestly, Lord Halston needed to take more interest in his ancestral home.

When Stella didn't reply, she went on. "What's been going on? How did you get all the way over there without disturbing me?"

"You were asleep."

"I was dozing, then I heard a click, and I looked up and saw you. You appeared out of nowhere like a ghost."

"I'm no ghost." Stella tried to sound dismissive, but a stutter gave her away.

Imogen stood and ventured closer, so that she could see Stella more clearly. Although she'd already seen enough to guess that her cousin had been up to no good.

She should be appalled. She'd grown up in a society where a woman's chastity was regarded as her greatest treasure. She was shocked, certainly, if only because ever since she'd come to live at Hamble Park, Stella had acted the soul of propriety.

She had to. If Papa detected any hint of her mother's waywardness, he'd throw his niece out on her ear. Only fear of adverse public opinion had made Lord Deerforth offer Stella a home in the first place, after she was forced to flee war-torn Italy.

But Imogen wasn't appalled. She was too fond of Stella to make harsh judgments, and, anyway, she'd had her own taste of how powerful the urge to share oneself with a lover could be. When it was the right lover.

"No. You're not a ghost. You're a woman returning at dawn from a lover's bed." Fear for her cousin lent her voice an edge. "Who is it? I can't see you with Ivor or any of his friends. Or Lord Lumsden, who is famously devoted to his wife. Not to mention that you wouldn't risk hurting Lady Lumsden. I know you like her. Lord Tierney is too old for you. So is Mr. Bilson. That only leaves..."

Stella extended a shaking hand toward her, but let it drop before she made contact. Her expression was stark with contrition and shame and something that looked very much like pity. "Imogen, don't."

Reality descended upon Imogen like a thunderclap. Reality. And the vile recognition of her own vanity and ignorance.

God forgive her, Harriet was right. Imogen was too wrapped up in herself to pay attention to anyone else. With that realization came a flood of sick remorse that tasted rancid on her tongue.

She slumped into a chair in front of the fire, as she reviewed the events of the last few weeks in the light of what she now knew.

Imogen had always assumed that she was at the center of things, but in this case, her conceit had made her imagine herself as a much more significant player than she was. It turned out that very little of what happened at Prestwick Place was about her.

"It's Lord Halston, isn't it?"

Stella didn't answer, but the truth was stamped on her features.

"I should have realized when I saw you dancing together." For pity's sake, she should have realized the day they arrived, when Halston gave Stella the best bedroom in the house. "Lord Halston has been pursuing you this whole time, hasn't he? The lilies were for you. And the note."

The day after Imogen was introduced to Halston, he'd sent an extravagant bouquet to the Lorimer Square house, addressed to "my fair stranger." Nobody had suggested that the flowers were for anyone but Imogen. That morning call and those flowers were what had first convinced Lord Deerforth that his daughter was about to bag the marriage mart's most elusive prize.

Stella was Imogen's dowdy, undistinguished companion. Who would notice her?

One of London's most eligible bachelors, that was who. What a dozy fool Imogen had been.

The flowers had arrived the day after Stella met Lord Halston in the garden, when she'd rushed out to save Imogen from scandal. Imogen couldn't help recalling how tight-lipped Stella had always been about that encounter.

"Yes," Stella said in a whisper.

Imogen hardly heard her. "And the house party. He didn't ask us down to Prestwick Place because he's going to offer for me. Papa had it wrong. Halston asked us here, he asked everyone here, because it was the only way he could have you to himself. It's not about me. It was never about me. It was always about you."

"I'm sorry," Stella said, still on a thread of sound. She dropped into the other chair, lighting her chamber stick from Imogen's and setting it on the low table between them. "I know you like him. I hate to think that we've hurt you."

Imogen shook her head. "I'm not hurt."

It was true. Her vanity was a little bruised, and she was discovering that self-knowledge wasn't always comfortable. But she'd never wanted to marry Lord Halston. She'd never in her heart believed that he wanted to marry her. As it turned out, she was right about that.

Stella waved her denial away. "You don't have to pretend."

"I'm not pretending." It wasn't hard to send Stella a reassuring smile. "He's too old for me and too sophisticated, and far too experienced."

What was odd was that once she got used to the idea, Stella seemed just right for Halston. She was clever, much cleverer on an intellectual level than Imogen, who had never been the slightest bit bookish. And Stella's sardonic sense of humor matched the earl's.

Imogen had a sudden memory of Stella and Halston dancing. Before she'd met Caleb, she wouldn't have noticed, but now she thought back, they'd moved to the music as if they were created to dance together.

The waltz had gone on for a terrifically long time, too. The orchestra seemed to play repeats of repeats. She'd quite run out of things to say to Ivor Bilson, Lily's brother, who had been her partner. Lord Halston must have arranged that so he could hold the woman he wanted in his arms without causing comment.

Scandal chased Lord Halston around the way a terrier went after a rat, but he'd taken enormous care to shield Stella from gossip. Imogen hadn't heard a whisper about his interest in a humble governess, a woman whose livelihood relied on a pristine reputation. It hinted that perhaps this affair was more important to him than his previous brazen liaisons.

Imogen only had to glance at Stella, who looked thoroughly compromised, to realize that she was right about the physical compatibility bit. Carnal satisfaction almost seeped from Stella's skin.

Would Imogen look just as satisfied when she and Caleb wed? If kisses were any indication, she suspected that she might. The thought made her pulse stir with anticipation.

Stella still looked troubled, as if she feared Imogen put a good face on romantic disappointment. "But you were so excited when he invited us to the country."

She shrugged. Of course she'd been excited. She had her own flirtation to conduct. "Anyone would be. He's a leader of society. I was flattered when he singled me out. Anyway, I wanted to see the gardens. You know that."

"Oh, Imogen," Stella said, shaking her head with familiar wry fondness and a hint of relief. "So you hadn't set your heart on marrying Gray?"

Gray? The easy use of Lord Halston's Christian name betrayed just how intimate Stella and the earl had become, even without the evidence of Imogen's eyes.

"No, although it was fun to hear people say I'd captured the elusive lord's heart, and it stopped Papa pushing me at Chippenham." Not to mention granted her five glorious days to meet Caleb.

Stella's distraction over her love affair with Halston had worked to Imogen's advantage. If her cousin had been her usual sharp-eyed self, Imogen suspected her erratic comings and goings would have sparked a few awkward questions.

A grunt of laughter escaped Stella. She might look like a wanton stranger, but as they talked, she started to sound more like herself. "Now *he* really is too old for you."

Imogen gave a theatrical shudder. "He's too everything for me." Once more, she focused on her cousin, wondering how she could have missed the signs that her governess conducted an intrigue. Stella wasn't the only member of the family distracted by a man's attentions. "So you've been a fallen woman since we came here four days ago? Or did it start in London?"

Stella avoided her eyes. "I shouldn't talk to you about this."

"I think you have to."

Stella sighed. "Or what? You'll tell your father?"

How could Stella imagine she'd betray her? If only she knew quite how much fellow feeling Imogen experienced at this moment. She responded with a trace of heat. "No, I won't tell Papa. You know how he'll react. He'll ban you from the house, which means I'll lose a friend and a cousin I love very much. Give me a little credit."

Self-derision turned down Stella's lips. "It might be better if you do tell him. I'm not fit to be your chaperone."

A dismissive snort escaped Imogen. "You're still you. You haven't murdered anyone. You've fallen for a rake's wiles. To be honest, I can see the attraction. If Halston made any serious attempt to capture my interest, I couldn't resist him either."

At least that might have been true before she met Caleb. Now that she didn't have to think of Lord Halston as a suitor, she could acknowledge his powerful appeal. No wonder Stella had succumbed.

What did this mean for her cousin's future? Stella hadn't said anything about Halston harboring honorable intentions.

Why would he? Imogen thought her cousin was brave and good and magnificent, and those qualities should make her a catch in any world that understood true value. But this world judged people on wealth and powerful connections and prestige.

Halston could look much higher for his countess than a penniless governess, a child of scandal. Not to mention a woman willing to come to his bed without benefit of marriage.

His loss, Imogen couldn't help thinking. She turned to her cousin, curious about how this secret love affair had progressed to this point. "I suppose it all happened when I went to the wrong gazebo."

Stella cast her an uncertain glance, but soon spilled the story. As Imogen listened, she couldn't help but recognize that her cousin hadn't just fallen for a rake's tricks, she'd fallen in love with him.

Poor Stella. Certain heartache loomed ahead.

Imogen felt for her cousin and pitied her dilemma. But even her new gift for empathy couldn't dismiss the questions rising in her own mind.

A happy ending to Stella's liaison seemed improbable.

Was a happy ending any more likely for Imogen and Caleb?

CHAPTER NINE

"You're late." Caleb rushed down the steps from the doorway of the summerhouse, where he'd been watching for Imogen. Despite the sun coming up earlier each morning, he'd arrived before dawn. Every other day that they'd met, Imogen had left the big house while it was still dark, too.

"I know. I'm so sorry." She was breathless and on edge in a way that she hadn't been since their first morning at Prestwick Place. "I've been with Stella."

Alarm hurtled through him, as he lashed his arms around her. "She knows about us?"

"No."

Relief soothed the alarm. He couldn't bear to think of Imogen facing punishment and disgrace for meeting him. "Thank God."

"But I couldn't leave until she went to sleep."

So far, he'd kept a rein on his passion, even if every moment in her company just made him want her more. Her agitation and his own fear that this might be the day when she decided that the risks were too great had him hauling her close. When his mouth descended to hers, there was no chance of preserving even a hint of distance.

Nor did Imogen's immediate surrender help to remind him that they needed to be careful. He respected her. He meant to wait for their marriage before he claimed her. He was always agonizingly aware of her innocence.

But this morning, all he knew was how warm and soft she was in his embrace, how well she fit against his aroused body, how sweet her lips tasted.

Somewhere in their hectic kisses, they crossed a barrier. Caleb forgot everything except how much he desired this girl and how much she seemed to desire him in return.

Before this, his caresses had been chaste, however compelling his need to take things further. His hands had touched her face, her hair, her neck, her arms, her back.

Now he cupped her buttocks. As his fingers sank into luscious female flesh, she made a muffled sound against his seeking lips. If he'd heard a protest, he would have stopped. Perhaps. Although every sense overflowed with Imogen, and his blood pumped hard and hot. But what he heard instead was an incoherent plea to continue.

On a groan of pleasure, he hoisted her up until she pressed against his hardness. Her grip on his shoulders tightened, and her squirming only sharpened his hunger.

Caleb stared down at her with wild eyes. Imogen was always lovely, but in the strengthening light, passion transformed her delicate features into vivid allure. The blue eyes were hazy with longing, and excitement flushed her cheeks.

He kissed her again, reveling in her passionate welcome. Then after some more excruciating wriggling, he swung her into his arms and carried her up the stairs.

"I feel...I feel strange," she murmured, nestling her disheveled head under his chin and curving her arm around his neck.

"Good strange?" He sank onto the seat beneath Diana's benevolent blind glaze and arranged Imogen over his lap. Her back rested against his arm, and her legs stretched along the stone bench. He was painfully aware of her hip against his cock.

"I think so. Those kisses were..."

Hot? Enticing? Wicked?

He couldn't bear it if she said they were frightening. In an agony of suspense, he waited for her to finish the sentence.

She sighed. "...heaven."

The sweet yielding in her voice made his heart expand until it threatened to crack his ribs. "Yes," he said in a low rumble. "But it's a dangerous heaven."

Heavy-lidded eyes, dark with awakening knowledge, rose to study his face. She lifted one hand to his cheek, her tenderness making him feel like a ravening beast for what he wanted.

"Can we play with danger a little more? I've never felt like this before. Untamed and free and...desperate."

"I don't think that's wise." How it hurt to say those words.

"I'm not sure I want to be wise." He hated the sadness that shadowed her features. "We've got one more morning, and because Stella and I are traveling early, we can only meet for a few minutes. After what we've done here, London will be—"

"Intolerable." He'd tried to avoid thinking about how fast these few stolen days with Imogen disappeared.

"I'll find a way to see you."

"But it will be much more difficult. I know."

To his dismay, tears brightened her eyes and her hand trembled against his face. "Why does everything have to be so difficult? When I'm with you, I feel like we're invincible."

A grim smile twisted his lips. "So do I."

"But when we're apart, I can't help thinking that we're going to cause an awful scandal if we run away together. Papa will be livid. He'll never forgive me. He'll blame Stella and throw her out to fend for herself, when she doesn't deserve that. The scandal will damage Eliot's political ambitions. Because everyone thinks he's such a saint, plenty of people would love to see him tarred along with the rest of the family."

Caleb regarded her in horror, even as his conscience reminded him that she was right. This very morning, hadn't he feared that she might decide that the risks of their engagement far outweighed the rewards?

He swallowed to dislodge the lump in his throat. Then swallowed again. Yet his voice emerged as if the words scraped across gravel. "Are you saying you want to end everything?"

Shock flooded Imogen's features. "No, no, never."

His turmoil eased and for a long moment, they clung to each other in fraught silence.

Imogen shifted to look at him. "I want to marry you, Caleb. Is that still what you want?"

"More than anything in the world."

Her eyes bored into his before she relaxed. Whatever she saw in his face must have convinced her that he was in earnest.

"That makes me happy." As her lashes fluttered down, delightful pink brightened her cheeks.

He gave a self-deprecatory grunt. "I just have to rein myself in until we wed."

"I know what happens between a man and a woman. At Hamble Park, I saw animals mate. And the laborers aren't always careful when they talk."

For pity's sake, they shouldn't be discussing this. Not when his honor hung by the thinnest of threads. "I can control myself," he said in a thick voice, although at times this morning, he wouldn't have wagered a penny on his restraint.

"Is that easy?"

Another bleak huff of amusement. "It's torture."

A troubled light entered her lovely eyes. "I'm sorry."

"Don't be. When we come together, all this frustration will fuel my immense satisfaction."

Her smile was uncertain. "Will you touch me, Caleb?"

He went rigid. All over. And stared at her in concern. "Imogen, we can't risk it."

"I don't mean…"

"I know."

She didn't mean to let him take her maidenhead. She didn't need to finish the sentence.

But those incendiary kisses had tested his willpower. Too many more liberties, and Imogen wouldn't leave this summerhouse a virgin. Especially as intoxicating experience had taught him that she was as lost to this attraction as he was.

If they made a child, their already challenging situation would become untenable. Although Caleb couldn't help picturing Imogen growing round and sleepily contented, as his baby increased inside her. It was a beguiling dream, but he wanted his ring on her finger first.

"This might be our last chance." Distress cracked her voice. "I want more to remember, more to dream about, when we go back to snatching a minute together here and there."

He stared into her pleading eyes and felt his never very staunch scruples waver. She was everything he wanted. How could he deny her? Especially when this privacy would be a thing of the past once they returned to London.

"If I do anything you don't like, tell me." He hoped to Jericho that he'd stop.

"I trust you, Caleb. I trusted you from the first."

He swore that whatever happened, however strong the temptation to take things too far, he wouldn't let her down. A young girl's trust was heartbreakingly fragile. And the most powerful obligation in the world.

Caleb gathered her up and kissed her again. The touch of her lips was as potent as brandy to a drunkard.

His heart beat faster than a clipper ship racing before a strong wind. Watching her with an unwavering gaze, he reached for the top button on her green pelisse.

Because he shook so badly, it took forever to release the fastening. Imogen's erratic breathing made her lush bosom heave beneath the prim covering. She was shaking almost as badly as he was. Heaven knew what state they'd both be in by the time he got her coat off. Then he still had her dress to contend with.

When the high collar parted, he caught a tantalizing glimpse of her pale throat. A visible pulse pounded between her delicate collarbones.

Fumbling fingers released another button. His blood thrummed so hard, that he felt light-headed.

His fingers moved faster, as his urgency to see her breasts grew.

After what felt like an eternity, the coat opened to the high waist. Caleb planned his assault on the practical blue gown beneath. So practical that it, too, buttoned down the front. He supposed that was how she managed to dress without a maid's help each morning.

Even as his excitement heightened, his hands learned the knack. Three delicate pearl buttons down the bodice of her modest gown parted with gratifying speed.

Imogen's breath emerged in gasps. Suspense and bristling sensual awareness weighted the air.

When he brushed the soft material aside, delicious curves mounded above a plain white corset and the top of her shift. The sight sent heat blazing through him.

She must know how aroused he was. Sitting on his lap, her body was in intimate contact with his.

"Dear heaven..." he sighed in a mixture of wonder and torment.

"I feel...I feel wicked," she said breathlessly, covering the creamy slopes of her breasts with an unsteady hand. Her cheeks were as red as ripe strawberries, and her eyes glittered with embarrassment and agitation.

"We really shouldn't do this," he said in a choked voice, catching her hand and bringing it to his lips.

Despite what he said, he couldn't look away. He'd spent hours imagining Imogen's breasts. They were even lovelier than his fantasies. Full and white, with pert nipples of rich pink that pressed against the shift's transparent material.

When he released her, he expected her to cover herself again. Instead, she raked her fingers through his hair in a caress that made him shake.

Caleb touched one breast. Immediate fire sizzled through him, made his cock swell. He fought the urge to rip away every shred of her clothing.

One day – the good Lord make it so – he'd see her naked body. But Caleb already knew that wouldn't be today. Not only because of the ever-present risk of discovery. But also because for Imogen's first time, she deserved better than a quick tumble without benefit of marriage.

Which didn't mean that he meant to pass up his chance to touch her. He was only human. His fingers curled around one perfect breast.

When he squeezed, she sighed with pleasure. "That's wonderful."

"You're so beautiful, Imogen," he murmured. "What chance did I have against you? I was enchanted from the first."

"So was I."

He loved to hear that this bond was a glorious mystery for her, too. He took the pearled tip between his lips, drawing on her through the fine cotton.

"Caleb!" He heard surprise and burgeoning arousal. This time, her sigh was louder and longer and she curved up to meet him.

Still suckling her nipple, he shaped her other breast, his thumb brushing its pointed peak. She made a longing sound deep in her throat and buried her hands in his hair, urging him closer. It was an unspoken request to keep going.

Soon, the barrier of fabric between his lips and her skin, frail as it was, became unbearable. Almost roughly, Caleb tugged down the edge of her shift to reveal the rosy nipple. More wonder crashed through him, jammed the breath in his lungs.

She was perfect Venus lying in his arms, lost in a voluptuous swoon, while her lovely white breasts spilled over the top of her stays. The image etched itself into his whirling brain. As long as he lived, he'd treasure this moment.

"I'd like to draw you like this," he muttered.

Her giggle expressed both horror and delight. "Goodness me, imagine if someone found it."

As he toyed with her nipple, he dropped a kiss on one pale breast. "Something for the lonely nights when you're not there."

"Caleb..." Poignant emotion weighted the word.

He caught her close, kissing her with desperate ardor. Every kiss, every caress, could be their last. The thought added an edge to their passion. He could never take such fragile happiness for granted. If they won through – and he knew enough of the elevated world she inhabited to question that they would – he'd bask in the victory forever.

Her innocent fervor threatened to melt the chains that he placed around his masculine impulses. Reveling in her soft gasps of enjoyment, his lips drifted down her throat to kiss that brazenly exposed breast.

She tugged his simple neckcloth free. Her hands curved around his bare neck, then traced his shoulders under his white shirt. The fevered caresses heightened his craving, and his kiss turned fierce.

Even as Caleb told himself to stop, even as he reminded himself that she was a gently born virgin, he laid her upon the bench and kneeled over her. The blue eyes that met his were cloudy with yearning. She bowed up to run her lips across the vee of bare skin revealed under his open shirt.

The touch of her mouth made him burn. Her attentions might be innocent, but they inflamed every sense. Imogen had a natural gift for pleasure that he thirsted to explore.

So as his lips descended to hers for a wild, carnal kiss, Caleb reached down to edge her skirts higher. He knew that it was wrong. He knew that he asked for trouble. He knew that if he wasn't careful, he'd shatter every good intention.

But how could he send her back to her world of suitors and wealth and glamour, without stealing a taste of heaven first?

As he rolled to his side, the narrow bench seemed another excuse to snuggle closer. Leaning on one elbow, he surveyed the glories that his seeking hand had unveiled.

A shapely pair of ankles in white silk stockings. Neat calves and pretty knees, gartered in embroidered pink silk. He insinuated his hand into the loose leg of her drawers, delighting in the feminine nonsense of her lacy underthings.

When his fingers encountered the satiny warmth of her thigh, she gasped. Caleb buried his head in her shoulder, as he told himself that he really couldn't venture higher. His nostrils flared to catch the rich scent of her rising excitement.

He should stop. He must stop. He couldn't expect Imogen to call a halt. Since he'd kissed her breast, she'd relinquished all thought of propriety. It was up to him to remember where duty and decency lay. Even as his hand crept upward, dragging at the fragile material of her drawers. She muttered encouragement and turned into his arms, wrapping herself closer until his whole world turned to sumptuous, perfumed woman.

He laid his cheek against hers and withdrew his hand. Not, heaven forgive him, to set her clothes right and place her out of reach, but to find the slit in her drawers and cup her mound. Satisfaction rumbled in his chest, as he felt silky wetness on the feathery curls.

"Caleb…" Her voice held surprise, but no denial. She dug her fingers into his arm and God bless her, tilted her hips up.

"By all that's holy, Imogen…" His balls ached with the need to thrust inside her.

Forgetting where he was, forgetting everything apart from how this girl fulfilled his every dream, he slipped his hand between her legs. Even now, she didn't resist. Instead, she spread her thighs wider to allow him access.

He stroked her cleft, glorying in her satiny heat. The scent of need rose higher, made him drunk as a sailor on fragrance alone.

The devil whispered self-serving questions in his ear. Questions that rose above the stormy pounding of his blood.

Where was the harm if he took this encounter to its natural end? They were going to marry. He only preempted what they'd do on their wedding night.

When he touched her with more purpose, she cried out in confused wonder and buried her face in his chest. Her breath was humid on his skin.

"That's…that's even more wicked," she muttered, her lips moving upon him like a kiss.

He withdrew his hand from between her thighs, although the urge to continue thundered through him. "Your father would horsewhip me for touching you like this."

"He'd horsewhip you for daring to look at me sideways," she said with a hint of wryness. "He'd flay you alive for what you're doing now."

Caleb's grunt of laughter was just as wry. "Should I stop?"

She crushed closer to the heart that drummed in ceaseless yearning for her. "You should."

Her voice was nigh inaudible, but he heard her. By Harry, she was right. He should stop.

Unjustified disappointment flooded him, although her decision was no surprise. It was getting late, and they'd already tempted fate too many times.

Yet again, his hand ignored his mind's command. His hand slipped back to tease the place that he knew would bring her the greatest pleasure. As his caresses became more intent, she made a faint muffled sound against his skin.

The war between what he wanted to do and what he must do was so painful that when she spoke again, he almost didn't hear her.

"You should stop, but I really don't want you to."

What in Hades? "Imogen, you shouldn't say such things. But by God, I'm glad you do. So very glad." He went on stroking her secret places. "I love you."

She went still, and after a thorny silence, pushed away from his hand. She tilted up on her elbow to stare at him in consternation. Although why on earth she was so astounded, he didn't know.

"What...what did you say?"

He frowned into wide, shining eyes. "I said I love you."

Her brow crinkled, as though she had to translate the words from a foreign language before she understood them. "You've never told me that before."

"Every breath I've taken since that fateful gazebo means I love you. What on earth did you think?"

Her gaze softened. "That's nice."

Nice again? That seem a dashed half-hearted reaction to a fellow's declaration of his feelings. He wanted to ban that tepid word from her vocabulary. "Nice that I love you?"

"No. Well, yes. Obviously. But I meant the bit about your breath."

"It's the truth."

She looked extremely pleased with herself. "It's still nice."

His impatience sharpened. "I'm not a man for poetic declarations."

"I know." Her lashes fluttered down with the natural coquettishness that would have got him all stirred up – if he hadn't already been so stirred up. "When we're together, it's so difficult to stop kissing and find time to talk."

She had a point. He was a practical man, more inclined to action than speeches. And kissing Imogen was such paradise, he often forgot that sometimes a fellow needed to take the next step and put things into words of one syllable. "I love you" certainly met that criterion.

Which reminded him of something important. "Don't you have something you want to tell me?"

She kept her eyes down, although a deepening at the corners of her kiss-reddened lips hinted that now she might be teasing. "Do you think so?"

Caleb released his breath in an audible puff. "I do indeed think so. Do you love me, Imogen?"

The heavy fringe of eyelashes lifted slowly. The eyes that met his were radiant with light. He was dazzled anew. He'd always thought her lovely. Now she took his breath away.

"I must. I'm lying here half-naked. I'm breaking every rule and risking a horrendous scandal."

It was a declaration of sorts. But having held back from saying the words, now that he'd told her how he felt, he wanted her vows in return. More than he'd ever imagined that he would.

"Do you think you could tell me?" He cringed at how needy he sounded.

She licked her lips, although how could she be nervous? Right now, the advantage was all hers. When her voice emerged, it was soft, but certain. "I love you, Caleb."

His longing heart gave a great thud of triumph. A triumph that contained its share of relief. He'd believed that she loved him, but the actual declaration contained a power far beyond its apparent simplicity. "Do you?"

Her smile was pure delight. "You must know I do."

"I hoped. But the words make a difference."

"Yes, they do." She stretched up and kissed him quickly. Before he could respond, she pulled free to study him with a serious expression. "I love you so much. I saw you, and I knew you were the one for me."

"It was the same for me. I love you, my darling."

This time, he took control of the kiss. He only drew back to ask her if he could touch her intimately once more.

Then all thoughts of dalliance scattered to the winds.

From outside, he heard melodious whistling.

For one horrified moment, he stared down at Imogen as the sound swelled. Someone approached the summerhouse along the lake path.

If Caleb didn't act fast, Imogen's reputation would end up in shreds.

CHAPTER TEN

Imogen was adrift in a glorious golden world where the man she loved was in love with her, and everything was heat and pleasure and perfect understanding. She hoped Caleb would touch her between the legs again. It was most improper, but his hand down there had sparked the most extraordinary sensation.

His kisses were always splendid, but those few forbidden moments when his fingers explored the hollows of her body had promised a universe of experience beyond anything she'd ever known.

So when he drew away to stare down at her with love in his eyes, she didn't understand straightaway that something had changed. "Imogen, someone's coming."

Sharper than a cold north wind, the whisper sliced through the sultry mist enveloping her mind. "Oh, no."

There was a moment of confusion, as she and Caleb struggled to sit up on the narrow bench. When she'd been in his arms, the bench had seemed big enough to encompass the whole world. Now it took a ridiculous amount of maneuvering for both of them to rise to their feet.

Fear jammed the breath in her lungs. Thank heavens, whoever it was had decided they wanted a song to accompany their stroll. Or else they might have stumbled without warning on Lady Imogen Ridley and Mr. Caleb Black doing lascivious things to each other.

Hauling at her dress's drooping bodice, she glanced around in alarm. "There's nowhere to hide."

The whistling was getting louder. She even recognized the tune, "The Lass of Richmond Hill," one of her brother's favorites.

Caleb gestured her forward to where he leaned out the open window facing the rear of the temple. "I can let you down through here. It isn't much of a drop. If we use the main doors, we'll run straight into whoever is coming."

"What about you?" she whispered, climbing up onto the sill and taking Caleb's hands. They were firm and steady. That confident grip rescued her from a headlong rush into panic. Caleb would keep her safe.

"If I'm here alone, there's no scandal. It's just Lord Tierney's American gardener taking in the famous beauties of Prestwick Place."

A quick kiss bolstered her hope that they'd emerge unscathed.

"Are you ready?" he asked.

"Yes." Then because if they were discovered, all this morning's sweetness would vanish in a morass of anger and shame and recrimination, she couldn't help adding, "I love you, Caleb."

His eyes brightened, even as determination set his jaw. "And I love you." He kneeled on the bench beside her. "Sit facing out, and I'll let you down that way."

Without another word, she obeyed. He hooked his hands under her arms and lowered her. There was a horrid sinking sensation when Caleb took her full weight. If he overbalanced, they'd both end up in a humiliating heap on the grass.

He held steady. "Ready to jump?"

"Yes." Although she tried to sound brave, the ground looked a long way away.

He let her go. For a sick moment, gravity caught her, then she hit the ground. She lost her footing and collapsed onto all fours, but she was safe.

"All right?" he whispered above her.

Imogen looked up and nodded. She was winded and afraid of discovery, but at least behind the temple, she had a chance of escaping.

The whistling paused. The walker must be nearby. The lake path continued as a circuit leading back to the house. Maybe whoever it was would wander straight past, imagining that they were alone in this part of the garden. It was still early, although later than the usual time when Imogen left Caleb. An excess of passion had made them forget the ever-present danger.

Her heart warmed when Caleb blew her a kiss. Then he moved out of sight.

Imogen crept close to the building. Only a few feet away, a thicket of trees provided cover, but she wanted to make sure that the new arrival wasn't looking for her and Caleb.

She squeezed into a shallow arched niche, one of a row carved into the foundations. Nobody who glanced out the window would see her.

"Good Lord, I thought I was the only early bird," she heard a man say in an unmistakable upper-crust drawl. One of the guests, not a laborer.

It took her a moment to identify Ivor Bilson, Lily's handsome older brother. She'd danced with him several times, most recently at Lord Halston's ball last night. He was an amiable fellow, who liked hunting and fishing. That was all he ever talked about.

Relief made her knees wobble. Ivor Bilson was likely checking the lake for trout. Lord Halston had invited his guests on a fishing expedition today.

"Good morning, sir." She could tell by the sound of Caleb's voice that he was heading for the steps. "I won't intrude on you."

Ivor laughed. "Indeed, sir, it is I who intrudes upon you. You're not one of the guests, are you?"

Rather than an accusation of trespass, it was a casual enquiry. She supposed Caleb's self-possession proclaimed his right to be in the summerhouse.

"Please allow me to introduce myself. I'm Caleb Black of Saratoga in New York State. I'm lodging with Mr. Perrett, Lord Halston's head gardener, while I study the layout of the grounds."

"Good Lord, you're Elizabeth's American." Ivor sounded in alt. "She told me you were here when we danced last night. I've always wanted to visit your country. Now the recent unpleasantness between our two nations is over, I might have a chance. I'm Ivor Bilson, by the way. I believe you've been introduced to my sister Lily. Lovely little thing with big eyes and feathers for brains. Mamma is as smart as a weasel, but we children take after Pater. Amiable chap, but no more sense than God gave a butterfly."

Despite everything, Imogen couldn't contain a smile. Ivor had it right about the Bilson family.

"Yes, I remember Miss Bilson," Caleb said.

"She thought you were likely to murder her, silly wigeon." Ivor was fond of his sister. Even if she didn't already know that, Imogen heard the warmth in his voice. "Anyway, I'm just out for a walk to see the day. Town tomorrow, and I can't say I'm looking forward to it, but my sister needs me there. Her first season, don't you know? I hope your visit to England goes well."

"I'm enjoying it very much, thank you," Caleb responded with a smoothness that had Imogen stifling a giggle. For a brief moment, she remembered his hands on her bare breasts. Caleb was indeed enjoying himself in England, however improperly.

Then she glanced down at her gown, and all amusement evaporated. Good heavens, she looked like she'd been tumbled in a field. In her agitation, she'd done the buttons up wrong. With shaking hands, she righted herself and for good measure, buttoned her pelisse up to the neck.

She and Caleb had come so close to exposure. Reaction set in, leaving her shivery and faint. Her stomach roiled with acrid nausea.

Nor was she safe yet. At this hour, she was sure to meet someone when she slipped back into the house.

Upstairs, she heard footsteps running down the stairs. Ivor or Caleb?

"Imogen, are you still there?" Caleb hissed from the window above.

She emerged from her hiding place and looked up. Despite all the fear and worry, she smiled. He was just so dear to her. And he'd told her that he loved her. That was worth any amount of risk. "Yes."

"I thought you'd be long gone."

"I needed to know if he was looking for us."

"I don't think so."

"I don't think so either, thank heaven." They were lucky that their intruder was Ivor. As he'd admitted himself, he wasn't the ton's sharpest mind. Someone a little more alert might have wondered at

Caleb's lack of a neckcloth. Or even noticed it draped over the bench or crushed on the floor.

She glanced about her. The day was well advanced. Too well advanced for her peace of mind. In such bright, warm weather, any number of guests could decide to explore the grounds. "I must go. I'll come to say goodbye to Mr. Perrett later."

"I'll be there. I love you."

Her tummy performed an adoring flip, and she felt quite giddy with happiness. Now Ivor had gone, her mind returned to this morning's momentous avowals. What joy could equal knowing that the man she loved loved her in return?

They would surmount the obstacles to their union. They had to. Imogen refused to spend the rest of her life with a broken heart. That wasn't her plan for the future at all. "I love you, too."

All day, Caleb waited in an agony of suspense to see Imogen again. But she only managed to escape her duties as a guest in the late afternoon. It was so damned unfair that Lord Halston could claim his darling's time when he couldn't.

He had trouble concentrating on George's advice about perennial borders, however magnificent the plantings around them. Most gardens caught his attention, and here he was in one of the world's greatest. But all he could think about was touching Imogen.

As he stood in the knot garden and watched Imogen approach, he admitted that he should be ashamed of himself. But he wasn't. His mind whirled with too many fiery memories. How it had felt to caress Imogen's luscious breasts. The charged seconds – too short, even though they should never have happened – when he'd touched her sex.

That good-natured ass Ivor Bilson had scared the living daylights out of him when he turned up out of the blue. But the interruption had saved Caleb from an almighty sin. He'd been on the point of ignoring everything but the desire flaring between him and Imogen.

"Mr. Perrett, I wanted to thank you for your kindness while I've been at Prestwick Place," Imogen said.

In her yellow day gown, she was the personification of spring. Caleb couldn't help but feel like a satyr for the lewd things that he wanted to do with this girl who looked so pure and untouched.

Except he'd already touched her, hadn't he? He itched to do it again. His bare hands curled at his sides, as he fought the urge to touch her now. With every day, the rules and regulations that kept his beloved away from him became more irksome.

"That's right nice of you, Lady Imogen," George replied, smiling at her in approval. "It's a pleasure to show a young lady like you around. A young lady with such an exceptional knowledge of the art of landscaping."

Caleb watched as gratification warmed Imogen's cheeks. The compliment was justified. Imogen's understanding of the principles of design was impressive. It would be enough to make him imagine himself in love with her, even if she hadn't kissed him all the way to the sky and back.

However fanciful the thought, he couldn't help believing that destiny had created her just for him. It was hard to resist the idea, every time he heard her discuss practical topics like drainage and soil acidity with George.

Caleb was turning bacon-brained with love, but he couldn't help it. She was just so damned perfect for him.

"Thank you. That means so much, coming from such a great man."

The compliment had George looking boyishly pleased in turn. "Away with you, my lady. I'm but a humble workman."

Imogen shook her head in emphatic disagreement. "No, you're an artist. It's been a privilege to enjoy your company."

"Well, in that case, thank you."

"I wish I could stay longer. I've learned such a lot in the last days, yet I've only just scratched the surface."

The sour thought assailed Caleb that if she married Halston, she could stay forever. Much as he'd like to deride the earl as an aristocratic idler, it was impossible when George mentioned his lordship with such respect. Every time Halston spoke to his head gardener, their mutual regard was clear.

George was no fool. If he liked Lord Halston, there was something worth liking.

Which did nothing to quash Caleb's jealousy. Imogen might love him, but he remained too aware that in a worldly sense, she could do much better when she chose a husband.

"You must come again, my lady."

"I'd like that." She turned to Caleb, although he knew that most of her attention had been fixed on him since she'd arrived. "Mr. Black, I wish you luck with all your projects."

The slight emphasis she placed on "all" had him hiding a smile. She wasn't just talking about gardens. The niggle of jealousy eased a fraction. Only that morning, Imogen had declared her heart was his. In his estimation, that was a prize greater than any rich estate.

He bowed, for once without resenting the servile gesture. Imogen was his beloved. He placed himself at her eternal service. "Thank you, my lady."

Caleb didn't dare to say more for fear of betraying his feelings, but he couldn't stop his eyes from devouring her. His hands itched to seize her, to hold her close, to stroke that thick hair, now mostly concealed beneath a charming yellow straw bonnet.

"I'm sure Lord Tierney's gardens in Cumbria will be spectacular, once you've finished with them."

"You're very kind."

She was. His words weren't just air. For a blazing moment, she met his gaze before she looked away. He hoped that George didn't notice her flushed cheeks. "Not at all."

Imogen's cousin appeared around the corner of the house. She was tall and striking, more so now that she'd stopped dressing so severely. Caleb saw no resemblance between the cousins, but from what Imogen said, they shared a strong bond of affection.

"Imogen, his lordship is waiting for you in his picture gallery."

Imogen's gaze flashed back to Caleb. In her eyes, he read reluctance to leave and a hint of mocking humor. He guessed that an hour or two looking at old masters was her idea of a great bore. She had no pretensions to being a bluestocking.

"Goodbye, Mr. Perrett." As if she addressed an equal, she extended her hand to George. "I'll always remember meeting you."

George's smile conveyed surprise, but he didn't hesitate to close his tanned, scarred hand around Imogen's.

Imogen turned to offer her hand to Caleb. "Mr. Black, it's been a treat to meet you, too."

Struggling to hide his heated reaction to her touch, he accepted her handshake. He held her hand too long, but even knowing that, it required a massive effort of will to release her. By Jericho, they should be together, not separated by outdated rules of birth and status.

"Imogen," Stella called again.

"I'm coming," she said.

Caleb watched her hurry toward her cousin.

"Be careful, lad," George said in a low voice beside him.

Heat rose in Caleb's cheeks, although unlike Imogen, he didn't often blush. He kept his eyes on her. "A man can look at a pretty girl," he said, trying to sound careless when careless was the last thing he was.

"Aye, he can look, as long as he knows that's all he's allowed to do. Even then, if the nobs catch him looking too close, he'll find himself in hot water."

Caleb prayed that he'd regained control of his expression. He and Imogen clearly hadn't been clever enough about hiding their attraction. He wasn't surprised, given that he was sure that he lit up like a torch in her presence.

"I'm not..." When he read the pity in George's eyes, the denial died unspoken.

"My house isn't so big that I can miss someone sneaking out before dawn every morning. And don't try and tell me that you're walking around alone, measuring out flower beds. I won't believe it. A man can make out precious little garden design before the sun comes up."

"It's just a bit of a flirtation." Caleb loathed lying to a man who had been so good to him and whose work as a gardener had sparked his own ambitions.

"A man of honor would think twice before he risks a lady's good name for mere amusement." George went on before Caleb could try to defend the indefensible. "Although for your sake, that's a better outcome than if your heart is involved."

He avoided looking at George, just stared blindly in the direction that Imogen had taken. It should seem strange to hear such a practical man talk of hearts. George was big and strong and looked like he could haul an elephant up a mountain.

But living in his house, Caleb had witnessed the love in the family. Anyway, in his experience, all great gardeners were romantics, however gruff their exteriors.

So while Caleb wanted to scoff at the suggestion that his emotions were involved with Imogen, he couldn't quite summon the dismissive words.

When he didn't speak, George went on. His voice echoed the compassion that Caleb saw in his eyes, now he dared to meet the older man's gaze. "If your heart is involved, you're set to have it broken."

"Lady Imogen is—"

"Is not for you. You're not from this country, and I imagine you've been brought up with talk of liberty and equality, and Jack being as good as his master. I don't know how that works – it seems to me that somebody has to be in charge to make sure the whole show doesn't land in the ditch. But that's neither here nor there. Over here, Jack bows his head to his master, and he knows his place, or he pays the price. You're lifting your eyes to a prize that can never be yours. She's an earl's daughter. You work for a living. There's no future for the two of you. She'll marry Lord Halston or some other bigwig, while you're left to lick your wounds and rue your recklessness."

"But—" Caleb began, before George spoke over him.

"Don't look outside your own class, Caleb. The great and the good of England aren't for the likes of us. They're different, and that can make them cruel. I have every respect for his lordship, and I appreciate that he mostly gives me a free hand here at Prestwick. But I'd no more want him falling in love with one of my daughters than I'd want to fill in the three lakes and turn them over to pigsties."

"You're making too much of this."

The words rang false in his ears. He suspected they did in George's, too, because he gave Caleb a sharp look that penetrated beneath unconvincing nonchalance to the hurricane of emotion beneath.

"I hope so, lad, I hope so. You have a brilliant future ahead, if you keep your mind on the job and not on winsome girls who are out of your reach. I'd hate you to ruin all that promise, to no purpose."

"She's going back to Mayfair tomorrow morning." This time, there was no hiding the misery in his voice. Because how was he to manage this affair, now that Imogen left Prestwick? In London, the risks of discovery were so much greater than they were here.

"That's for the best. You're with us all next week and maybe that will convince you that there's nowhere for this dalliance to go. If you had any sense, you'd never have started it."

When George turned away, Caleb thought that he'd reached the end of his lecture. A lecture, to his regret, packed with painful common sense and hard-earned wisdom.

But the man paused before he left. "She might be as pretty as a picture, but she'll end up destroying you if you don't finish things here and now. I'd be sad to see that. You're a good man, Caleb, and a talented landscaper. But even if you become gardener to the king himself, you'll never be good enough for Lord Deerforth's daughter. You're a looby to imagine that you might be. If Lady Imogen doesn't bring you to grief, her father will. And you deserve better. Think on it, lad, while I go and check the men working on the rockery."

"I appreciate your advice, George," Caleb said in a dull voice.

George shot him another of those sharp looks. "See that you heed it."

As George left him alone in the knot garden, Caleb's heart was heavy. Nothing he'd heard came as news. He'd said most of it to himself at one stage or another, especially in the early days of his romance.

But what was he to do now, when he was so deeply in love that he was likely to drown?

It was too late for caution. All he could do was follow his fate to its end and pray that the voyage didn't leave him wrecked on a desolate shore.

CHAPTER ELEVEN

It felt odd to return to London and find the place exactly the same. Busy with parties and gossip and scandal. Nothing in Town had changed, yet Imogen felt like she'd lived through an entire lifetime since she'd left Lorimer Square almost a week ago.

She was now betrothed to Caleb. She loved and was loved in return. She knew how it felt to kiss a man until she floated free of earth and up to the stars. She'd become acquainted with physical desire, too, and widened her repertoire of sin.

It was all terribly shocking. Even more shocking, because so much of what she'd done with Caleb had seemed so natural, even as it astonished her. Perhaps most shocking of all: more than anything she wanted to be alone again with Caleb, so he could lure her further down the path to ruin.

The descent into damnation was so thrilling. The angels would despair of her.

Worse than the angels, her father would have an apoplexy, if he guessed what she'd been up to. The thought of his explosive temper blunted the pleasurable edge to her musings as she strolled through Hyde Park with the Bilsons.

She and Stella had arrived back in Town yesterday, after a very quiet trip up from the country. Both of them had been nursing aching hearts, and both had been tired, not only from the house party, but also from their extracurricular activities. Imogen had slept most of the way. Stella said she had, too, but Imogen suspected that she'd spent the journey tormenting herself instead.

The fateful visit to Prestwick Place had also changed her relationship with her cousin. Even amidst Imogen's obsession with Caleb, she couldn't help but feel terrible that Stella's passionate affair with Lord Halston had ended. Her cousin knew that keeping the liaison secret in Town would be impossible, and she'd broken the connection.

That severing of relations had left Stella almost catatonic with grief. It had also chased her lovely cousin back into looking as dreary as a November sky. At Prestwick Place, she hadn't hidden her natural vitality.

To Imogen's eyes, Stella had always seemed to play a part as a downtrodden governess, like a princess in disguise. But the woman who now drifted around the Lorimer Square house was beige all over, as if the life had been sucked out of her. A couple of times, Imogen had broached the subject of Halston, but Stella was still too lost in her sorrow to want to talk.

Imogen could imagine how desolate she'd feel if she could never be with Caleb again, and her cousin and Lord Halston had taken things much further than she had. It was frightening to witness Stella's misery. Frightening, and also bracing. Imogen swore that she wouldn't let anything come between her and Caleb. Whatever it cost her. Real love was worth any sacrifice.

Caleb remained in Buckinghamshire another week. Already she missed him like the dickens.

What were they to do? Where were they to go? She didn't even know how to contact him. She couldn't trust Nancy, her maid, to carry a letter without betraying her to Papa.

Her only certainty of seeing Caleb was the Tierney ball at the end of next week. Everything that she was engaged to do in the interim seemed pointless. Tonight she attended the Pollock ball. She'd much rather stay home and read a good book.

Luckily today in this talkative group, Imogen's distraction didn't cause comment. Harriet might have noticed, but Harriet wasn't here. At Prestwick Place, the coldness between them had faded, but Imogen shrank from confiding in her best friend. Partly because things with Caleb had reached such a pass that a full confession would horrify Harriet.

Heavens above, what she'd done would have horrified her, too, mere weeks ago.

"There's your brother, Imogen," Lily said. "Goodness me, what a stylish rig. Those horses are the last word."

"Don't point, Lily," her mother said sharply. "It's common."

Imogen stopped woolgathering to see Eliot bowling along in a new carriage with a spectacular pair of gray thoroughbreds in the shafts. He must have been shopping while she was away, and what superb purchases he'd made. Even from a distance, it was clear that his new horses were the best in the park – and the park contained some of the finest bloodstock in England. Not to mention that stylish yellow curricle was right up to the minute.

Her brother had a reputation for dignity and always doing the right thing. Imogen loved him dearly and recognized that there was more to Eliot than his pristine reputation might suggest. But even she would never have called him dashing.

Until now. Handling the ribbons with such panache and dressed in a smart bottle-green coat and biscuit pantaloons, dashing was the only word she could come up with to describe him.

"I'm sorry, Mamma," Lily said. "But Lord Colville looks so handsome."

Imogen spared Lily a curious glance. Had her friend developed a *tendre* for her golden-haired brother? Her immediate reaction was to scoff. Then with a shock, she realized that Lily Bilson was just the sort of girl her brother was likely to marry. Pretty. Virginal. Well-bred. Rich. She wasn't even a complete nitwit, despite Ivor's fond if disdainful description of her intelligence. Most of her gaffes originated in naivety rather than stupidity.

Lily's mother was still nagging her. "It's also common to show particular preference for a gentleman."

"But if she doesn't show her preference, how is the gentleman to know that a girl likes him?" Lily asked with what struck Imogen as both unusual spirit and some justification.

"It's not a young lady's place to like a gentleman until he's proposed and she's preparing to spend her life with him."

Imogen smothered a giggle when Lily rolled her eyes at her behind her mother's back. Lily was finding her feet in London at last. She might even be able to meet Caleb without shaking in her shoes.

As Eliot steered toward them, Imogen noticed a slew of admiring glances cast in his direction. He usually played down his good looks, and focused his attention on his parliamentary career instead of acting the beau. Imogen found his friends dull and rather starchy. This season, because of her debut, he'd attended more events than usual. As a habit, though, he avoided fashionable hour in Hyde Park.

But it was a perfect spring day, and he wanted to show off those horses. She could see why he was out and about.

Last night he'd dined with her and Stella. Papa had been out somewhere, which was a relief. He dominated any gathering and was inclined to lecture Eliot and put Stella down. As it was, Imogen had carried most of the conversation. Stella had been monosyllabic, and she looked like she'd spent the day crying. Eliot, too, had been distracted. The striking man attracting the ton's approval this afternoon seemed like a different person.

"Good afternoon, Mr. and Mrs. Bilson, Miss Bilson." He tipped his hat to them. Imogen noticed that it was set at a more rakish angle, too. "Imogen, have you settled back into Town?"

"I'd rather be at Prestwick Place." She smiled at Eliot, even as she couldn't help acknowledging the truth of that remark. "The gardens are so magnificent."

It was Eliot's turn to roll his eyes, which made Lily giggle. A giggle that earned her another disapproving glare from her mamma.

"First-class rig, Colville," Mr. Bilson said, and Imogen heard envy as well as appreciation in the older man's voice. "If I'd known those nags were for sale at Tattersall's, I'd have bid on them. I fancy a high-perch phaeton, and they're just the thing to pull it."

"Herbert, you're too old and fat for a sporting carriage," Mrs. Bilson said in a flat tone. "Don't be absurd."

Mr. Bilson flushed with humiliation at the insensitive comment. Imogen couldn't help but feel sorry for him. His wife ruled the roost in their family, and she wasn't the kindest of women.

"Would you like to come up beside me and see how these cattle handle, sis?" Eliot asked.

"I'd love that." She stepped forward and extended her hand so her brother could help her into the seat.

Eliot raised his hat to the Bilsons once more. "I'll bring her back in a few minutes."

He urged the grays to a high-stepping trot. Imogen caught a glimpse of Lily looking disappointed that there had been no invitation for her to ride with the handsome viscount.

It appeared that her friend had set her heart on Eliot. Imogen wasn't sure what she thought about that. Although Eliot had danced with Lily several times, he hadn't shown her any special favor. If Lily caught Viscount Colville, society would call it a triumph. And at least Lily, unlike her mamma, was kind.

"They're topping horses," Imogen said. "If you're not careful, people will guess that there's more to you than good manners and political nous."

Eliot turned to her, his glance unreadable. "It's about time they did. I'm rather tired of the ton treating me like I'm old before my time."

The intensity of his tone surprised Imogen. "Do they?"

"Yes," he bit off between straight white teeth. "I'm starting to find that my sterling reputation is more a burden than a pleasure."

"But you need a good reputation if you hope to become prime minister. Or at least that's what Papa says."

"Papa can go to the devil."

Imogen's eyes rounded, and she took a moment to study her brother. There were nine years between them. She'd always realized that however much she loved him, she'd never really had a chance to know him.

Until now.

Or perhaps her recent experience with profound emotion allowed her to look at the brother she'd always imagined certain of his path, and see signs of long-term discontent. Eliot, she realized with a surprise, wasn't a happy man. The weight of parental and societal expectations was onerous.

When she'd arrived in London, she'd viewed the world in simple, selfish, and optimistic terms that now struck her as fatally childish. She'd led a blessed life that had largely worked to her advantage.

Since then, she'd fallen in love with a man her father would scorn, and Stella, her proper governess, had turned out not to be proper at all. Now Imogen discovered that her paragon of a big brother wasn't content with his pristine reputation.

Imogen was so caught up in these not altogether welcome ponderings, that she didn't realize Eliot was directing the carriage with some purpose. She didn't notice that they drove toward a high-perch phaeton of the kind that Mr. Bilson had thwarted ambitions to drive, until they were almost upon the stylish carriage. Even more astonishing, the people in the phaeton weren't at all Eliot's usual company of punctilious, unexceptionable fellows with ambitions to run the country.

Instead, they were two of society's less respectable members. The acknowledged rake Lord Shelburn, who had a reputation with the ladies to rival Lord Halston's. And even more scandalous, the wildest woman in London. Or at least the wildest woman who was still considered good enough ton to attend society events.

Imogen had heard so much about Lady Verena Gerard, which was another thing that her father wouldn't like. But how could she help but be aware of the dazzling widow? Gossip buzzed about the duke's daughter who claimed the freedom of a man: taking and discarding lovers; bowing to nobody's authority but her own; breaking every rule without giving a fig for public opinion.

Papa despised her because he thought that she was a wanton. Even more, Imogen suspected that he couldn't bear to see a woman living life on her own terms without submitting to male suzerainty.

"Lady Verena, Lord Shelburn." Eliot doffed his hat and bowed with a style that startled Imogen. "The park is busy this afternoon. The fine weather must have brought everyone out to enjoy the sun."

"No doubt." Those two simple words in Lord Shelburn's lazy drawl expressed a world of insolence. Imogen gained the impression that Shelburn and Eliot weren't exactly friends, which made this encounter even more perplexing.

Unless...

Imogen's curious gaze settled on the lady sitting beside Shelburn in the elegant carriage. The shocking, scandalous, wicked lady with her beautiful, cynical face and her lush body.

A pair of intelligent brown eyes surveyed Imogen in turn. Their expression wasn't exactly friendly, but not hostile either. Perhaps watchful was the best description that she could think of. Although why Lady Verena should be wary of a girl just up from the country, she couldn't imagine.

Imogen had seen Lady Verena several times from a distance and thought her dauntingly sophisticated. Now she was close, the notorious widow's loveliness took her breath away.

With every second, an impossible idea gained purchase in her reeling mind. The impossible, disastrous, inevitable thought. The thought that would crush Lily Bilson's romantic pretensions to rubble.

Because however suitable Lily might be as his viscountess, it turned out that her brother had his sights pinned on a most unsuitable lady to fill that position. The last woman Imogen had ever imagined that her saintly brother would set his heart on.

Wondering, puzzled, Imogen glanced back at her brother. He was doing his best to hide his turmoil, but he wasn't succeeding.

Good heavens, Eliot was in love with Lady Verena Gerard. If Papa got wind of this development, he'd explode like a volcano. Eliot was in line to inherit the Deerforth title. Papa took great pride in his lineage. He'd abhor the thought of an unchaste woman darkening the family escutcheon.

Abhor? He'd be absolutely livid.

When Eliot spoke, his tone was as smooth and polite as ever. Or almost so. "Lady Verena, may I present my sister, Lady Imogen Ridley, who is enjoying her first season in London?"

In response to Eliot's polite request, Lady Verena nodded at Imogen. "I'd be delighted to make her acquaintance."

With a guarded smile, Eliot turned to Imogen. He would know that he risked a scandal just by bringing his innocent sister to Lady Verena's notice. That alone spoke to the power of his emotions. "Imogen, this is Lady Verena Gerard, who is one of society's brightest ornaments."

Yes, he was definitely in love with her. And that fact threatened to place all his political hopes out of reach. When Papa learned about this meeting, he'd froth at the mouth.

Imogen could already see heads turning in their direction. The way talk spread through society, Papa would probably hear about this improper introduction before Imogen got home from the park.

"Good afternoon, Lady Imogen," Lady Verena said. "I hope you're enjoying your time in London."

Imogen struggled to keep all these bewildering revelations to herself. "Good afternoon, Lady Verena. Good afternoon, Lord Shelburn." She already knew Shelburn. They'd danced together several times. "Thank you for asking, my lady. It's all been so exciting. Not a bit like Gloucestershire."

It struck her as unfair that a lady who kicked over the traces attracted such opprobrium, while a man with a bad reputation was welcome wherever he went. Shelburn was considered a catch on the marriage mart. Not that he showed any sign of seeking a bride.

Imogen went on, even as the taut atmosphere made her skin itch. She was amazed to notice that while Eliot might be burningly conscious of Lady Verena, Lady Verena was at least as conscious of him. How fascinating. On the surface, one couldn't imagine two people with less in common.

"I'm sure," Lady Verena responded with a wryness that Imogen liked. "I hear you've just come back from Buckinghamshire."

"That was exciting, too." Nobody except Imogen and Caleb knew just how exciting.

It suddenly struck her that all three of Papa's nearest relations pursued secret lives. Imogen with Caleb, Stella with Halston, and Eliot with Verena. "Lord Halston was a wonderful host, and Prestwick Place is quite magnificent. Do you know it?"

"Yes, I've been there several times. The grounds are glorious."

Next to Imogen, Eliot gave a theatrical groan. "Don't mention the grounds, my lady. Imogen has been waxing lyrical about terracing and water features since she came back to Town yesterday. If she gets started now, we'll be here until next week."

Imogen cast her brother an unimpressed look. She was used to his teasing.

"I'm sure you exaggerate," Lady Verena said.

That derisive snort was an unsuitable response from a correctly behaved debutante. But then, Imogen wasn't a correctly behaved debutante. "I'm sure he doesn't, my lady."

Lord Shelburn observed his companions with a sardonic expression. Now he laughed. "Talking about gardens would make a nice change. The last young miss I danced with entertained me with a long discussion about lace on bonnets."

Lady Verena's glance was disapproving, as if she couldn't commend the unkindness in his remark. With that, Imogen decided that she liked this unconventional woman who had gained her brother's love. The outlandish stories about Lady Verena had led Imogen to expect someone hard and brash and licentious. That wasn't what she found.

Lady Verena spoke. "I hope we can discuss Prestwick Place on some other occasion. I see Lady Edgecombe over there, and I have something particular to say to her."

Imogen sat close enough to Eliot on the narrow seat to feel him bristle, the way her collie used to bristle when another dog intruded on his territory. Then Imogen noticed that Lady Verena clung tight to Shelburn's arm.

The grays shifted, sick of standing still so long. Or perhaps because of a change in tension on the reins. Eliot's bow was stiff. "I'll see you tonight at the Pollock ball. Perhaps you'll keep me a waltz."

For a betraying moment, Verena's face froze. Imogen caught a flare of powerful but indescribable emotion in her fine eyes, before she adopted an expression of polite regret. "I'm sorry. I'm otherwise engaged this evening, my lord."

"What a pity," Eliot responded with an urbanity that struck Imogen as just as false as Lady Verena's regret. "Some other time?"

"Perhaps." Lady Verena's expression softened as she glanced at Imogen. "A pleasure to see you, Lady Imogen."

Once, Imogen might have peppered Eliot with questions as he drove her back toward the Bilsons, who stood under the trees talking to the Tierneys. The subject of their conversation, she guessed, was Eliot's shocking and uncharacteristic action in introducing his sister to a woman infamous for her profligacy.

Curiosity gnawed at her. She wanted to quiz him about his relationship with Lady Verena. But something about the line of his jaw warned her to stay silent.

Eliot was entitled to his secrets. After all, didn't she have secrets of her own?

Because Imogen had to rush to prepare for the Pollock ball when she returned from the park, she escaped a scolding from her father about unwise associations. The next morning, she wasn't so lucky.

She and Stella loitered in the sunny morning room after a late breakfast. Both of them looked heavy-eyed. Stella in fact looked more than heavy-eyed, she looked ashen and dismal.

It was hard to believe that this was the glowing, sensual creature Imogen had caught returning from her lover's arms at Prestwick Place. While last night's ball had been the usual crush, Lord Halston hadn't been there. After his guests left, he'd remained behind on his estate for a few days.

Imogen wondered if he missed Stella anything like the way that she missed him. Imogen hoped so. Her cousin mightn't be in line to become the next Countess of Halston, but she deserved better than for his lordship to treat her like a passing fancy.

Imogen had her own longings to contend with. The need to be with Caleb was a constant itch. Their meetings at Prestwick Place had been wonderful, but always too short. Now, back in London, she faced yet another day without seeing Caleb at all. That turned the lovely spring sunshine to dull gray.

She made a show of writing letters at the pretty satinwood desk in the corner, but the truth was that she daydreamed about Caleb's kisses and hearing him say that he loved her.

"Get out."

At the sound of her father's voice, Imogen stiffened and turned. She couldn't say that she was pleased to see him. Right now, nothing that he wanted to talk to her about meshed with her inclinations.

Nor did she like how he spoke to Stella. For a long time, she'd noted his rudeness, but it struck with particular harshness when her cousin was in such a low state.

Not that Deerforth noticed Stella's distress, which was probably a good thing. He was oblivious to emotional undercurrents. Imogen hid a wince, as she wondered if Harriet had been telling her that she was too much like her father.

"Yes, my lord," Stella said in a toneless voice, rising from her chair and curtsying before scuttling out. She rarely called Deerforth uncle, and suddenly that struck Imogen as wrong. Stella was his sister's daughter. Deerforth owed her much more respect than he ever paid her.

"Good morning, Papa." Imogen rose and crossed to kiss his cheek. She was the only person permitted such liberties. No wonder she was spoiled. "I hope you're well."

"Good morning, Imogen. I'd like to say I'm well, but I'm seriously displeased."

That answer was no surprise. His face was ruddy, and his small mouth was pinched with temper. More than ever, he looked like Henry VIII in a huff.

For one frightful second, the alarming thought crossed Imogen's mind that somehow he'd discovered her meetings with Caleb. Then she looked more closely and sucked in a breath of relief.

Over the years, she'd become an expert on her father's tantrums. If Papa thought that she'd been conducting an illicit flirtation with the Tierneys' garden designer, he'd be incandescent with rage. He was seething about something, but it was at one remove from Imogen herself, thank heaven.

"I'm sorry to hear that," she said, guessing what this was about. She sank into the chair that Stella had vacated and prepared for a tirade.

"It has come to my notice that your idiot brother has been careless with your reputation. I intend to reprimand him most strongly on the issue."

Yes, she was right about the cause of her father's anger. Eliot and her father had a difficult relationship at the best of times. It had become even more fraught since Eliot and Imogen's godmother had left them both a large share of her fortune. Imogen had to wait until she was twenty-five to gain access to her inheritance, but Eliot had used the money to establish a life separate from his overbearing father.

In his understated way, Eliot had always carved out a certain amount of independence. Now that he had a generous income of his own, he didn't have much to do with the family.

Eliot's rebellion infuriated Lord Deerforth, but there was little that he could do to bring his son to heel. The title fell as a matter of course to the oldest son, and most of the estate was entailed, so disinheritance wasn't much of a threat.

"I'm sure Eliot only does what he thinks best." Imogen knew, even as she said it, that her father would pay no attention.

Papa's eyebrows crunched together in a fearsome scowl. "You give him too much credit, my girl. You're too young and inexperienced to understand that a lady's good name is fragile. That's to your credit. But I won't sit by and allow your brother's unconscionable behavior to besmirch your reputation."

"I'm sure he didn't do—"

Her father spoke over her, as he was wont to do. "Part of that good reputation is founded on the company a lady keeps. So imagine my horror when Lady Pollock informed me last night that your muttonheaded brother had forced you to speak to that wanton harpy Verena Granger."

"Lady Verena was very gracious." Most of the time, Imogen accepted her father's scoldings without argument, but today something inside her rose in revolt and made her want to defend the woman Eliot loved.

As she should have expected, she wasted her breath. Her father went on in the hectoring tone that always made Imogen feel the size of an ant. "Poison always tastes sweet at first."

As a gardener, Imogen had her doubts about that, but this time, she remained silent.

"You must promise me that you will never again associate with that woman. You will never acknowledge her existence. You will act as if the introduction didn't take place, because if that damned pup of mine had an ounce of common sense, it wouldn't have. She's a soul-devouring witch, who would like nothing better than to drag a decent lady's name through the mud. She wants company in her degradation."

Imogen couldn't imagine that was the case. "But, Papa—"

Her father raised his hand. "Already I can see the rot is setting in. You will obey me on this, Imogen. I will not hear one word of protest. Verena Granger is a whited sepulchre, beauty on the outside, but death and decay within." Her father always turned all fire and brimstone when he was exercised about something. Lady Verena clearly had him exercised. "I can't expect you to understand, but I expect you to bow to my wisdom on this matter."

"Yes, Papa," she said, glad that at least she'd escaped giving her oath to shun Verena. But by heaven, if by any chance, Eliot and Verena wed, there would be trouble in the family like never before.

"You are to take special care just now, Imogen. The moment is critical. One false move, and we could lose everything we hope for."

Actually, Imogen agreed with her father that her whole future hung in the balance, but she doubted very much that they wanted the same thing. "I'm always careful, Papa," she said with a show of meekness that would have Stella rolling her eyes. Especially as the statement was far from true.

Everybody wanted girls to be careful and sweet and biddable. The problem with that situation was that all the really interesting stuff happened when a girl dared to overstep the barriers of duty and society. Goodness, if she hadn't taken a risk at the Lumsden ball and sneaked out to the gazebo, she'd never have met Caleb.

The thought of her life without him sent a chill rippling down her spine. She'd never have married Lord Chippenham, no matter how her father nagged, and Lord Halston wasn't interested in courting her, despite Papa's unrealistic hopes.

But she probably would have accepted someone like Ivor Bilson or Anthony Comerford, consigning her to a dull, predictable existence. Whereas every moment with Caleb was an adventure.

Papa didn't approve of women with a taste for adventure. The contempt in his voice when he mentioned Lady Verena was proof of that.

The self-righteous rage drained from her father's face. "Yes, you're always careful." Confirmation enough of how little her father knew her. "Several people at the Pollock ball last night told me how Halston paid you particular attention at the house party."

Imogen frowned. Knowing that she wasted her time – her father was impossible to convince otherwise, once he fixed an idea in his head – she spoke up. "I really don't think he did."

"He danced with you, didn't he?"

"No more than he danced with Lily or Harriet or Elizabeth." And all that, she now knew, was to hide his interest in Stella. Her father hurtled toward disappointment, if he imagined that the wealthy earl planned to court any of the season's debutantes.

Disquiet knotted her stomach. Her father was terrifying when he was disappointed.

The patronizing smile that greeted her statement made her cringe. "It's a credit to your modesty that you believe that, Imogen. But I hear he went out of his way to make sure that you saw the grounds of Prestwick Place."

"Yes, he did, but—"

"Why else would he do that, unless he planned to make you the chatelaine of his estate?"

"I told him I was interested in gardens. He was just being kind."

Her father's glance was pitying. "Men like Halston are rarely kind, unless they want something in return."

What a ruthless view her father took of life. Imogen knew it reflected his stony heart. She couldn't contain another premonitory chill, as she imagined how he'd react if his daughter ceased being of use and pursued her own agenda.

She'd always known that her association with Caleb put her very pleasant life at risk. But only now did she realize that the choice she made was stark and permanent. If she threw in her lot with Caleb, she'd be dead to her father. There would be no reconciliation ever. She'd be cast adrift upon the world with only her love and her wits to support her.

Her love, her wits, and in a couple of years, her inheritance from her godmother. But right now, that thought provided little comfort.

It would be bad enough when Halston didn't offer for her. And she knew for a fact that no such offer was coming. Stella had told her that Lord Halston had no interest in Imogen, apart from as a way to get to her governess. Imogen believed her.

Her lips felt like they were made of wood when she responded. "I don't wish to marry an unkind man."

Her father subjected her to another of those patronizing smiles that made her want to stamp her foot in protest. When that would only confirm her father's opinion that she was a brainless little flibbertigibbet. "He'd never be unkind to you. He'd respect you as his wife."

Imogen had seen enough of the world to know that a wife wasn't guaranteed either her husband's esteem or his care. But then her father was more concerned with access to Halston's power and influence than he was with Imogen's happiness. She'd always known that.

"Yes, Papa," she said with manufactured docility, while rebellion rioted in her soul.

That earned an undeserved nod of approval. "I'm expecting Lord Halston to ask for your hand soon, perhaps even this week when he returns from the country. Most probably, he's remained behind to settle a few things on his estate in preparation for bringing back a bride. But until you're wed, I want you to be additionally cautious not to attract any untoward notice. It would be the outside of enough if unfortunate gossip marred your chances at this juncture. I'm just hoping your meeting with that highborn slut doesn't cause his lordship to question his choice."

"Lord Halston doesn't seem high in the instep, Papa."

Her father's indulgent expression only made her more irritable. "Every man is high in the instep when it comes to choosing a wife, kitten. But if you steer clear of trouble over the next few weeks, we should sail through. His lordship is smart enough to understand that the inappropriate behavior was your brother's, not yours. In fact, your biddability may even recommend you. It's clear that you need a strong, steering hand to find your way in the world. After all, female weakness is hardly a mystery to his lordship."

Imogen struggled to stay silent, as the urge rose to hit her father with the silver inkwell.

CHAPTER TWELVE

$\mathcal{B}$y the time Imogen attended Elizabeth Tierney's coming-out ball, her longing for Caleb had reached an excruciating pitch. It was over a week since their last hurried moments together in Lord Halston's summerhouse. Since then, she hadn't heard a word from him. Not a rendezvous at a party. Not a note. Not even a sighting at the Tierneys' house in Lorimer Square.

Had he changed his mind about loving her? Did he regret his proposal? She dearly wanted to trust him, but every empty day widened the gap between them.

Not even the discovery that Lord Tierney had sent Caleb to Cumbria to make some adjustments to his designs for the garden reassured her. The only things that could console her were Caleb's arms around her and his voice in her ear, whispering his eternal devotion.

Because Stella was so sunk in grief, Imogen's uncharacteristic fit of the megrims didn't spark her cousin's curiosity. Lord Halston had returned to Town, but mostly avoided ton functions. Imogen had glimpsed him a couple of times, but he hadn't danced with her.

Everyone in the Ridley family was out of sorts. Her father and Eliot had had an almighty row about Lady Verena. Now Eliot had left London for the Wiltshire estate that he'd inherited from his godmother.

Imogen hoped that Eliot won his battle for his lady, but she wasn't optimistic. The tattle was that Lady Verena's first marriage had been a disaster, and she was determined never to wed again. So even if Eliot decided to sacrifice his political hopes and break with his powerful father, he still needed to persuade Lady Verena to accept any proposal.

Imogen was more convinced than ever that her brother was in love. If that was the case, marriage would be his goal. He wasn't a fickle man, and a passing affair wouldn't satisfy him.

Stella was just as deeply in love – and her chances of happiness with Lord Halston looked even more impossible than Eliot and Verena's. Real love seemed to bring as much pain as joy.

Halston was at the ball tonight. He'd requested a contredanse and the supper dance as well, so Imogen would have to do her best to pretend that she didn't know about him and Stella. She started to feel like she kept too many secrets.

At least her father wasn't here. Instead, he attended some political dinner in Belgravia. She disliked his avid interest in whether Lord Halston singled her out for special attention. A girl was only permitted two dances with any partner, so at least Papa wouldn't harangue her tomorrow about neglecting the earl.

Stella was delegated to sitting with the chaperones again. For the few days at Prestwick

Place, she'd joined the company as befitted her birth, but that ended back in London.

Lady Verena was here, too, sparkling and flirting with Lord Shelburn. If she missed Eliot, it didn't show.

Poor Eliot. Poor Stella.

And while she did her best to act as if she enjoyed nothing in the world more than her good friend's party, she couldn't help adding poor Imogen to that list.

She'd arrived at the ball wearing her favorite new dress, a spangled white sarsenet in the latest style. She was in a lather of expectation that at last she'd see Caleb. Not only see him, but for the first time, they'd dance together. She'd saved both waltzes, although even she wouldn't dare to devote two dances to the Tierneys' garden designer. Which was ironic, given that she looked forward to devoting the rest of her life to him.

That was if he still wanted to marry her.

She'd imagined that if he cared, he'd be just as eager to see her. But so far, although she studied the crowd the way she'd once studied the book about Prestwick Place, there was no sign of him.

She wanted to ask Elizabeth about Caleb. But Elizabeth, pretty in sky blue, was the center of attention and besieged by partners. Right now, she was incandescent with excitement as she danced with Lord Halston. And why not? The ball was a triumph.

The time approached for the first waltz. Several gentlemen had invited Imogen to partner them, but she'd put them off in the hope that Caleb might arrive. If he didn't, she'd have to hide in the retiring room to save causing offense.

Although if Caleb wasn't going to appear, she'd rather go home and sob into her pillow. She could imagine how her father would react to that! It became more and more of an effort to pretend that she was having a wonderful time, when a great clump of sour disappointment settled in her stomach.

Why aren't you here, Caleb? Don't you want me anymore?

Ivor Bilson glanced back at her with a smile as he held her hand in the circle of the *boulanger*. "Can you spare me another dance after supper, Lady Imogen?"

She smiled, even as she feared that it looked like a rictus grin. She liked Ivor. He wasn't the cleverest man in London, but he had a good heart and even better, he didn't want to marry her.

She tried to sound enthusiastic. "That would be lovely."

"Capital. This is a topping party. I hear Lady Tierney hired the orchestra from Paris."

"Did she?" Elizabeth had told her this weeks ago, and so had all Imogen's dance partners. Every time, she'd expressed pleased surprise. "They're very good."

"She'll set a fashion. The London fiddlers will riot for lack of work, I vow."

Imogen wasn't too concerned about the city's musicians. The Tierneys were fabulously wealthy. They'd spared no expense to ensure that Elizabeth's ball counted among the most talked-about events of the season. Imogen doubted that many other hostesses would invest in importing an orchestra, when perfectly adequate ensembles already existed in London.

The Tierneys were spending to impress on their Cumbria property, too. Caleb had told her about his lordship's plans. They were grand – and sure to cost a fortune. The contract was a huge coup for Black &

Sons. Perhaps Caleb had thought better of jeopardizing that project through his unwise association with Lord Deerforth's daughter.

Her heart, already weighted down with Caleb's absence, cramped a little more. She couldn't blame him for choosing prudence and prosperity over romance. But nor could she contain her flaring pain, as she struggled to come to terms with a future that contained no more of Caleb and his kisses.

Ivor was still talking. She nodded and murmured and somehow managed to follow the dance steps, but she was scarcely aware of where she was. Instead, a vast emptiness opened up before her, as she wondered how she'd get through the rest of her life.

First, she had to get through the rest of this dreadful evening. At least without bursting into tears. If she broke down, she'd attract all the gossip that she'd done her best to avoid.

If Stella felt like this, her cousin was wretched indeed.

Imogen stared blindly ahead, as Ivor swung her across the circle. Then she realized that she was looking at a tall man with dark hair who stood beside Lord Tierney.

A tall man in perfect black and white evening dress, who appeared familiar – and beloved.

Her heart, so shrunk and aching only a second ago, swelled to the size of a pumpkin. He was here. He was here! She made a faint sound of pleasure and missed her step.

"Lady Imogen, are you all right?"

Ivor's concerned question wrenched her back to reality and reminded her that if she followed her natural inclinations and flew across the room to Caleb's side, the game would be up. Not to mention any hope of having a life with him.

Still, it took far too much effort to drag her gaze away from Caleb and meet her partner's eyes. Her face must be as red as a radish. With luck, Ivor would blame her fluster on embarrassment at the stumble.

"I'm sorry. I lost my concentration for a moment." Because the sight of the man she loved, when she'd given up all hope of him, sent her quite demented.

"Never mind. It can happen to anyone. Good heavens, I was a clodhopper when I learned to dance. None of the girls wanted to be my partner, so poor Lily was stuck with me. I don't think she's forgiven me yet for how I bruised her poor feet."

Imogen summoned a smile, thinking not for the first time, how kind Ivor was. And also an excellent dancer. She couldn't believe that story about Lily was true. He only told it to make her feel better. "Now I've walked all over your toes. I'm sorry."

"Didn't even notice," he said gallantly. "You're light as thistledown, my lady."

Imogen laughed at that. Not to mention that she most definitely wasn't as light as thistledown. Her recent dejection had driven her to seek comfort from the bonbon box. "You're a nice man, Ivor."

It was his turn to blush. "Not at all."

With his usual skill, he guided her through the last few sets of the dance, then brought her across to his parents. The first waltz was next. Would Caleb dare to approach? She was too aware of the curious crowd to check if he was looking at her.

The last time they'd met – which felt like a hundred years ago – she'd told him that she'd keep a waltz for him. Would he remember?

She had one chance to dance with Caleb. Even that might put the high sticklers into a flap. So she wanted it to be a dance where she didn't have to change partners, and they'd share a few private words. And he'd touch her. The need to feel his hands on her was like physical pain.

"Are you engaged for this waltz, Lady Imogen?" Ivor asked. "If you can bear my inept partnering again, I'd be delighted to take you onto the floor."

Lily and Anthony Comerford had already moved into position. A quick glance around the ballroom revealed that Lord Halston had disappeared. Perhaps he'd left. At the few events that he'd attended since he'd returned to Town, he hadn't lingered.

"Thank you, Ivor, but your toes are safe."

"Lady Imogen was kind enough to grant me this waltz," a deep voice with an intriguing accent said from behind her.

Yes. Yes. Yes. Yes.

Struggling to hide her jubilation, Imogen turned and extended her gloved hand. "Mr. Black, shall we?"

Her heart pounded so hard that she had difficulty speaking. She directed her gaze past his shoulder, because she feared that if she met his bright eyes, everyone would guess how much she loved this superb but woefully unsuitable man.

He took her hand and tucked it into his crooked elbow. "With pleasure."

His touch, even through her glove, made her blood surge. Nothing but Caleb existed in this crowded ballroom. As she clutched at him, she felt quite giddy.

"I thought you weren't coming," Imogen muttered under her breath. The music would cover her whisper from anyone inclined to listen.

His quick glance seared like fire. "The carriage lost a wheel on the way south. I nearly didn't make it."

"That's terrible." She faltered and couldn't help stealing a quick look at his face. "Are you all right?"

"A bit knocked around, but nothing short of death could stop me from dancing with you. We've never danced together before, you know."

"I know." Caution made her look away, although she longed to stare at him and let his presence soak into her bones.

Her dazed gaze roamed across the ballroom. Nobody seemed to pay her undue attention, thank heaven. She supposed most people here wouldn't know that Caleb worked for Lord Tierney. As her attention fell on the chaperones sitting along the wall, she wondered whether Stella might guess something out of the ordinary took place.

But Stella's chair was empty.

"Dear God, I've missed you, Imogen." His voice vibrated with urgent emotion.

Releasing his arm, she turned to face him and allowed herself to meet his eyes for a blazing second. The heat there made her tremble. It was as powerful as a kiss. It said all the things that they could never speak in public. Her idiotic insecurities disappeared as if they'd never existed. Caleb still loved her. Of course he did.

"For heaven's sake, don't look at me like that," she hissed. "We're supposed to be strangers."

"You're the other half of my soul," he murmured, even as he masked his intense expression.

The difficulty now was hiding her own reaction to his impassioned statement. Imogen wanted to fling herself into his arms and beg him to make her his. She wanted...*him*.

Throughout his absence, she'd languished with loneliness. Now, his company, much as she gloried in it, left her aching with frustration. She chafed at having to conceal her love.

But however much she might kick against the restrictions, she retained some grip on reality. Now that society saw her with Caleb, she needed to be more careful than ever. She prayed that any onlooker would observe nothing more momentous than a handsome young man partnering one of the popular debutantes.

The musical introduction reached its end. The waltz was everyone's favorite dance, so the floor around them was crowded. Under the beau monde's sharp, uncharitable gaze, it would be so easy to spark a scandal.

Caleb set his impressive jaw, and a muscle flickered in his cheek. He slid his hand around her waist and despite her counsel to be careful, she couldn't contain an incoherent murmur of pleasure. She bent forward, then made herself pull back.

Since she'd left him over a week ago, everything had been wrong and out of tune and irritating. With her beloved far away, the mere act of breathing had jarred. Just having him here, whatever the peril, smoothed away all those rough edges.

His lips curved in an exultant smile, as he began to move to the music. "Now you should stop looking at me like that."

The physical compatibility that they'd always shared translated to the dance floor. As Caleb whirled her around in graceful circles, her feet seemed to fly an inch above the ground.

A giggle escaped. "I should take my own advice. But it's so long since I saw you."

That was the alchemy of love, she supposed. Once upon a time, a week had passed quickly, day following day in a flurry of activity. But every minute without Caleb extended for an hour, every day a month. Now that they were together, the seconds raced away faster than the latest Derby winner. She struggled not to spoil her current happiness with dwelling on how fleeting this meeting must be.

"I know," he said with such emphasis that she laughed again. He lowered his voice. "We need to find a way to communicate, now we're back in London. It's not enough to hope that Elizabeth will mention where I am or what she saw you doing the night before."

Imogen frowned, before she recalled the need to pretend that this dance was nothing out of the ordinary. "I don't trust my maid. We can't use her to carry messages."

Not that she could blame Nancy. Like most people in the house, the girl was terrified of Lord Deerforth. She wouldn't risk violence and dismissal, just because Imogen wanted to pursue a forbidden flirtation. On the other hand, Nancy's laziness meant that Imogen had little trouble escaping her observation, so the girl had her uses.

"I checked the garden in the middle of the square. There's a hollow in one of the elms. The one with the burl."

"I know it." Paying attention to growing things was what she did. "We'll have to be careful."

"No names."

"No names. But we can leave a scrap of paper there. It seems mad that we live yards apart, yet it may as well be a hundred miles. Speaking of being apart, you're holding me too close."

He muffled a groan, but retreated a fraction. "One day, I'll dance with you and nobody will raise an eyebrow."

"One day," she said with a hint of wistfulness. "One day, we won't have to leave secret messages for each other."

"One day, I'll show you off to the world as my cherished wife."

"One day," she said in a dejected murmur.

When she'd sneaked out to meet him at Prestwick Place, she'd been optimistic about their chances of success. Now that she was back in London and surrounded by society's glamour and power, she recognized the difficult task ahead of them.

"Chin up, Imogen." Caleb read her darkening mood. He shared it, she guessed. "It's you and me against the world. We'll beat them all. You'll see."

The feet that had seemed as light as air now felt like lead, although fortunately, they kept time to the music. "I hope so."

They danced in fraught silence. They had too much to say and neither time nor seclusion to say any of it.

The waltz approached its end. Which meant that she and Caleb must separate again. She could hardly bear it. She'd longed for this moment to arrive, and now it was nearly over. She'd wasted most of it stewing on their problems, instead of reveling in this chance to feel Caleb's arms around her. It was enough to make her want to wail like a lost soul.

She noticed Elizabeth glancing her way. Or perhaps she checked on Caleb and how he coped in this unfamiliar world. It was enough to remind Imogen to plaster on a carefree smile. She suspected that it was as unconvincing as her attempt to sound as if she believed they'd win through against the forces ranged against them.

"Will you come onto the terrace?" Caleb's voice was low and urgent.

She stared up at him in consternation. "I shouldn't."

His beloved features were sharp with longing. He knew as well as she did that their opportunity to talk and touch and bask in each other's company dwindled with cruel rapidity.

"Just for a minute."

"People will still watch us out there. It's not like the gazebo at the Lumsdens'." She paused. "And the gardens will be crowded. It's a nice night."

The weather had blessed Lady Tierney's ball. Tonight it was warm enough for the air inside to be close and overheated.

"Don't...don't make me let you go yet. Who knows when we'll be together again?"

He sounded on edge and unhappy. However unwise Imogen knew it was to agree, she couldn't resist. Not when she hungered for a moment of what passed for privacy as much as he did.

"Oh, Caleb," she sighed in surrender. She realized that she leaned toward him. Against every female instinct, she straightened. To remind him to keep his distance, she pushed back at the hand upon her waist.

Triumph glittered in his eyes. "You'll come."

"For five minutes, then I need to find my next partner. Nobody can guess that dancing with you is special." So special that the rest of this extravagant evening stretched ahead like a desert.

"Lord Halston?"

She heard a trace of jealousy. If only Caleb knew that Lord Halston had no interest in her. But she couldn't betray Stella's secret, even to him.

"No, Lord Chippenham. Then Anthony Comerford has requested the quadrille."

"He's handsome, too. And rich. And eligible. He's in line to become the Earl of Lumsden, once his father passes away. I've heard Elizabeth talk about him."

Once Imogen had delighted in Caleb's jealousy. No more. "He's like a brother to me. You have no need to worry about him."

"I don't," Caleb said gloomily. "I just hate that these overbred numbskulls have the right to your company when I don't."

The coda had the couples around them turning faster and faster. Caleb paused beside the row of French doors and whisked Imogen outside. She drew in a breath of cool air, tinged with the smoke of London's coal fires.

The night was lit bright by rows of flaming torches and full of watching eyes. She saw Ivor and Harriet, leaning on the parapet above the garden. Harriet glanced up with a quick smile. Then, oh, no, her friend said something to Ivor and they approached.

"I hate that I haven't got you to myself," Caleb growled under his breath. He held her arm with outward propriety. Only Imogen felt the possessive weight of his touch. "This is torture. I want to kiss you."

"I want to kiss you, too, but it could never happen at Elizabeth's coming-out ball."

"I know. But that doesn't stop me wanting."

"No." Her own frustrated longing weighted the short word.

"Imogen—"

"I'll organize something," she responded in a hurried whisper. "I'll leave a note in the tree."

"Isn't this the most marvelous party?" Harriet's enthusiasm grated, when Imogen felt as if she was being ripped apart. "Good evening, Mr. Black. What do you think of your first London ball?"

"It's very festive, and Lady Elizabeth seems to be having a wonderful time." Caleb sounded composed and polite, not at all like the man who had pleaded with Imogen to come outside.

Imogen struggled to remind herself that it worked to her advantage that Harriet and Ivor joined them. If she was with other people, nobody would question the handsome American's presence.

"She looks so pretty in that blue dress, too, like a princess."

One of the things that Imogen had always loved about Harriet was that she didn't have a jealous bone in her body. She talked about her friend's social triumph without a trace of envy.

But then Harriet had grown up with better examples than she had. Harriet's family life was stable and loving. The Comerfords were a happy couple, and they'd raised their children in an atmosphere far removed from the strain and conflict reigning in the Ridley household. Imogen realized that if the life that she created with Caleb reflected the Comerfords', she'd feel she'd succeeded.

"Yes, she does." Imogen tried to sound as if she gave a fig for Elizabeth and her happiness. "Madame Lisette has outdone herself."

She didn't pretend to be nearly as unselfish as Harriet, not now when parting from Caleb would leave her forlorn. Who knew when they'd meet again? And now she must share these last few precious seconds with Harriet and Ivor.

It just wasn't fair.

"You looked very pretty at your ball, too, Lady Harriet," Ivor said with his usual chivalry.

Harriet gave a snort of laughter. "Thank you, but my party was weeks ago. Nobody remembers that."

Imogen couldn't help sharing a quick look with Caleb. As long as she lived, she'd never forget

Harriet's coming-out ball. "It was a great success, too."

"It was a freezing cold night, and everyone was stuck inside," Harriet said in cheerful dismissal.

Not everyone, Imogen couldn't help recalling. As if he had the same thought, Caleb's fingers flexed on her arm.

"Lady Imogen, I beg your pardon, but I have a message for you."

The respectful interruption seemed to emerge from another world. Imogen turned to see a footman bowing and extending a silver salver in her direction.

Caleb let her go. The minute that steady clasp was gone, she missed it. "Oh?"

"I believe it's urgent," the servant said in a low voice.

She frowned, even as she reached for the note and edged closer to the line of torches to read it. Caleb, Ivor and Harriet stepped aside to offer her privacy.

It was from Lord Halston, of all people. Although given what Imogen knew about his lordship's interests, the surprise didn't last long. She raised her head and caught Harriet's curious stare. Out of politeness, the other two pretended not to be interested.

"Stella has been taken ill and has left in our carriage."

Her poor cousin. She'd looked peaky and out of sorts. The separation from her lover affected her more powerfully every day.

"I'm sure Mamma won't mind taking you home with us," Harriet said.

Imogen glanced at Caleb. "I could walk. It's only across the square."

Perhaps Caleb could accompany her, and they'd be together for a few more minutes.

"Lady Imogen, it's not done," Ivor said.

No, it wasn't done. She knew that. This was London, not the country. Even in the country, she wasn't allowed to wander around late at night.

She hid a sigh. She'd been silly to make the suggestion.

Not for the first time, Imogen chafed at the restrictions placed around her, just because she was female. She understood that London was full of unspoken dangers – and plenty of spoken ones, too. But she wasn't talking about flitting around the city on her own. She was prepared to accept an escort.

"It's such a nice night, it seems a pity that we all have to squeeze into a carriage to go a few hundred yards."

"Anthony isn't coming back with us," Harriet said. "He's off to find more exciting company than a crowd of debutantes."

"There you are, Lady Imogen."

It was Lord Chippenham, seeking her out for the next dance. That placed the icing on the rather bitter cake of having to leave Caleb, when she'd said hardly anything to him and she had no idea when she'd see him again.

Dancing with him had been as wonderful as she'd hoped, but it had passed in a flash. She was greedy. She wanted more than just one waltz.

"I needed a breath of air, my lord." Lack of enthusiasm flattened her voice.

In the fire-edged darkness, her eyes met Caleb's and she passed on a silent message of devotion. He answered with an almost imperceptible nod, which was all Imogen could expect, before her uninspiring suitor took her arm and guided her back into the ballroom.

CHAPTER THIRTEEN

Caleb still stewed on the pleasures – and frustrations – of dancing with Imogen when he left the Tierney house the next morning. The weather continued fine, and the capital was dressed for spring. It was late. The ball had extended into the early hours, and he'd been invited to share a tipple with the family before they retired. The sign of favor was unexpected, although he knew that Lord Tierney was impressed with the designs for his Cumbrian estate.

Since he'd returned from Prestwick Place, the barriers of rank had started to crumble between him and his patron's family. He found it hard to put a finger on the exact difference, but it was there.

Last night, he'd danced with Elizabeth and Lady Harriet, and both had treated him like any other gentleman. If he was an acceptable partner at a ball, did that mean he might rise high enough to court Imogen? It was a nice dream, but he doubted it.

A long evening of minding his manners and watching Imogen spin from one noble partner to another had left him restless and discontented.

Seeing Imogen set like a jewel in the world she inhabited was a painful reminder that he was an outsider.

He'd tossed and turned until dawn, then snatched a few hours of sleep, disturbed by horrid dreams. Over and over, he held out his hands to catch Imogen, only to watch her recede out of reach.

As he made his way toward Hyde Park for a long walk among growing things, he felt out of sorts. Being outdoors always improved his humor. If only he could stretch his legs amidst wild scenery, instead of along London's graveled paths and manicured gardens.

Caleb didn't usually court difficulty, but last night's ball was a graphic illustration of everything ranged against him when it came to marrying Imogen. He didn't usually suffer low moods, but a grim weight lodged in his gut, as he feared that every dream must fail.

Because he wasn't as sharp as usual, he'd reached the park before he was certain that someone followed him. A quick glance behind revealed that in fact several someones followed him.

He'd first noticed the men in plain, respectable clothing when he crossed Lorimer Square. They were too large to escape notice. And Lorimer Square didn't attract much passing traffic.

They were still there as he wended his way through streets and squares toward the park. But he only decided that their presence was no accident when he checked back as he walked along Rotten Row, mostly empty at this unfashionable hour, and saw four men a hundred yards behind him.

Caleb frowned. This seemed odd. They didn't look like footpads. They looked like merchants' clerks, if the merchant hired for size.

Caleb was in the center of the world's richest city. He had powerful protectors. He was handy in a fight, although he preferred negotiation over violence, if he had the option. There was no indication that these unknown men meant him harm.

But nonetheless, some atavistic instinct warned him to avoid a confrontation. He turned down a shrub-lined path that would take him out onto the Paddington side of the park. With luck, he could lose the men in the maze of streets there and make his way back to Lorimer Square.

He'd spent a lot of time wandering London, while the Tierneys slept the mornings away after a late night at some ball or other. He also had an excellent sense of direction, honed in his homeland's forests and mountains.

He cursed the fact that at this hour, the park contained so few people. In the afternoon, he could lose himself in the crowds. Or at worst, appeal for help, if things got nasty.

To his dismay, his pursuers – because now he knew that was what they were – must have guessed his strategy.

He came around the corner of the path into an area of thick bushes and found two men blocking his way. A glance behind offered the not entirely surprising sight of two more bruisers closing off his escape to the rear.

Caleb was young and strong and had a few tricks up his sleeve. But he had little chance of prevailing against four men. Instead of trying to fight his way out, he faced the two thugs in front of him. "If you want money, I only have a few coins on me. I doubt I'm worth the trouble of robbing."

Except these men didn't look like thieves. He was close enough now to see that they wore identical suits in good plain English wool. Their hats and boots were of similar quality. Apart from the lack of insignia on their clothing, they could be servants.

"We're not after your money, Mr. Black," the largest man said. The hint of insolence in his voice chilled Caleb's blood. As did hearing that they knew his name. He couldn't pretend anymore that they'd targeted him by chance. Whoever they were, they'd set out this morning with Caleb Black as their quarry.

"So what do you want?" he asked. "You've followed me all the way from Mayfair, after all."

"Aye, we knew you'd clocked us when you turned into Piccadilly."

"You're quite noticeable," Caleb said in a dry tone, although he wasn't amused. He was afraid. Even at a distance, these men stank of menace.

He was trapped. They'd chosen a perfect site for an ambush. The hedges of pruned yew on either side were impenetrable and tall enough to hide him from view. The path was too narrow for him to get past the men, unless he battered his way through.

He could already tell that he was no match for his assailants. Up close, they didn't look like respectable servants. They looked like retired prizefighters, who now worked in protection or extortion. The spokesman's battered features spoke of a long acquaintance with violence. His gaze was cold and flat in a way that told Caleb he wouldn't hesitate to carry out the orders he followed. All the men sported flattened noses and scars.

"Aye, well, that wasn't our intention."

Caleb hid his disquiet under an easy tone. "What is your intention?"

"Someone wants a word with you, Mr. Black."

Caleb's mind scurried to work out who might bear him a grudge. Many local garden firms would resent Lord Tierney's commission going to a foreigner. But that was the way of business, and he doubted that they'd resort to brute force to express their displeasure.

The only other person likely to desire his destruction was Lord Deerforth, but he and Imogen had been so careful, he couldn't imagine that her father knew of the flirtation. Imogen certainly believed that her father remained in ignorance of her love for a middle-class American, and surely she'd know.

"Does this someone have a name?"

"Aye, he does." The man's smugness boded ill. "But he said he'd rather introduce himself."

Caleb already knew that bravado would do him no good, but be damned if he'd cringe before these ruffians. "So do we wait for him?"

The smugness intensified. So did Caleb's foreboding. "No, you're to come with us."

If Lord Deerforth had set these bully boys on his trail and now awaited an interview, Caleb's prospects were bleak indeed. And not just because he faced a beating today – these men were primed to do him injury. Imogen had always insisted that if her father learned of her indiscretions, he'd whisk her out of reach forever.

"I have another appointment."

"I'm afraid you'll have to miss it, Mr. Black. My employer was most insistent on seeing you this morning, and he's a busy man unaccustomed to waiting on lesser fellows' convenience."

Lesser fellows? Caleb's stomach cramped with dread. It must be Lord Deerforth.

How the devil had his lordship discovered their affair? Who in hell had betrayed them? Someone at Prestwick Place? It must be. Apart from last night's ball when they'd followed all the rules, he hadn't seen Imogen since then.

Damn it, did this mean that his every hope crumbled away? He'd lay good money that these polecats were going to rough him up. He could survive that. He wasn't sure that he could survive losing Imogen.

"And if I choose to pursue my original plans?" he asked, although he already knew the answer.

The smile that curled the man's lips was more like a sneer. "If you'll heed a friendly warning, Mr. Black, that would be most unwise. I have my orders to take you up in the carriage that's waiting through the park gates, and I'm a man who always obeys orders."

For a fleeting moment, Caleb considered trying to fight his way out of this predicament, but what was the point? He nodded. "In that case, I'm at your disposal, gentlemen."

The man's head dipped in a mocking bow. "A wise choice."

He signaled to the men behind Caleb. Soon two massive rogues grabbed Caleb's arms on either side.

"I've said I'll cooperate," he protested.

"Aye, well, just in case you change your mind, once you get a bit more room to run and a chance to call for help from a passing stranger. Don't get any clever ideas. My companions are armed, and our instructions are to deliver you to our master. Nothing was said about whether you needed to be alive."

"You can't commit murder here in the middle of Hyde Park," Caleb said, not even believing himself that they couldn't.

"Are you willing to chance your life on that opinion, sir?"

No, blast them to Hades, he wasn't.

The silence extended, then the man's sneer reappeared. "I thought not."

He turned and strode along the path. Beefy hands circled Caleb's arms and compelled him into a stumbling walk.

Caleb was right about who had ordered his abduction. It was Lord Deerforth.

The men in the park had bundled him into an unmarked carriage with a speed and efficiency that in other circumstances might have been impressive. Even if he'd wanted to call for help, he didn't see anyone else on the way.

They'd driven for a good while through London's busy streets, but because the blinds were down, it was only when the odors of sewage, salt and rotting fish thickened the air, along with an incongruous hint of exotic spices, that he guessed their destination.

They'd left the glamorous western part of London far behind and traveled to the docks of the East End. He'd been afraid the whole way. Only a fool wouldn't have been.

Now that he stood in front of Imogen's father, dread made his belly knot. If Lord Deerforth wanted to get rid of his daughter's inconvenient suitor and balked at murder, it would be easy enough to send Caleb back to America. Or have him impressed into the navy so he didn't set foot in England for years.

That would be a more effective punishment than murder for daring to court a daughter of the aristocracy. Years of brutality, suffering and longing would be his lot, while Imogen went on to a life without him. A life where she never discovered what had happened to the American who she had so unwisely loved.

Caleb surveyed the hulking man behind the large and elaborate desk. It dominated a spacious office on the top floor of a bustling silk warehouse. Outside, he saw the tops of masts on the ships moored at the quays and the rows of warehouses on the other side of the river.

The area was chaotic, crowded and noisy, as loading and unloading proceeded and carts and drays rolled over the cobbles. But tense silence reigned in this high, airy room, however inescapable the stench of Thames mud.

"You are Caleb Black?" Deerforth eventually asked, after taking his time to inspect his captive with a contemptuous gaze.

"I am, Lord Deerforth," Caleb said.

He should bow, but to blazes with that. The four men who had snared him in Hyde Park ranged around the room, he presumed to stop him from breaking free. Or from attacking Lord Deerforth.

He made no move to run. He knew that he wouldn't set foot outside this room until his lordship was ready to release him.

The man across the desk arched his eyebrows with a haughty disdain that was clearly meant to put him in his place. "You know who I am?"

The Tierneys and the Ridleys were neighbors, so he'd seen his lordship around Lorimer Square. "Yes."

Lord Deerforth looked to be about sixty, heavyset, jowly, red-faced. Even if Imogen hadn't warned Caleb about her father's temper, he'd know by looking that this man brimmed with anger and he rarely saw the need to control it. Not only anger, but arrogance and entitlement. Right now, Caleb could tell that every inch of the man's large body vibrated with outrage.

He must have discovered those secret meetings with Imogen. But how in Satan's name had he found out? Caleb was sure that nobody but George had known about the dawn trysts, and he trusted his mentor not to break his confidence. He supposed Ivor Bilson could have said something, but he'd swear that Ivor hadn't seen Imogen.

"Keep a respectful tongue in your head when you address his lordship," the man who had so far done most of the talking said sharply, lurching forward with chastisement in mind.

Deerforth waved one plump white hand to stop him from striking Caleb. "It's all right, Mr. Gibbs. He's an ignorant colonial, too stupid to know his place."

"Very good, my lord." Gibbs retreated to his former watchfulness, but Caleb felt the man's hostility from where he stood. If it came to violence between them, at least one of them would enjoy it.

Caleb was no fool. He didn't need to hear Gibbs's subdued response to know that the only really dangerous man in this room was Lord Deerforth. Despite everything, part of him had dismissed Imogen's warnings about the dire consequences if her father learned of their love.

Now that he finally stood in Deerforth's presence and met those flat, inimical eyes, he no longer underestimated Imogen's fears.

"Even an ignorant colonial has rights in this kingdom," Caleb said in a steady voice, while apprehension swam in his belly like a barracuda in a lagoon. "What reason can you have for kidnapping me, my lord?"

Until he knew what his enemies had found out, he'd play ignorant. He had his doubts that he'd be able to bluff his way out of this mess, but by Jericho, he'd give it a damned good try.

Deerforth's eyebrows lifted further toward his receding hairline. "Kidnapping?"

"What else would you call it?"

"I'd call it a chance to teach an insolent underling a few manners. You'll get on much better in this country, once you have a better understanding of our ways. You'll thank me, I'm sure."

"I'm sure," Caleb said with equal dryness. The promise of physical harm reeked worse than the filthy river outside the open windows.

"It's come to my attention that you had the temerity to ask my daughter to dance last night. Then, even more improperly, you invited her out onto the terrace."

Dance? All this was over one waltz? Relief flooded him. Deerforth didn't know about his meetings with Imogen.

"I was Lord Tierney's guest, and I danced with a number of ladies apart from Lady Imogen, including his lordship's daughter. I was introduced to Lady Imogen several weeks ago at the Tierneys' house. I can't see that I've broken any rules."

"It's precisely because you don't see your *faux pas*, that we're having this little chat." Temper flared in Deerforth's eyes. "If Tierney wants to act the fool and let riffraff run tame about his house, I can't stop him. But any right-thinking person knows there's no benefit to be gained from mixing the classes."

"Every man in his place?" Caleb asked with more dryness, even as he couldn't help recalling George Perrett's lecture on how life worked in England.

"Indeed. And your place, sirrah, is the servants' hall, not associating with your betters."

"We fought a war to prove that there's no such thing as a man's betters. And I believe we won."

Caleb had cause to regret his defiance. Deerforth glanced at Gibbs. Suddenly Caleb found himself in the clutches of his former captors. He struggled to free himself as Gibbs planted a brick-like fist in his solar plexus.

Pain exploded through him. For a moment, his vision turned gray.

By the time he'd regained his breath, Gibbs was back standing by the wall. Deerforth's piggy little eyes expressed a distant satisfaction, as he flattened his hands on the blotter. "I won't abide any treasonous talk, Mr. Black."

Caleb struggled to stand on his own two feet. By Harry, Gibbs had fists like granite.

He fought to keep his voice steady. "I can't imagine Lord Tierney will be pleased to hear that you've taken it on yourself to chastise his garden designer. I'm not without friends in London, my lord."

Deerforth sneered. It was an even more impressive effort than Gibbs's. "I'm not intending for him to hear."

Dear Lord, did this overbred ruffian intend to send him back to America? For a sin as minor as dancing with Imogen at a ball to which Caleb had been officially invited? His mind boggled at the penalty this man would inflict if he ever guessed the intimacy that existed between his daughter and Caleb. "How are you going to manage that?"

Caleb braced to hear of his removal from England. Or even his upcoming murder. The thought of everything coming to an end filled him with helpless rage. He loved his life. He always had. He particularly loved it now, when he'd found the girl for him.

A gloating smile curved Deerforth's lips. Caleb was fast learning to loathe the man who he hoped one day to call his father-in-law. How on earth had this bastard produced a child as exquisite as Imogen? He could see no similarity between this pompous windbag and the girl he adored.

"I believe that your own self-interest will keep you silent."

"Oh?" The tightness in his chest eased, although he wasn't fool enough to imagine that he was out of trouble. At least this didn't sound like Deerforth intended to kill him, even if there was little question that Gibbs would get another chance to use his fists.

"I am a man of influence, Mr. Black, and I gather you're here to tout for business as a landscaper. If I hear one word that implicates me in your unfortunate...accident, I'll ensure that you never get another contract in this country. The same goes if I hear a whisper about you approaching my daughter, or mentioning my daughter, or even so much as looking at my daughter. She's too fine for the likes of you."

At last, Caleb agreed with this overweening bully about something. "The Tierneys will notice if I turn up looking as if I've been in a battle."

The smile didn't falter. "Such a pity that their American visitor encountered some local footpads. London can be so dangerous these days. Someone should do something about it."

"You could let me go. I've been suitably rebuked," Caleb said, with no hope at all that Deerforth would exercise mercy. If only because the man couldn't hide his relish for the situation.

His lordship's outrage wasn't feigned. But he was eating up this opportunity to put an uppity colonial in his place, the way he'd hoe into an omelette at the breakfast table.

Deerforth's reply was no surprise. "Not yet, my dear fellow, not yet. But you will be. And I'll see that it's a lesson you remember."

To his regret, Caleb was sure that would be the case. The other four men in the room bristled with eagerness to beat him to a pulp.

Deerforth rose. He was taller than Caleb had expected, and his weight conveyed power rather than the softness of mounds of fat. It would be a rash man indeed who underrated this rattlesnake's venom.

For a moment, Caleb wondered if Deerforth meant to do the honors. But the man picked up a stick with an elaborate silver dragon's head on its handle. He placed a stylish gray hat on his head, and crossed toward the door.

His voice was cool and uninvolved, as though he'd lost all interest in what was about to happen. Caleb, who was under no illusion of just how unpleasant his morning was about to become, suspected that was true. Lord Deerforth dismissed him with no more thought that he'd squash a flea. Not that any flea would dare to suck that blue blood, Caleb was sure.

"I don't imagine we'll meet again, Mr. Black. If you didn't know it before, you know it now – you and I move in different social circles. Remember that before you start making wild accusations of ill-treatment at my hands. With a mere word in the right ears, I can have you deported as an undesirable alien. I'm sure you're not a stupid man. Although you did a stupid thing at the Tierney ball last night. I assume that you'd like to survive to enjoy a successful future. Tierney may be a damned fool in many ways, but he's known as an arbiter of taste. If he says your notions for his flower beds are first rate, they are." Deerforth's contempt for Caleb's profession dripped from his words. "Now I'll leave you in my servants' hands. Good day to you, sir."

Gibbs rushed to open the door, and everyone bowed to his lordship as he left. Everyone except Caleb. The insolence might add a few extra blows to his ordeal, but be damned if he'd show that swine Deerforth an ounce of respect.

Gibbs closed the door with a care that seemed more ominous than force and faced Caleb who remained in his cohorts' hold.

"Now it's time for some fun, lads. Pretty boy won't be so pretty by the time we finish with him, by gum. Just be careful you don't go too far. His lordship don't want to have to explain no dead Yank."

Confirmation that Caleb was meant to survive at least. Although that wasn't much consolation, as the thugs holding him firmed their grasp on his arms and Gibbs approached with an intent expression. Caleb braced for what was about to happen, but not even the last blow prepared him for the force of Gibbs's fist plowing into his stomach.

Red-hot pain ignited, and his vision failed again. He told himself that he'd stay on his own two feet, but when he returned to awareness, he was sagging, only semi-upright because Gibbs's associates maintained their bruising hold on his arms. He opened bleary eyes to see Gibbs surveying him the way a hungry man looked at a plate of bacon and eggs.

"This is going to be amusing, Mr. Black. His lordship said to give you a good going-over, and it's too long since I've used my fists on anything but a punching bag."

Caleb's lips turned down in grim acknowledgment. "Not amusing for me."

Gibbs dipped his head in agreement. "Aye, well, that's as may be."

Caleb was right. The next little while wasn't amusing at all.

CHAPTER FOURTEEN

"My goodness, Imogen and Harriet, did you hear what happened to Mr. Black?"

At the sound of Elizabeth's breathless question, Imogen turned from where she was talking to the Comerfords under the shade of the plane trees along Hyde Park's Rotten Row. It was three days after Elizabeth's triumph at her ball. It was also three days since she'd seen her friend, as they'd attended different events the last two nights.

More significantly, it was three days since she'd seen Caleb for such a frustratingly brief interval. Since then, she'd slipped out of the house before dawn each morning, in the hope of finding a message in the tree and to leave a message of her own. But this morning, she'd taken her third message home with her, as well as the previous two that she'd left.

She was nearly sick with worry and longing. After those glorious days at Prestwick Place, this lack of communication made her frantic.

"No, what happened?" Harriet asked, and Imogen took a moment to envy the way that her friend felt free to express her curiosity without worrying about betraying deeper feelings.

Elizabeth rushed up to them, while her mother lingered behind to talk to Lady Pollock. Her pretty face was flushed with excitement. "It's just too awful, I can hardly tell you."

Too awful? The world of fashionable London promenading through the park receded down a long black tunnel. Imogen struggled to hide the way her stomach compressed into a painful lump.

"Tell us, Elizabeth." In her own ears, her voice sounded high and artificial, but nobody seemed to notice, thank the Lord. They were all too focused on Elizabeth and her news.

Elizabeth looked around her audience, her expression a mixture of horror and pleasure in being the focus of attention. "The day after my ball, Mr. Black went for a walk, and a gang of thieves jumped on him. They did the most awful damage. His poor face is black and blue, and the doctor says he's broken a couple of ribs and fingers."

"Imogen! Imogen, what's wrong? You've gone as white as a sheet."

Imogen came back to herself to find herself slumping against Lady Lumsden, who held her up while Harriet fluttered around her in a panic.

"Imogen, I'm sorry," Elizabeth said. "I should have thought before I spoke. It's shocking to hear of the criminal element coming so close to Mayfair. You must tell Eliot. He might be able to get his powerful friends in the government to arrange some extra patrols."

"I'm sure that you're quite safe, Imogen," Anthony Comerford said in his calm way. "There's no need to worry."

There was every reason to worry. Imogen bit back the urge to cry and shout. She burned to rush to Caleb's side. The thought of him hurt and suffering cut like a knife.

But as her panic receded, she realized the danger. Fear for her beloved rose in her throat like vomit, but she needed to remember where she was and who she was with. This was the most gossip-obsessed society on earth. If she fell into a fit of hysteria over the Tierneys' landscaper, all her secrets would come out.

So far, she and Caleb had managed to preserve the illusion that they were the merest of acquaintances. If she displayed too much concern for the young American, she'd arouse her friends' suspicions. Word would get back to her father.

Her knees felt like water and her sight remained blurry, but she shifted away from Lady Lumsden and somehow managed to sound almost like herself. "It's such a shock to think these villains are brazen enough to attack a respectable man like Mr. Black. I've always felt so safe in Lorimer Square."

Luckily, curiosity about Caleb's misadventure occupied everyone, so nobody looked too hard at her.

"I don't blame you for taking on so," Elizabeth said. "No, he wasn't attacked in Lorimer Square. It was here in Hyde Park."

"Here?" Harriet looked around, as if expecting marauders to leap out from the trees.

"Yes." Elizabeth paused. "Well, not precisely here. Apparently Mr. Black was walking along the Serpentine, when a gang of cutthroats demanded his money and his watch, then assaulted him. Somehow, he managed to stagger back to the house, where he collapsed on the front step."

"That's just appalling," Lady Lumsden said. "Poor Mr. Black. For pity's sake, a man should be able to visit the capital without fearing for his safety. It's outside of enough."

Imogen let the tide of outrage flow around her, as she struggled to maintain an expression of cool concern. Inside, a violent storm raged. She needed to see Caleb, but how could she? Even if he was from her class, she couldn't call on an unmarried gentleman in his sickbed. The rules that hemmed her in had never chafed so badly.

Poor, poor Caleb. The thought of his pain made her feel sick. What a frightful thing to have happened.

"Where is Mr. Black now?" Harriet asked.

"He can still hardly move, although we've had such trouble getting him to rest. It's so sad seeing him like this. He's become like one of the family. One almost forgets that he's here to do a job for Papa."

Fortunate Elizabeth. At least she could see Caleb. At least she could talk to him. Propriety locked Imogen away from him as securely as a dungeon door.

"What did the doctor say?" Imogen asked, at last trusting her composure enough to formulate a sensible question.

"He's called every day. He was rather concerned at first, but he says Mr. Black is young and healthy and should soon be as good as new. I believe there's some doubt about the use of his hands, though. He must have fought back like a tiger. They were a mess."

Another wave of nausea overwhelmed Imogen. This time, she managed to hide it, even as her stomach heaved. "But he needs his hands to draw his designs."

"I know. It's just too ghastly." Elizabeth looked at her without a trace of suspicion. "Papa has assured him that he's happy to wait for the final plans."

"That's good of him," Lady Lumsden said.

"It's the least we can do. As Mr. Black's hosts, we should have kept him safe."

"Will you tell Eliot about this?" Lady Lumsden said, turning to Imogen. "It really is unacceptable."

Imogen shoved aside her agonizing worry. She was lucky that she hadn't betrayed herself just now. It was imperative that Lady Lumsden didn't guess the depth of her reaction to Elizabeth's news. "Eliot is down in Wiltshire right now, but I'll speak to him when he comes back to Town."

"What a pity he had to go away at the height of the season," Lady Lumsden said.

"Yes, he missed my ball," Elizabeth said with a hint of pique. "I'd saved him two dances."

Imogen had difficulty dragging her mind from Caleb to her brother. She was worried about Eliot, too. Most of the time, he looked like some golden angel, but when he'd called to tell her that he was leaving London for an indefinite period, he seemed to have aged twenty years. Lady Verena hadn't been mentioned, but her invisible presence had dominated the meeting like a miasma. Imogen guessed that her brother's love affair didn't prosper. "His trip couldn't be delayed."

"When will he be back?"

Surprised, Imogen looked at Elizabeth properly. Perhaps Lily wasn't alone in setting her cap for rich, handsome Viscount Colville. Imogen couldn't fault her friends' taste. Eliot was kind and nice and altogether a good man. Which made it even sadder that he couldn't persuade the woman he wanted to have him. "I'm not sure."

He hadn't admitted as much, but she knew that Eliot was licking his wounds. It was possible that he had no immediate plans to leave his estate, although with parliament sitting, his political career required his attention. For once in his life, she suspected his abiding interest in the governance of the country failed.

Elizabeth and Harriet started to talk about what they were wearing to tonight's ball. Lady Lumsden and Anthony wandered back to speak to the Bilsons. Imogen stayed where she was, as she tried to think of some way to see Caleb.

Nothing came to mind that wouldn't result in scandal, and her swift exile to Hamble Park. How could she bear this separation, now that Caleb had been hurt? But bear it she must.

"Good morning, Lady Imogen," Nancy said with a brightness that chimed ill with Imogen's aching head. Lack of sleep marked her love affair. For weeks, a whirlwind of emotions had stolen her peace. Excitement. Joy. Desire. Doubt. Fear.

But since hearing about the attack on Caleb, she'd hardly slept a wink. She almost looked as haggard as Stella. Last night, they'd both stayed in. It had been a relief not to pretend to carefree gaiety, but she hadn't slept any better.

According to Elizabeth, Caleb recovered well, and the doctor was pleased with his progress, but he remained bedridden. Imogen imagined that he was an uncooperative patient. Something they shared was a low tolerance for inactivity.

"Good morning, Nancy." Imogen heard the crabby note in her voice. She'd fretted into the early hours, then fallen into a restless doze that hadn't refreshed her.

Now the time approached eleven, and she was due to go back to playing the sparkling debutante. She felt a million miles from sparkling. There was something grotesque about enjoying herself while Caleb suffered.

"One of your admirers has been busy – and nobody will thank him for it, I vow."

Imogen pushed herself up against the pillows, while Nancy placed the breakfast tray on her knees. "What's happened?"

Nancy shook out the napkin and dropped it across Imogen's lap before she poured the chocolate. "There were handfuls of flowers scattered over the front steps this morning. Tessie found them when she went out to scrub the steps first thing, so whoever did it must have been at work last night."

Flowers? Who on earth would do such a thing? "They left no note?"

"No, just flowers."

Imogen took a sip of her chocolate and felt the sweetness ease her weariness. "That's an extravagant gesture."

Nancy moved around, straightening the room. "It turns out that it wasn't extravagant at all. It was a matter of thievery, pure and simple, whatever name the person who did it might choose for his actions. Mr. Brent told us all at breakfast that one of the square's garden beds has been cleared. Not a flower left. Your admirers won't be popular with the people in Lorimer Square – it's an awful mess now, which is a pity because it was so pretty before. I went over to see, and it looks like a tornado has hit it. It's the garden bed directly opposite this house, too, so we can't miss it."

Brent was their straitlaced butler. He wouldn't approve of this aristocratic vandalism in tribute to the daughter of the household. As a gardener, Imogen couldn't condone such wanton destruction either. During the season, well-bred young men were wont to behave in very ill-bred ways. Night watchmen were often assaulted, or damage was done to people and property, as a result of excess spirits, both personal and potable.

She drank some more chocolate, and her sluggish brain started to work. Another explanation arose for the floral tribute.

Could Caleb be trying to attract her attention? If his hands were as bad as Elizabeth said, writing would be difficult.

"It's coming to a point where a girl isn't safe to walk about Town. Did you hear the Tierneys' gardener was attacked in broad daylight a few days ago? I don't know what to make of it all."

Imogen hardly listened as Nancy wittered on. Instead, her certainty grew that the destruction of the flower bed was a message. Her heart, laden with worry and longing, rose at the thought that Caleb was well enough to devastate the gardens. Not to mention that if he'd managed to escape the Tierneys' house long enough to rip up a mass of spring blooms, he might be able to escape to meet her.

Imogen drew her father's black greatcoat closer around her. As May advanced, the weather had warmed up, but she was trying to blend into the night, and the bulky wool garment was her best hope of that.

She stood in the thicket of trees in the center of Lorimer Square, near the elm where she'd left messages for Caleb. It was well after three. It had been just on two when she returned home from the Castellaine ball, and she'd had to wait for the household to retire before she ventured outside. She might be wasting her time, but she couldn't pass up a chance to talk to Caleb and see for herself how he was.

All the houses around the square were dark. She'd carried a candle with her, but blown it out when she reached the trees. The darkness was kind to the square. It hid the ruin of what had been a beautiful bed of tulips . She wished she'd seen the flowers left on the steps, but Brent with his usual efficiency had everything cleared away by the time Imogen came downstairs.

Waiting for Caleb here had seemed like a good idea this morning, when she'd eaten her breakfast and convinced herself that only he could have left the floral message. Now, with the world silent and black around her, she wasn't quite so sure. She felt dreadfully alone, and she couldn't help thinking that thieves had attacked Caleb in Hyde Park. Lorimer Square didn't feel nearly as safe as it once had.

She sucked in a deep breath and told herself to be brave. The square employed a watchman, who she suspected was asleep in his booth. If she screamed, he'd come to her rescue. Then all hell would break loose, when her father discovered that she'd been wandering around outside in the middle of the night.

The air smelled of London. Coal smoke and river mud and the flowers that Caleb hadn't picked. If indeed, Caleb was behind the devastation. The longer she loitered here, the less convinced she became.

When she heard a shuffling footfall on the paved path, she shivered. She shrank into the shadows and strained to make out who approached.

"I'm armed," she said in a shaky voice, edging closer to the nearest tree.

"I'm glad to hear it."

Her breath escaped in an audible gasp when she heard Caleb's voice. Relief flooded her. Relief and sheer pleasure. She hadn't seen him since Elizabeth's ball. It felt like forever.

She rushed out from under the trees just as the clouds cleared, and the gibbous moon shone down on him. "Oh, Caleb…"

Her heart clenching into a painful fist, she faltered to an unsteady halt. He moved like an old man, and he leaned heavily on a walking stick.

"I hoped that you'd understand my message. I had no idea how to get in contact. There were no notes in the tree, and I can't write. Those bastards concentrated on my right hand."

Imogen noticed that he held the stick in his left hand. "My love." Her voice cracked, as she took a faltering step closer. "It's very bad, isn't it?"

She caught a flash of white teeth as he smiled. She couldn't read his expression, but something about his awkward stance told her that he was in oceans of pain.

"It's better than it was. At least I can walk now. Just seeing you helps." His voice sounded thicker than usual. It might be emotion, but she suspected it resulted from physical discomfort. "Let's move into the shadows in case anyone is looking out their window."

When they'd shifted back under the trees, she spread her shaking hands in a helpless gesture. "I want to kiss you, but I'm afraid I'll hurt you."

"If we're careful, we should manage."

She took one more step and curled her fingers around his arm to support him. Also because she was desperate to reassure herself that he was here with her. "Does this hurt?"

"No."

"Liar." Her voice was thicker than usual, too, as she released him. "I felt quite sick when Elizabeth told me."

"I couldn't get word to you that I was all right. I knew you'd worry."

"But you're not all right."

When he shifted to face her, she noticed again how gingerly he moved. She was used to Caleb's animal vigor. Seeing him in such a state was devastating.

"I'm all right, now I'm with you. Kiss me, Imogen."

She cradled his face between shaking hands. He flinched under her touch, however gentle she strove to be. She jerked her hands away. "I wish I could see you."

The soft huff of wry laughter wasn't reassuring. "It's better that you don't."

"Caleb..."

"It will heal. At least I've still got all my teeth. And the doctor reset my nose. By Harry, I was never the handsomest fellow. I can't afford to lose what looks I have."

She blinked to dispel the mist in front of her eyes. "I think you're the handsomest man in the world. I'll always think that. But I loathe that this happened to you."

"The bruises will fade."

"It's not just bruises, though, is it? You've broken ribs, and your hands are damaged, too."

"I'll be fine."

"I pray you will be."

"Imogen, don't cry," he said urgently.

"I'm not crying."

"Yes, you are."

Yes, she was.

"My darling..." Unable to bear waiting any longer, she rose on her toes and placed a swift kiss on his lips. She pulled away after an instant, unsure whether she'd caused him pain.

He reached out to bring her closer, then recoiled as his bandaged right hand met her shoulder. The tears she battled so hard to hide fell even faster.

He hissed through his teeth. "Damn it, I'm so blasted decrepit, I can't even kiss you properly."

She glanced around to make sure nobody in the square was stirring. All seemed quiet. "There's a bench under the lilac tree. Would you like to sit down?"

"Yes, I believe I would."

Caleb always moved fast and with purpose. Or at least he had before this. It sliced at her heart to see what it cost him to cover the couple of yards to the wrought-iron bench. As he sank onto the seat with a long sigh of relief, she supported his weight.

Her pity was excruciating. It was almost impossible to sound normal, although she knew that he'd hate her fussing over him. Which was a shame, because she wanted to flutter and commiserate and soothe. "It must have nearly killed you, picking those flowers."

Another wry grunt of laughter, cut short because she suspected his broken ribs objected. "It did. Destroying a garden bed goes against all my principles. But I was so desperate, I overcame my scruples."

She struggled to smile. She'd actually meant the physical strain of gathering the flowers. Only now that she saw him did she realize the toll his injuries took. "It was a clever idea."

"You were clever to realize what I meant by it. I didn't know what else I could do if this failed."

Her laugh was even less convincing than her smile. Seeing him, she had some small idea of the misery he'd undergone to send her that message. It was clear that every movement he made caused him pain, hard as he tried to hide it.

She slumped down beside him. It was dark here under the trees. A delicious scent almost overpowered the capital's less pleasant odours. "At least you left the lilacs alone."

"I couldn't reach them."

He rested his stick against the edge of the bench and curled his hand around hers. His left hand. "Please don't cry, Imogen. It's not that bad, really."

She gave up all pretense to calm. "I can't help it."

"My dear…" He released her hand and turned her face toward him. This kiss was considerably more satisfying than the last one.

When Caleb lifted his head, they were both trembling. She felt him staring at her through the darkness. "I've missed you so much."

Light as air, she touched his cheek. "Tell me what happened."

"Didn't Elizabeth say?"

"Yes, but I want to hear it from you."

He was so close that she felt him stiffen up again. "I haven't got much to add."

She frowned. That seemed an odd response, and his voice flattened as if he told a lie. "Are you uncomfortable? Should we stand up again?"

"I'm fine."

"You're not. We both know that. You should be in bed."

"I've been stuck in bed for days on end." His sigh conveyed resentment of his confinement. "That's the last place I need to be when I can be with you instead."

She took his left hand again, gently because he still hurt. The thought of his suffering made her want to cry again. She fought the tears. She'd cry later, in the privacy of her own room. "Caleb, what is it? Are your injuries worse than I heard? Elizabeth said that you're likely to make a full recovery."

"The doctor is hopeful."

"Are you worried that you may not be able to draw again?"

"I'll damn well make sure I can draw again," he said with some heat. "This isn't going to turn me into an invalid."

Imogen admired his courage, but she'd seen enough accidents at Hamble Park to know that sometimes determination wasn't enough. "I'll draw for you, if you can't manage it. I've done landscape plans before."

He lifted her hand to his lips and kissed her knuckles. "I love that you're still looking to our future."

"Of course I am." She paused. "Now stop beating around the bush. What aren't you telling me?"

"You don't need to hear all the grisly details. It was a chance encounter. I was in the wrong place at the wrong time."

She caught the false note in his voice. "Who were these men?"

He shrugged, then stopped on a groan. "I keep forgetting that I shouldn't make any sudden movements."

She wasn't distracted. Her instincts with Caleb had always been excellent. Now they shouted that he hid something. "Tell me."

"Don't fuss, Imogen. Some random footpads tried their luck in a wealthy part of London. I don't like to relive the attack."

Now that really didn't sound like Caleb. She frowned again, as she released his hand. "Hyde Park seems an odd place to waylay you, and you'd hardly be the richest pickings there."

She'd been in such a fever of fear and worry since she'd heard about the attack, that she hadn't thought much past her urgent need to see him. Now in his presence, so much about the whole story struck her as unlikely. Not least the way that Caleb shirked answering her questions.

"Lord Tierney is furious. Given that the upper classes gather in Hyde Park, it should be safe, according to him."

He still sounded like he lied. Why?

"Caleb, tell me the truth." Her voice hardened. "What happened?"

"You know what happened." He started to sound annoyed, but she hardly noticed as she pieced the clues together, only to reach an unacceptable conclusion. Although the conclusion explained why Caleb was hedging.

Imogen had felt sick to her stomach when she learned that he'd been injured. Now sour bile rose in her throat. She pressed an unsteady hand over her heaving middle. "It was my father, wasn't it?"

CHAPTER FIFTEEN

Caleb cursed her quickness. "Imogen—"

"Don't bother trying to deny it." He felt her gaze burning through the darkness. "I know."

He sighed and tried to take her hand. "It's not your fault."

"Yes, it is," she said in a brittle tone, as she pulled away. "But I don't understand. If Papa knows about us, why hasn't he said anything to me? Why am I still in London and free to sneak out to see you?"

"He doesn't know about us."

"Then why did he hurt you?"

"Because I danced with you."

"Oh, Caleb..." The unnatural harshness of her voice dissolved, and he heard tears in her response. "How can you ever forgive me?"

"You've done nothing wrong."

"I should never have danced with you. But I assumed that because you were the Tierneys' guest, Papa wouldn't like it, but he could have no real objections."

"He made it very clear that he did." He paused. "It was worth it for the chance to hold you in my arms."

"No, it wasn't," she said. "I'm not going to make this romantic. It's horrid. Vile and cruel and unfair."

"My darling..." Caleb turned on the bench to take her into his embrace, then groaned. He kept forgetting that he was such a useless crock.

"I hate my father," she said in an implacable voice.

"He loves you." Caleb didn't know why he defended the swine. He'd spent most of the last few days wishing Lord Deerforth a swift trip to a permanent residence in hell. But he couldn't bear to think of Imogen suffering, and an estrangement from her father would distress her.

"In his way, which doesn't mean much. He loves me the way he loves his dog or his favorite pistol, or anything that's useful and doesn't have plans of its own."

Caleb hated to hear her sound so tired and cynical. "You love him. That counts for something."

"Not a lot." When she reached for his hand, he hissed in reaction. She released him with a horrified gasp. "I'm sorry. Every time I touch you, I hurt you."

"You don't mean to."

"Stop being such a hero, Caleb. You don't have to be. Not with me. Yes, because he's my father, part of me will probably always love him. The little girl who he made such a fuss of and who he spoiled. But I'm not that little girl anymore. I've seen how he treats Eliot and Stella, and what harm he's done to them. He's not a good man, although he's mostly been good to me. Now I can never forgive him for coming close to killing you."

"Nowhere near." Although Caleb suspected that if he hadn't had the Tierneys' backing, Deerforth would have dropped him in the river after the beating.

"I told you not to be so cursed brave, Caleb."

He started to shrug. His ribs didn't like that at all. "I'm trying to impress the girl I love."

"She's impressed, you gallant fool. Tell me what happened."

"You don't need to know."

"Yes, I do." Her tone was uncompromising. "You can't shield me from life's bitter realities. That's what my father would do."

"I love you. That means I want to protect you."

"And I want to protect you, but I can only do that if we're honest with each other. I've been torturing myself with dreadful imaginings. The truth can't be worse."

He sighed again. "You won't like it."

"I don't expect to like it," she snapped. "But if you were strong enough to endure the pain, I'm strong enough to hear about it."

So he told her, although he kept the worst of it to himself. He suspected that she guessed that.

By the time he finished, he heard the hitch in her breathing. "You're crying again."

"No." But her voice gave her away.

"Kiss me, Imogen."

She turned and very gently kissed his bruised jaw and his forehead then finally his lips. He tasted tears, as revitalizing warmth seeped through him.

"You should have believed me when I told you Papa was dangerous."

"I believed you."

Although he hadn't. Not really. He'd been stupid and arrogant, and far too sure of his ability to win out over the forces ranged against him. Perhaps back in New York, he could justify his self-confidence. But here in a country that wasn't his and where he had few defenders, he'd asked for trouble. In London, all the advantages were Lord Deerforth's.

Cursing his shaky legs, he managed to stand up. Sitting so long was making him stiff and sore. He staggered to find his balance. With swift grace, Imogen rose and took his arm to keep him upright. Another gasp of pain escaped him.

"I'm sorry," she whispered, letting him go. "Why don't you hold onto me instead?"

"I hate that I'm such a wreck." He caught her shoulder and waited for the panicked rush of his blood to ease. It would be the last straw if he fell flat on his face in front of Imogen. He felt unmanned enough as it was.

"I hate that my father hurt you," she said in a small voice.

He sucked in a shuddering breath and straightened his spine. "We can't keep on like this. We've been lucky to escape discovery, but we can't expect that to continue."

She spoke in a rush. "I don't blame you for changing your mind about our engagement. If my father ever learns that we've been more than dancing partners, he'll kill you. I'm not worth your life."

"No, you misunderstand." His grip stopped her from moving away. "You're worth the whole world to me."

She peered through the darkness. "And you're worth the whole world to me. You know that."

Despite his pain, her ardent response made his heart expand. "I do know, but it's still nice to hear you say it."

She twisted her head and placed a clumsy kiss on his fingers. "So you don't want to end things?"

"Never." He paused. "But our meetings have become dangerous. Nor are they enough for either of us. We need to take the next step. You turn twenty-one on the third of June, don't you?"

"Yes."

"After that, you can marry without your father's permission?"

"Yes."

He heard excitement in her voice. She must guess where he was going.

"Once you're of age, I'll arrange a marriage license."

"Papa will find out."

"Not if we're quick and clever. Once we're married, you're free of him."

"He'll seek revenge."

"If we're on our way to America, he can't touch us."

"What about the Tierneys?"

Damn it, he kept forgetting that he shouldn't shrug. "I doubt that I'll be working for anyone in England, after you and I elope. Lord Tierney will have to find someone else to build his garden in Cumbria."

"But Mr. Perrett says your designs are brilliant."

"You're more important than any garden, Imogen. I want to marry you. I want to claim you as mine. I want to spend every day with you. I'm starving to death, only seeing you for a few minutes here and there. I want to start our life together."

"Caleb..." She stretched up and kissed him properly this time, a deeply carnal expression of her faith in him.

It hurt to put his arms around her, but he did. Although when he forgot everything but the heat of the kiss and hauled her closer, his broken ribs reminded him that he wasn't fit for amorous play. He swore against her lips and pulled away. "Tarnation, I hate that I can't hold you the way I want to."

She stroked his cheek with a tenderness that set his heart aching with longing. "We'll have a lifetime for kissing."

"So you'll run away with me?"

"Yes, I will."

Triumph flooded him, briefly made him forget his injuries. "We need to be careful. I'd hate to fail at the last minute."

"You're going to say that we shouldn't meet here again." Her tone was somber.

"It's not what I want, but it's wise."

"It means you'll get some sleep at night, too."

That roused a huff of grim amusement. "Thoughts of our wedding night will spur my recovery." He paused. "Although it's an exaggeration to say that I'll run away with you. It will be more like a totter."

He hoped that his weak joke would make her laugh, but when she responded, her voice vibrated with intense emotion. "I'll never forgive Papa for hurting you. I once felt guilty about embroiling him in a scandal when I marry you. But I'll never feel guilty again."

Imogen had spent so long afraid that her recklessness would tarnish the Ridley name. But over the next fortnight, she turned out to be little more than an observer while a series of scandals battered the family.

The very day that she'd met Caleb in the early hours, Lord Halston called on the Lorimer Square house to propose to Stella. The union of a penniless governess and one of the marriage mart's prizes would have caused talk in any case. When Imogen's father created a violent scene and disowned his niece, gossip went wild. It turned out that Lord Deerforth had been all over London, boasting about Imogen becoming the next Countess of Halston.

Papa wasn't popular. His bombastic manner and caustic tongue had made him many enemies. So society went on a spree, deriding his misplaced ambitions and lack of dignity. The news that he and Halston had nearly come to blows in a noisy confrontation in Deerforth's front hall was the icing on the cake.

Then to Imogen's joy, Eliot and Verena married. Again sparking her father's public fury. The wedding of the wildest woman in London and a man nicknamed the Saint caused even more of a flurry than Halston's wedding to Stella. Especially as the Saint hadn't lived up to his saintly reputation in the days leading up to the engagement.

Not that Imogen was present at either wedding ceremony, to her regret. Her father forbade any contact with Eliot or Stella.

Even worse, he packed her off to the country to save her good name. The people who sniggered about Lord Deerforth were no kinder to Imogen. Gossip painted her as a vain, empty-headed harridan, who had set her sights too high when it came to choosing a husband. Society didn't just gloat over Papa's comeuppance. They gloated over the downfall of one of the season's most admired debutantes.

Once, she might have smarted under the nasty tattle. Now, all she cared about was that she and Caleb were soon to wed and start their life together.

In the mad scramble to get away, Imogen managed to leave a vaguely phrased message in the tree for Caleb. Not that she needed to. She had no doubt that Elizabeth would share the latest *on-dits*.

Now she just had to wait for Caleb to come for her after her twenty-first birthday. She had no doubt that he would, but time hung heavy on her hands. She couldn't muster any interest in restoring the gardens at Hamble Park. What was the point, when she was leaving for America?

As lovely summer's day followed lovely summer's day, Imogen's spirits, initially bolstered by the news about Stella and Eliot, flagged. After the excitement of the last few months, the hours slowed to a trudge.

She missed her friends, especially Harriet, but most of all, she missed Caleb. This was worse than waiting for the Tierney ball, because at least then she had the hope of seeing him or hearing about him – and at the very least, the knowledge that he lived just across the square.

Here, he might as well be a thousand miles away. Worse, Imogen felt as if her old childish life sucked her back. Everyone at Hamble Park treated her like she'd never been to London. She was spoiled, pampered Lady Imogen, with her eccentric interest in gardens and her plentiful but insignificant activities.

Her secret love began to seem like a distant dream. Nor did it help that while all her friends wrote to her, her least diligent correspondent was Elizabeth.

In one of her early letters, Lily said that Caleb remained bedridden, then didn't mention him again. Why would she? Caleb was nothing to her, apart from an interesting oddity. And if Lily had harboured a *tendre* for Eliot, she had her own problems to deal with.

Imogen didn't just yearn for Caleb's company, she thirsted for news about his recovery. When they met in the square, she'd been appalled at his injuries. He'd done his best to conceal his pain, but she knew that it was much worse than he admitted.

Could Caleb draw again? Had his ribs healed? She burned to know, but had no way of finding out, plague take propriety.

During her remaining days in London, she'd had difficulty being polite to her father. Perhaps it was fortunate that after Stella's engagement, he hunkered down at his club to escape the scandal.

Her birthday passed quietly and had been a rather miserable day. Papa stayed in London, scrambling to save his political career. His wayward behavior and the family upheavals had eroded his influence in parliament.

As days lengthened into weeks, Imogen took to sleeping late. What was there to get up for? After existing for so long on a couple of hours a night, now she turned sluggish and inactive. At least in the privacy of her bedroom, she could indulge in a good cry when her pining became unendurable. Nobody must suspect that Imogen, too, had taken up with an unsuitable amour during those turbulent weeks in London.

"Good morning, Lady Imogen," Nancy said with a cheerfulness that grated.

"Let me sleep," she said grumpily, keeping her eyes closed.

She'd woken at dawn, but she'd been drowsing for a couple of hours, reliving every one of Caleb's kisses. How she regretted that there weren't more to remember.

"I don't know what's got into you, I really don't." Nancy ignored the bad-tempered grumble and pushed open the curtains with a loud rattle that played on Imogen's overstretched nerves. "You're usually up with the birds. Goodness me, when we visited Lord Halston's house, you were out at sunrise. You were that keen to be out in the gardens. Yet since you've got back from London, you've turned into such a lazybones. Are you sickening for something?"

Imogen was lovesick, but she had no intention of confessing that to Nancy. "I'm just tired," she said in a dull voice.

"A girl your age shouldn't be this tired. I worry that you might be ill, indeed. You haven't shown any interest in your little projects. Once you never shut up about them."

With a sigh, Imogen pushed herself up against the pillows. It was clear that Nancy wasn't going to leave her alone. "You were never very interested."

"No, I wasn't, God bless you, my lady." Nancy lifted a loaded tray from the chest of drawers and placed it on Imogen's lap. As Imogen was the only member of the family in residence, she'd taken to eating breakfast in her bedroom. It wasn't worth setting up the morning room for one person.

Imogen was surprised that she'd been left on her own for so long. It wasn't precisely proper for her to live here without a chaperone, despite a household full of servants to keep an eye on her and report back to her father.

Papa hadn't written, but she assumed that he kept himself informed of her activities. Or perhaps he was so busy maneuvering to restore his prestige, he couldn't spare the time to worry about his daughter.

These last weeks were the closest that she'd come to being unsupervised in her entire life. Stella had always been with her before. If Caleb was here, they could have met every day.

But he wasn't here.

That knowledge always hurt, but something about the sunshine and Nancy's nagging made it sting more than ever this morning. Without much enthusiasm, Imogen contemplated the congealing eggs on her plate, then started to butter a roll with listless movements.

"But if it means you returning to your old self, you can talk to me about seeds and compost and drainage for the next month. I won't say a word of complaint."

"Thank you." Imogen sighed again as she picked up the roll, then put it down. She wasn't hungry. Her stomach was too full of unhappiness to leave room for food. "Life in the country seems very flat after London."

Nancy tidied the pile of books that Imogen had brought up from the library and was yet to open. "Aye, well, you thought life in London was too busy when you first went there."

She had, hadn't she? But once she'd met Caleb, lightning had charged every second.

"Nothing seems to happen here." She knew that she sounded like a brat. In fact, she sounded like the selfish little miss that she used to be. She didn't want to go back to being that girl.

Save me, Caleb.

"Fie, my lady. Lots of things happen in the country. Lizzie the dairymaid is going to marry Harry the head groom next month, which has put John Coachman's nose out of joint. Tilly the stable cat just had a litter of nine kittens. You should go down and see them. They're such sweethearts. Mrs. Tate from the home farm ran off with the farrier. And that's only in the last week."

"Goodness," Imogen said, despite herself impressed with the litany. She'd been so wrapped up in her troubles, she'd missed all of it.

"Mr. Tate is that angry, he threw all of her dresses on the fire. And you wouldn't believe what else has happened."

"Oh?" Imogen managed to take a bite of her roll.

Nancy stopped fidgeting and came up to stare at her over the base of the bed. Her eyes were round with excitement. "There's an American staying at the Dog and Duck."

When Imogen choked on her roll, Nancy ran up to stand beside her.

"My lady, I'm that sorry for giving you such a surprise." Nancy spoke in rhythm with her pounding on Imogen's back. "What on earth a Yankee is doing here in Little Hamble, nobody knows. Mr. Baker at the inn says he's a quiet, well-behaved gentleman, but very close about himself. He's on a tour of the Cotswolds, but that doesn't seem right to me. Why would someone come so far, just to look at the countryside around here? I ask you."

"I'm all right now, Nancy," Imogen managed to say through her coughing. Sudden joy turned the previously mundane day to molten gold. "You can stop hitting me."

He was here. He was here!

"Are you sure?"

She managed to catch a breath at last. Her mind was in a whirl. Through watering eyes, she looked at Nancy. "Yes, very sure."

"All at once, Americans are everywhere. I heard the one Lord Tierney had running tame around his house was a nice gentleman, too, although he was in a bad way after those ruffians jumped him in Hyde Park."

Imogen's surge of happiness stuttered to an end, as caution kicked in and reminded her that she wasn't safely away with Caleb yet. She needed to be careful, or Nancy might guess that Lord Tierney's American was the same American lodging at the Dog and Duck.

Because it must be Caleb. Imogen was certain to her bones that he'd come for her at last.

"That was such a pity." She struggled to sound disinterested. "Where did Mrs. Tate go?"

Nancy's eyes brightened, as she sat on the bed. "Lordy, my lady, it's set the village on its ears. Nobody knows a thing. And her always a most respectable lady, although the word is that her man used to knock her around after he had a few pints."

"She might be better off with the farrier."

Disapproval pursed Nancy's lips. "It's not God's law, though, is it? Where would the world be if females just up and follow their inclinations, without worrying about wedding vows and the rules of society and such?"

In Imogen's opinion, it would be a good thing if women took an independent line. Although she could imagine what people would say about her, once she turned her back on her class and her family and ran away to America. "They don't have children, do they?"

She had a vague memory of Mrs. Tate, a subdued blonde. She definitely recalled Mr. Tate, who reminded her of her father. While it would shock Nancy if she voiced the thought, she applauded the lady's courage. She hoped Mr. Jones, the farrier, made her happy. He'd always been kind with the horses. That hinted that he'd be kind to a wife.

"No. At least there's that. But what's to become of us, now there's no blacksmith? Harry is that cranky about it."

"Harry, at least, has been lucky in love."

That launched Nancy into a long description of Harry's courtship of pretty Lizzie. To Imogen's relief, the romantic intrigue in the servants' quarters overshadowed the novelty of a foreigner visiting the village.

Imogen came back to herself enough to pretend an interest in the local gossip, but her mind churned with how she could make contact with Caleb.

She'd woken this morning, facing yet another dreary day without her beloved. Now he was mere minutes away, and her heart danced.

"That's Mr. Rose there, talking to Mrs. Allery," Nancy hissed to Imogen, who walked beside her along the village's single paved street.

She'd told Nancy that she wanted some ribbon from the haberdasher to decorate an old bonnet. Nancy had been so pleased to hear that she was ready to do something other than mope around the house that she hadn't questioned Imogen's sudden interest in such a feminine activity. Usually Imogen was so busy in the gardens that she scorned pastimes like sewing.

Imogen had already spied him. It was over a month since they'd last met, and he looked like the handsome man who she remembered. She felt as if the world filled with birdsong. The hardest part of all was stopping herself from rushing forward and flinging her arms around him.

The stick he carried hinted that he still hadn't returned to full health. He hadn't used one before the attack. But it was fashionable to sport a walking cane, so nobody except Imogen would note the oddity. He wore gloves, so she couldn't see how his hands had healed.

Imogen battled to hide her elation. "He looks very respectable."

He looked like the answer to her every prayer. Nancy told her that he'd booked into the inn as Richard Rose. Rose seemed appropriate for a man who loved gardens so much.

"I told you he was." Nancy giggled. "I knew you were curious about him. You've never sewn a ribbon on a bonnet in all your days. You wouldn't know where to start."

So much for her subterfuge. It was a reminder that she needed to be careful with Nancy, who had been with her all her life. Yet again, she wished that Nancy was the kind of servant who was seen and not heard. Even better, one whose allegiance she could trust.

Maids in novels were always happy to carry secret love letters for their mistresses. But Nancy's first loyalty remained to the Earl of Deerforth.

"Nobody interesting ever comes to Little Hamble. I was intrigued."

"Lady Imogen! Lady Imogen!" Mrs. Allery was the local notary's wife and had little grasp of social niceties. She should wait for her betters to acknowledge her, rather than shriek down the street to attract Imogen's attention. Imogen usually did her best to avoid the woman, but today she was grateful for her rudeness.

"That woman!" Nancy muttered. "She's got the manners of a wild boar."

Imogen stifled a laugh. Mrs. Allery, right now, might be one of her favorite people, because it was clear that she meant to introduce Imogen to Little Hamble's exotic visitor. She was also Imogen's best chance for speaking to Caleb without the world guessing that she and the dashing American were already acquainted.

Mrs. Allery fluttered in her direction, ribbons and lace flying from her over-ruffled dress. Caleb moved more slowly, and Imogen winced when she saw how he tried to hide his reliance on the stick.

Oh, my darling... The proof of his pain soured her delight in seeing him.

"Good morning, Mrs. Allery." Imogen struggled to sound as if nothing out of the ordinary took place. "Lovely weather we're having at the moment."

Mrs. Allery dipped into a quick curtsy, as her two horse-faced daughters wandered across to inspect the baker's window. "We haven't seen you in the village lately. There was talk that you might be ill."

There was talk that she'd been embroiled in a scandal rather, Imogen was sure. Little Hamble might be in the middle of nowhere, but some of the local ladies subscribed to the more gossipy London papers and quite a few of them had correspondents in the capital.

Imogen was under no illusion that her family's fall from grace remained a secret from her father's tenants. They'd enjoy hearing of Papa's woes. Lord Deerforth wasn't a diligent landlord.

"No, but thank you for your concern." At her side, she heard Nancy muffle a laugh.

"I believe congratulations are in order."

"Oh?" For a sizzling instant, Imogen met Caleb's dark eyes and hoped to heaven that she wasn't blushing.

Mrs. Allery's smile turned very cat that got the cream. "Miss Faulkner made an excellent match, I hear. Who would ever think of such a...humble lady rising to become the Countess of Halston?"

The woman's false sincerity held a world of meaning. Everyone in the village knew that Lord Deerforth despised his niece and treated her as a dogsbody. Mrs. Allery clearly assumed that Imogen, her father's pet, suffered a hell of jealousy, now her cousin had wed the man that gossip had designated as Imogen's beau.

Imogen was glad that she could respond with utter candor. At least now Mrs. Allery and Nancy could blame her blushes on the lady's spite. "I'm delighted for her. She and Lord Halston are perfect together."

Mrs. Allery looked disgruntled, then fixed a bright smile to her face. "Where are my manners?"

A question that Imogen would dearly love to answer, but she restrained the impulse as the woman gestured toward Caleb. "May I present Mr. Richard Rose of Virginia in the United States? Mr. Rose is visiting Little Hamble, while he makes a tour of nearby beauty spots. He's staying at the Dog and Duck, although Mr. Allery and I have offered him a room with us. He's a most superior person, too fine for our local hostelry."

At last, Imogen could turn to Caleb. She had difficulty containing the broad smile that threatened to break out. "Mr. Rose, welcome to Little Hamble. I hope you're enjoying your stay."

She extended her hand, and Caleb bowed over it. His touch made her feel alive in a way that nothing else had since they'd parted in London. She grit her teeth against a murmur of disappointment when he released her.

"Lady Imogen, your servant."

When he stared deep into her eyes, she saw a mirror of all her love and longing and loneliness. It was a wrench to look away.

"I hoped that your housekeeper might show Mr. Rose around the public rooms at Hamble Park while he's here," Mrs. Allery said.

"That seems an imposition," Caleb said.

"Not at all. We regularly welcome visitors to view the house and the art in the gallery," Imogen said, surprised that she sounded so normal when her heart performed a drunken steeplechase inside her chest.

"That's very generous."

"Not at all. Would tomorrow be convenient?"

He shook his head and smiled. Even a smile that veiled his true feelings made her silly heart launch itself over a triple jump.

"Unfortunately much as I'd like to take in the glories of Hamble Park, I'm leaving very early in the morning. My view of the house will be restricted to what I see when I pass the gates at dawn."

"What a pity," Imogen said, piecing together Caleb's message without difficulty. Tomorrow, they would run away together. She'd soon be on her way to America. She felt like laughing and doing somersaults. And wouldn't that surprise Mrs. Allery?

"Needs must, I'm afraid."

"Where do you go next?"

"I have an appointment further north that won't wait, although it's been a treat to visit the Cotswolds and meet such a kind welcome here at Little Hamble."

"I wish you happy travels, then," Imogen said, fighting to keep her expression blank as a powerful tide of anticipation raced through her.

CHAPTER SIXTEEN

Caleb drew his curricle up in front of Hamble Park's gates. The sun just peeped over the horizon, and it promised to be a fine day. Perfect for travel.

"You understood my message," he said in pleasure, as he watched Imogen let herself out the smaller wrought-iron entrance beside the impressive metalwork of the main gates.

The sight of her made him happy. Over these last weeks, he'd missed her like the devil. For longer than that. Since the day they'd met, any moment that he didn't spend with his darling felt wasted.

"How could I not?" She smiled at him with unconcealed joy, although like him, she kept her voice low. There was a lodge about a hundred yards along the drive, so they needed to be careful. He couldn't bear to think that having reached the point where he and Imogen eloped, they still might come to grief.

"Have you been waiting long?"

"I've been here since three." Self-deprecating humor turned her lips down. "Not that I could sleep before that. I was too excited. I'm getting very good at slipping out of houses in the dark of night. Perhaps I should consider a career as a burglar."

He muffled a laugh and looped the reins around the rail at the front of the neat little vehicle. "Let me step down and help you."

She shook her head. "If you give me your hand, I can manage. It can't be easy for you to get in and out of the carriage."

It wasn't. Even now, six weeks after his beating. He had to commend the efficiency of Lord Deerforth's henchmen.

"Love gives me wings," he said with theatrical fervor, although right now, he really felt as if he could fly. His whole existence led up to this moment, when he and Imogen embarked on a life together.

"Romantic fool," she said with such fondness that he couldn't resent her mockery. She placed two small bags next to his valise in the space behind the seat.

"Is that all you've got?" he asked in surprise.

Any of his sisters would have brought half a household. He'd feared that Imogen's luggage mightn't fit in the curricle, which was built more for speed than capacity. But a large carriage needed a driver, and he wanted as few people as possible to know his destination.

"I thought it best to travel light. Although we'll need to go shopping before we leave for America."

This time, he spoke sincerely. "You're the perfect companion in crime."

She stood beside the carriage and extended her hand. "Not just in crime, I hope."

He helped her up beside him. Then, even though at any moment, the gatekeeper could appear and sound the alarm, he drew her into his arms and kissed her. He hadn't kissed her properly since those temptation-soaked mornings at Prestwick Place, and he hungered for the taste of her lips.

She melted into his embrace and kissed him back with all the passion that was so natural to her. Their separation had gnawed at him. Now they were together, it was as if they'd never been apart.

Only with the greatest reluctance, he drew back to meet hazy dark blue eyes. "I needed that."

"So did I." With an unsteady hand, she straightened her stylish chip straw bonnet. Their enthusiasm had pushed it to the side, to what Caleb thought was a charming angle. In her dark green traveling ensemble, she looked charming altogether.

"The last time I kissed you, I didn't do you justice."

"Well, that was lovely." He saw her mind shift beyond the mist of pleasure. With sudden intent, she surveyed their surroundings. "We really should go. There's so much that I want to know, not least how you are, but we can talk on the road. We just need the horses to kick up a fuss, and we'll wake Mr. Graham at the lodge."

Caleb couldn't help smiling. He was just so damned elated to be with her. "Are you ready to become a runaway bride, my lady?"

She leaned in and kissed him again, far too quickly for his liking, although he, too, realized that they couldn't linger outside her father's house. Legally, she could marry where she liked, now she was twenty-one. But a couple of broken ribs and a month and a half of recovery had taught him a healthy respect for Lord Deerforth's determination to have his own way. And his own way didn't involve his daughter marrying a middle-class American.

"I've been ready for weeks." She cuddled against Caleb's side, as he took the reins and urged the horses into a canter.

As his heart swelled with hope, he glanced down at her. "Then let's not wait, sweetheart."

They'd got away. Nobody had come out to stop her. Nancy hadn't appeared while Imogen packed. Mr. Graham hadn't stirred from his dreams to challenge Caleb's arrival at the gates.

Imogen couldn't believe that their escape had been this easy. Not after all the difficulties that had dogged their affair.

But they'd surmounted those difficulties. Against all the odds, she now set out for a new life with the man she loved.

She'd left a note on Papa's desk in the library, so nobody would think that she'd been stolen away against her will. Although when the servants discovered that she'd taken clothes and other necessities, they'd guess that she'd run off of her own volition.

The note didn't say much. She knew how relentless her father could be, although his violence against Caleb still shocked her. She might be of age, but Papa wouldn't quibble at forcing her back under his control. When she reached America, she'd write to her family and let them all know that she was safe and happy.

"What are you thinking about?" he murmured, as they headed onto the turnpike.

The tollgate was just ahead. It was now full daylight. The summer days were long. Where would she be by sunset? She had so much to ask Caleb. It gradually dawned on her that their frustrating, curtailed meetings were in the past. They could talk to their hearts' content.

They could kiss and touch whenever they wanted, too. Heat flooded her cheeks, as she thought of other things that they could do. She was about to become a bride, after all.

She firmed her hold on his arm, feeling the subtle movement of his muscles as he controlled the two horses. The seat was narrow, crushing them together. She didn't mind at all. His warmth radiated along her side, and her nostrils filled with his spicy scent.

"I'm thinking about how happy I am." She paused. "And how I feared this day might never come."

He glanced down, his eyes grave under the brim of his high-crowned hat. "You always seemed so sure and brave."

"I haven't felt brave this last month," she admitted.

He kissed her gently. "It's been too long since I saw you."

"But now we're together."

"Yes, forever."

"Forever."

He drew the horses to a stop, and for a profound moment, they stared at each other. Without speaking, they made vows as eternal as the promises that they would soon make before a minister.

By the time Imogen glanced toward the tollhouse in the distance, she felt as if something inside her had changed. A wedding loomed ahead, but she'd already made a silent pledge of lifelong devotion to Caleb, just as he pledged his faith to her.

"They'll know you here, won't they?"

"Probably."

"I think you should make your way through the trees. I'll meet you further along the road. Once the household discovers you're gone, they'll search high and low. I don't want to make it easy for anyone to track us."

"Good idea."

Caleb helped her down, although she could tell that it hurt him. He waited until she disappeared into the thick woodland lining the road. Then she heard him urge the horses forward.

She picked up her skirts and rushed ahead, keeping out of sight. Soon, she stumbled upon a path, probably a poacher's track. It brought her out on the road, well past the gatekeeper's cottage. Caleb was already waiting, the horses straining in the shafts. They were fresh and eager to run. From here, the open road stretched ahead.

She climbed up into the carriage and this time, their kiss was longer and more passionate. She was trembling by the time he stared down at her with wonder in his eyes. "We're going to make it."

"We are."

"Let's go. We have a long journey. We're getting married the day after tomorrow."

"So soon?"

"I need to make you my wife as fast as I can."

"Because of Papa?"

A wry smile twisted his lips. "Because I can't keep my hands off you."

Was it wicked to find that answer enormously satisfactory? "Oh."

"Are you nervous?"

"A little. But I've liked everything else we've done. I imagine I'll enjoy...that. Especially if it's along the lines of what you did at Prestwick Place."

He groaned. "Don't remind me. You have no idea how many sleepless nights that has caused me."

A blush rose in her cheeks. "Not just you."

He held the reins with one hand and curled his arm around her shoulders. "At least I didn't suffer alone."

From the warm shelter of Caleb's embrace, she viewed the countryside. The road was in good condition, and now that the trees had thinned, fields dotted with sheep lined the way. This wasn't the main North Road, which even at this hour would be busy.

When Caleb gave the horses their heads, Imogen approved. The greater distance that they put between themselves and the discovery of her disappearance, the better. In June, no housemaid would enter her room at dawn to stoke the fire. Because she'd become such a slugabed, Nancy wouldn't bring her morning tea until after nine.

By then, Imogen would be hours away, thank goodness. With luck, it might take the servants even longer to work out that she wasn't out walking in the gardens. It was what she used to do before she went to London.

Once the staff knew that she'd gone and informed her father, hordes of people would hunt her. But getting a message to London from Gloucestershire took time and given the servants' reluctance to spark Lord Deerforth's formidable temper, they might delay alerting him until they were sure that Imogen had run off.

She was grimly aware that her optimistic predictions of a good head start relied on too many maybes. To distract herself from the disturbing thought, she turned to Caleb. "This is a nice carriage. Is it hired?"

"No, it seemed more practical to buy one."

Several times, Caleb had told her that the American business was thriving, but even so, she was surprised that his funds extended to such a sporting vehicle. "It's new?"

"Not quite. One of the men I met when I was interviewing contractors to work on Lord Tierney's project was buying a landau, and he had no further use for such a dashing rig. I offered to take it off his hands. He lives in Preston, so it was easy to make a small detour and pick it up on my way north. I'll sell it before we go to America."

"You've thought of everything."

"I've always known that to win you, I needed to be cleverer than my opponents. This carriage is fast and well-sprung, and I don't have to worry about getting it back to its owner."

"So where are we going?"

"A village called Barrowford near Kendal."

Kendal was a couple of hundred miles north. "So far?"

"It's out of your father's reach and too obscure for anyone to pay attention to what happens there. Lord Deerforth will start looking for you closer to home or in London, I suspect, or he'll try and track you to Scotland. Going to Barrowford should give us breathing space. It's also within easy reach of Liverpool. I booked us passage to New York next week."

The future rushed toward Imogen even faster than this swift little carriage flew across the miles. The prospects opening before her left her breathless. "Goodness me."

He glanced at her. "Now are you nervous?"

"I'm a little taken aback, although I shouldn't be. It just seems so...real all at once."

"You can change your mind."

A short laugh escaped her. "Don't be a clodpoll, Caleb. I've waited for this day almost from the first."

"Good." Masculine contentment weighted the short answer.

"What did you tell the Tierneys?"

"That I want to see more of the Lake District before I settle on a final design. They thought it was a good idea for me to get out of London for a while. His lordship still feels as guilty as blazes."

"He shouldn't feel guilty. Your injuries aren't his fault."

"No, but it gave me an excuse to get away and arrange our escape. I chose Cumbria for our wedding, because it's the part of Britain I know best. The vicar at Barrowford seems a good man, and he's looking forward to meeting the bride. I told him you've been caring for a family member in the south."

"Lying to the clergy. How dastardly."

Her gentle jibe made him smile. "Think, my darling, soon we won't have to lie or pretend or hide away ever again."

As his hold firmed, she snuggled closer. "I can't wait."

"I couldn't risk buying a special license from Doctors' Commons in London. Your father would be sure to hear if I had. I got our marriage license from the Bishop of Carlisle. But then I needed to settle somewhere for four weeks so they could call the banns."

"That explains why you were away for so long. I was worried sick that your injuries had worsened. Plague take Elizabeth, she isn't the world's greatest correspondent, and I couldn't ask my other friends about you without betraying an improper interest."

"An improper interest sounds good."

She didn't smile. Instead, she wriggled out of his embrace so that she could see his face. "Caleb, are you better?"

"I get the occasional twinge, but I'm healing well."

That didn't reassure her. Imogen would wager that he played down both the twinges and their frequency. When he'd helped her into the carriage, the blood had drained from his face. "Will you always need the stick?"

"I hope not. I'm more limber every day."

"When we met in the square, I couldn't see you very well."

A grunt of wry amusement. "I was quite the hideous monster, although the damage looked much worse than it was."

"I doubt that." She glanced down to where both hands now held the reins. "How are your hands? Can you draw?"

"Not yet, but the doctor has given me exercises."

Guilt stabbed her anew. She should never have danced with him. She'd been a reckless fool to put momentary satisfaction ahead of good sense. "How will you work?"

He shrugged. In London, moving his shoulders had been agony. Now he showed no ill effects. Perhaps not everything that he said was well-meaning lies.

"If I have to, I'll learn to draw with my left hand. Or as you said, you can draw for me. I'm hoping you'll join me in the business, once we're set up in Saratoga."

Pleasure flooded her. "Really?"

"Only if you'd like to." He cast her a quick glance before he returned his attention to his driving, although surely he knew that she'd jump to work with him. "But both Mr. Perrett and I liked your ideas. As it seems that American style isn't going to take over England, perhaps English style might appeal in America."

"Partners in work as well as love?"

"If you like. You don't have to decide now, although you may need to help me with drafting until my hands get their old skills back."

She didn't need to think about it. A chance to be with Caleb every day? A chance to prove that she wasn't just another aristocratic hobbyist when it came to her passion for gardening? A chance to seize a future beyond the bounds of feminine domesticity? "I'd love to work with you."

After a pause, he spoke with affectionate impatience. "Don't tell me you're crying, you goose."

She fumbled in her pocket for a lace handkerchief. "It's mad, isn't it?"

"I thought you'd be happy to join me."

"I am."

"So happy that you're sobbing your eyes out."

"A slight exaggeration," she said in a clogged voice as she wiped her cheeks. "For so long, I've hoped that we'd have a life together. Now that it's actually happening, my emotions are in complete disarray."

"In a good way?"

"Yes. It all sounds so wonderful. A person can cry with joy, you know."

"It's always struck me as absurd not to make use of the skills and intelligence of half of humanity, just because that half happens to be female."

"A lot of women work. Only rich women have the luxury of leisure."

"I'm not saying you need to work. Hell, you can spend your days embroidering and taking tea, if you like. As I told you, I'm not a poor man."

"You're giving me the chance to use my talents."

"My mother has always worked with my father. Most successfully, too."

"They never argue?"

Caleb burst into laughter. "Like cat and dog sometimes, but it never seems to change how much they love each other."

"In my family, nobody except Eliot argues with my father, and I doubt that there's much genuine love between them."

He reached across to squeeze her hand. "Genuine love thrives on healthy debate."

"I agree." She blew her nose and surveyed her surroundings through blurry eyes.

Caleb was right. It was stupid to cry when she was so happy. But she couldn't help it. A world of freedom and opportunity opened up before her, and her gratitude was too powerful to suppress.

It was still light when they stopped at a small coaching inn south of Manchester. Imogen knew without asking that Caleb avoided large towns in an attempt to cover their tracks. With regular changes of horses, they'd driven more than a hundred miles from Hamble Park.

Once she'd gained control over her chaotic emotions, she'd enjoyed the trip. In so many ways, her life had been restricted. She knew the corner of Gloucestershire around Hamble Park. She'd visited a few aristocratic estates with her father. She'd been to London and Prestwick Place.

Now she traveled through unfamiliar country to the Lake District, which she'd always wanted to see. In a few days, she'd leave England for America.

It was difficult to come to terms with so many radical changes over such a short period.

Servants rushed out to unload their modest luggage and help her out of the carriage. She and Caleb had snatched a couple of hurried meals on the way, but she was stiff and tired after long hours in the curricle. She was looking forward to a wash and a hot dinner and a bed.

She glanced up at Caleb, who remained in the seat. He looked drawn with exhaustion and, while he hadn't mentioned it, pain. She'd offered to take the reins, but he'd done all the driving. Now she was sorry that she hadn't insisted. She noted the unhealthy pallor of his skin and the deep lines etched between his nose and his taut lips. He'd been remarkably quiet over the last couple of hours, too.

"Mr. Rose, we've put your instructions into place." The landlord bustled out to greet them, using Caleb's alias from Little Hamble. "Two bedrooms for you and your lady wife, and a parlor in between. We've got hot water waiting and a good dinner on the way."

"Excellent. Will you please show Mrs. Rose to our rooms? I'll be with her presently."

Imogen heard how Caleb struggled to conceal his discomfort. Annoyance rose, along with agonizing pity. "Let me help you down."

"I'm fine," he said with a hint of a snap.

"You're not." She came closer to the curricle and lowered her voice. "Don't be such a proud fool."

A remorseful smile curved his lips. "I'm not sure I can stand."

"Then I'll hold you up. Or ask a servant to help. I told you before that you don't have to play the hero with me. I love all of you. In sickness and in health, remember?"

She waited for an argument, wondering if she and her beloved were about to have their first constructive quarrel, along the lines of his parents' interactions.

"I hate that I'm less than I should be." His voice was so soft that she had to lean in to hear over the yard's noise.

"You're everything I want. I couldn't love you more. A few stumbles here and there don't change that." She kept her voice soft, too. "Now come inside and stop being an idiot."

With a short laugh, he shifted in the seat. "As my lady commands."

Imogen wrenched her gaze away from Caleb to save his pride. She understood it, even if she didn't approve. She addressed two brawny grooms with all the hauteur that a daughter of the Earl of Deerforth could muster. "You there, my husband is recovering from an injury. Assist him out of the carriage."

"Aye, my lady," the stockier one said, as they leaped to obey her as fast as any servant at Hamble Park would.

Most fine ladies wouldn't travel without at the very least a maid to accompany them. But she knew that the tone of authority, not to mention her expensive and fashionable clothes, would impress the staff at this small country inn. Nobody would question her right to take charge, despite her youth.

With the men's help, Caleb made it to the ground, but she was appalled at the effort it cost him. The long day's travel had taken its toll.

As he found his feet on the cobblestones, she retrieved his stick from under the carriage seat. "Here, my love."

"Thank you."

Earlier, she'd cried for joy. Now, she wanted to cry with compassion, as his knuckles whitened over the stick's ebony handle. Each time they'd stopped, he'd been awkward getting out of the carriage, but he'd pushed on into the late afternoon to reach this inn. She'd been tired herself, and hadn't observed him as closely as she should. She wouldn't make that mistake again.

Moving to his side, she took his arm. He trembled under her hand and while he tried to hide it, he was panting after climbing down from the carriage. She wanted to scold him, but she beat back the urge. "Shall we go?"

"Yes," Caleb said through his teeth. To Imogen's relief, he didn't protest as she helped him upstairs to an airy chamber at the rear of the inn.

CHAPTER SEVENTEEN

Caleb broke away from Imogen and collapsed into a chair, as his stick clattered to the ground. He felt like all kinds of hell.

Through the blood thundering in his ears, he listened to Imogen give the servants orders in a voice that he'd never heard from her before. It was absurd, but he'd never before believed in his heart that she was a great lady who had been chatelaine of her father's house since she was a young girl.

Every time he told himself that he knew her, she presented him with a new facet of her character. No wonder she was so fascinating.

Right now, as she took immediate and natural authority over their arrangements, he couldn't help admiring her strength. In his bleaker moments over the last few weeks, he'd wondered whether he was cruel to rip this girl from everything she knew and steal her away to a new life among strangers.

He didn't doubt her love, and the idea of leaving England without her made him feel like someone tore out his liver with red-hot pincers. But in accepting Caleb, Imogen accepted a thousand other changes. He couldn't bear to think that one day she'd look at him and regret that an excess of youthful romanticism had denied her the advantages she was born to enjoy.

But as he listened to her now, he realized that she was strong enough to survive anywhere. His last niggling doubt about their decision vanished.

He heard the door shut, and he realized that he must have fallen into an exhausted doze. He watched Imogen fall to her knees beside his chair. She'd taken off her bonnet and her stylish pelisse to reveal a matching green travel dress beneath.

"You asked too much of yourself today."

He had. But he'd been determined to carry her as far as he could from her swine of a father. He took off his hat and set it on the floor. "I'm so damned keen to marry you."

Her smile was rueful. "I'm keen to marry you, too. But I'd rather have you alive for the ceremony. Call me odd, but I'd prefer not to pledge my troth to a ghost."

He managed to laugh, although it hurt his ribs. Right now, everything hurt.

Caleb thought that he'd manage the travel. He'd been north and back again since Imogen left London. But he'd completed those trips in sensible increments. Today, he'd started driving before the early dawn, and it was going on eight now. "I promise I'm nowhere near dead."

"I'm not convinced."

"Kiss me and I'll come alive."

Amusement sparkled in her eyes. "Like a fairy story?"

"The sleeping prince."

"I haven't heard of that one."

Nonetheless, she leaned over the stuffed arm of the chair and kissed him with heartbreaking gentleness. He'd been joking about her kiss restoring his failing strength. But by God, her lips performed sorcery. His aches became bearable. "You're the princess in this particular story. Just now, you sounded like you commanded an army. If I was capable of standing, I'd salute you."

She gave a soft laugh. He was relieved to see her concern fade as they spoke. He could imagine what she must have thought when he had such trouble moving. "My countess training came in handy for once."

"I'm sorry I frightened you." He caught her gloved hand. "It truly isn't anywhere near as bad as it looks."

"And you intend to do it again tomorrow." Her disapproval of that plan was clear. Also her skepticism about his assessment of his travails.

"I want my ring on your finger, Imogen. Until then, all the advantages are your father's." He paused. "Which reminds me – will you open my valise? There's a small box in the bottom."

Curiosity lit her eyes. Instead of asking what he was up to, she rose with a grace that all those hours of travel hadn't marred. Within minutes, she stood at his side, extending a small velvet-covered box toward him. "Is this what you want?"

"Yes, that's it." He stripped off his leather gloves and dropped them to the floor before he accepted the box. "You might want to take your gloves off, too."

Imogen removed her gloves and shoved them in her pocket. He struggled to his feet, trying to hide what it cost him to move. By Jericho, he'd hoped to be in better form than this. He wanted to cut a dashing figure on what he hoped would be a memorable occasion.

"Caleb, what are you doing?" Imogen asked with a frown. She reached out to hold his elbow as he took a second or two to find his balance.

"I owe you a birthday present," he said, once he'd caught his breath.

All his life, he'd been vigorous and strong. It wounded his vanity to be such a blasted lame duck, when more than ever, he wanted to be the lover that Imogen dreamed of.

"It can wait." Her hold tightened. "Until my next birthday, if need be. Having you here is the best present you could give me."

"No, it can't wait." He pulled free. "Hold out your left hand."

He waited for her to insist that he sit down, but she must have recognized his determination. The hand she stretched out trembled, and powerful emotion glowed in her eyes.

Caleb wasn't altogether steady either. And not entirely because of the beating's aftereffects.

He fumbled as he opened the box and took out a ring. "Happy birthday, my darling."

Cringing at his clumsiness, he caught her hand and slid the delicate ring onto her slender finger. His hands had healed remarkably well, with only a few scars to show for Gibbs's ingenuity. Full dexterity hadn't yet returned, but he had a greater range of movement with every day.

"Oh, Caleb," she said in wonder, as she stared down at her hand lying in his.

The sparkle of moisture through her heavy sweep of eyelashes warned him of her powerful reaction. "You're crying again, aren't you?"

Those eyelashes fluttered up to reveal blue eyes glazed with tears. "I can't help it. It's beautiful. It seems..."

He slipped the box into his pocket. "A promise that we're going to have the life we want?"

"Yes." Her voice thickened with feeling. "That's exactly it."

"You like it?"

With a dazzled expression, she gazed down at the ring. "I love it."

"I chose a sapphire to match your eyes." When he saw the ring in a curio shop on a narrow medieval street behind York Minster, he'd known immediately that he wanted it. It wasn't just the rich blue stone. The buttery gold and the subtle chasing around the band were unusual and beautiful, just like Imogen herself.

"Oh..."

He went on, guessing that she struggled to frame words to express her reaction. He didn't mind. By now, he knew her well enough to understand that she was pleased.

"I know it's not terribly fashionable. It's at least a hundred and fifty years old. If you'd like a more modern setting, I can—"

"Don't you dare." She snatched her hand back and pressed it to her breast, as if he'd threatened to steal the ring. "It's perfect."

He'd chosen right, then. He thought he had. "It's a poesy ring."

Imogen tugged the ring off and peered down at the tiny cursive writing around the inside of the band. "I can't..."

"It's French. It says '*Toujours à toi.*'"

"'Always yours?'"

"Yes."

"Oh, Caleb..." The tears overflowed at last, and she leaned forward and kissed him with a poignant yearning that seeped into his bones. "Thank you."

"I've been carrying it around since May. I found it on one of my trips north. I'm so happy you love it, too."

"I do. I'll treasure it forever."

The success of his selection made him feel stronger. Caleb slid his hand into his pocket and brought out the box again. He opened it. "There's also this."

She looked at the plain gold band, then met his eyes. "Part of our disguise?"

"If you like, although in a few days, it will mean that you're my wife. But for now, it will preserve your reputation. You can't keep your gloves on all the time. Will you wear it?"

"I will." She pulled off the engagement ring, to allow him to slip on the wedding ring.

"Once we're wed, you'll wear it forever."

"Yes." The moment felt strangely solemn.

She replaced the sapphire on her finger and held out her hand to admire the effect. Caleb was relieved to see a smile, if a little misty, curving her lips. "It's mad, but these make me feel as if we're already married."

"In my heart, we are." He drew her against him, ignoring the complaint of his ribs, and kissed her. While recovering from his injuries, he'd had far too much time to imagine what he'd do to Imogen when he got her to himself. Now despite injuries and exhaustion, his body reacted with predictable enthusiasm.

He curled his hands around her bottom, shaping the lush curves through layers of skirts and petticoats. With a groan, he brought her close. She was so warm and soft, and her kiss extended a gilt-edged invitation to paradise. With a soft sound of approval, she flicked her tongue against his. Heat flared, made a mockery of caution and pain and weariness. He flexed his hands against that luscious rump and tilted his hips forward.

The knock at the door emerged from another universe. A second knock made Imogen pull free with a grumble. "I've ordered baths for us."

"Damn it..." Caleb stepped back and ran an unsteady hand through his hair. "I forgot everything, except how much I want you."

Her cheeks were pink when she crossed to open the door. The army of servants who invaded the room lowered their eyes, as they carried the tub and cans of steaming water through into one of the bedrooms. Caleb had no doubt that they guessed they'd interrupted a romantic interlude. Imogen looked flushed and ruffled and well-kissed. And heartbreakingly beautiful.

Caleb stirred to the click of the latch. A hot bath, a lavish dinner, and several glasses of good claret had sent him to bed early. Imogen had been just as tired.

Imogen poised in the doorway in the circle of golden light cast from her chamber stick. He should be surprised. But he wasn't. Not really. He'd tried to play by the rules. He'd intended to leave her untouched until their wedding. But neither of them was much good at doing the proper thing.

When he sat up, he bit back a groan. He kept forgetting his injuries, although he felt much better now than he had after a day in that mobile torture chamber disguised as a curricle. The bath had smoothed the stiffness from his muscles, and a couple of hours' sleep left him refreshed. He almost felt like his old self.

While he guessed why she was here, he gave her the benefit of the doubt. "Are you all right?"

Her eyes devoured the bare chest revealed above the blankets. "I missed you."

He was naked. She wore a pretty pink and white silk robe. Despite the shadows, he had a feeling that she, too, might be naked beneath the flimsy wrap.

Shining black hair tumbled around her shoulders. That conveyed its own message. He'd dreamed of seeing that gorgeous hair cascading about her. He'd dreamed of burying his hands in that extravagant mane and twining it into a silky rope as he thrust into her body. By Harry, were those dreams about to become reality?

"I'm prepared to wait," he said, although that wasn't nearly as true as it had been before Imogen hovered mere feet away.

She took a step into the room and let the door close behind her with a soft snick. Flickering candlelight transformed her into a creature of beguiling mystery. The silk clung to her body, hinting at other feminine mysteries concealed beneath.

Caleb's heart raced so hard that his ribs ached anew. His blood thundered hot and strong. Every male instinct clamored for him to jump out of bed and grab her before she changed her mind.

She studied him with more of that unconcealed hunger that set his nerves leaping with irresistible desire. The light wasn't strong enough for him to see if she blushed, but he'd wager good coin that she did. "Should I go away?"

A grunt of self-derisive laughter escaped. "Don't be a silly wigeon, Imogen. I wanted you from the first moment I saw you. It's a miracle that you're still a virgin."

She took another step forward and set the candle on the deal table against the wall. "Until we're on the ship to America, I won't be certain that we've won. We've overcome separations and the fear of discovery and other people's interference. Now at last we're alone. We should take our chance, whatever old people and society and the church say."

Imogen's passionate declaration stole his breath. She had such courage. He shifted across the bed to make room for her and pushed the covers aside to reveal his bare body. He was already hard and ready.

Her fascinated gaze centered on his erect cock. Even in the uncertain light, he read shock on her face. Shock and unmistakable curiosity.

Anticipation tightened his every muscle. "Come here, beloved."

CHAPTER EIGHTEEN

Imogen gave an incoherent gurgle of happiness and darted forward to join Caleb in the big four-poster bed. Once she was within reach, he seized her and tugged her down over him. The welcome in his kiss made her pounding heart expand to bursting.

The sight of his aroused body had surprised her. So many times, she'd felt his hardness through his clothes, but it was different when he wasn't wearing anything. Now that male part of him rubbed against her stomach. Nervous anticipation shuddered through her. Soon he'd put that massive column of flesh inside her, and she'd belong to him at last.

Still kissing her in a frenzy of desire, he rolled her beneath him and crushed her into the mattress. He squeezed the air out of her – or perhaps she should blame her breathlessness on her feverish excitement. She wriggled until she cradled him between her parted thighs. Trembling hands ran over his back. Under her palms, his muscles tensed and released. His skin was hot and smooth.

He groaned and rose on his elbows. The candlelight barely reached this corner, so she couldn't read his expression. "I was right. I thought it was too good to be true, but by Jericho, you're naked under this ridiculous confection of silk."

The awe in his voice made her laugh through her blushes. "It seemed easier."

"My Imogen! Always practical."

He kissed the skin revealed under the gaping edges of the robe. He'd touched her breasts before, when they'd both come so close to losing control at Prestwick Place. Nothing however prepared her for the wild sensations sizzling through her veins, when he took his time to discover what pleased her. A great weight of arousal settled in the pit of her stomach, a throbbing demand that only Caleb could answer.

"You're so beautiful," he whispered, nibbling a path across her bosom. Her flesh swelled under his lips, and her nipples peaked with aching need.

"You can't see me."

"I don't need to see you." When his lips closed around one beaded point, she felt the most delightful suction. Her breath escaped in a broken moan of surrender, and she arched up, instinctively seeking more.

He increased the pressure on her nipple, until that weight of desire inside her dissolved into hot liquid. She cried out and tangled one shaking hand in his rumpled hair.

His hands were busy, pushing aside the silk robe. Her skin was so sensitive that the brush of soft material made her shiver. He shifted from her breast, but before she could express disappointment, he took her other nipple into his mouth. When his teeth scraped across the sensitive tip, she squeaked with surprised pleasure.

He growled his satisfaction and began to kiss a line down her stomach, pausing along the way to explore the ticklish dip of her navel. Her stomach quivered under his lips, as circles of heat rippled out from where he tormented her. Then his lips retraced the path until they met hers.

Imogen shifted in restless demand, feeling his hardness against her skin. She lifted her knees to frame his hips. Every steamy moment intensified the heat between her legs. The air she gulped had a salty edge. Caleb's skin smelled different, too, earthy and musky.

Another of those disturbing surges inside her. Caleb's hands trailed along the top of her thighs and glanced across the place where she ached for him. She jerked at the contact and felt another rush of pleasure.

"Oh, no," she muttered, reaching down to check if she was as wet as she feared. She was. "How embarrassing."

With a muffled grunt of amusement, he nipped a thrilling line down her neck. "It's natural, sweetheart. It means you want me."

"I do want you," she choked out. With Caleb's every touch, her body became more of a stranger. "It still feels odd."

When he'd touched her before this, she'd felt wonderful and daring. But fear of discovery had inhibited her responses. Tonight nobody would interrupt them, and it turned out that her earlier reactions were a pale reflection of what she was capable of experiencing.

He slid his hand between her legs and traced the slick folds, provoking more of that melting sensation. "Your body is getting ready for me."

As the world reeled, she clutched his shoulders. "This is so bizarre," she panted.

His hand paused in its brazen exploration. "Should I stop?"

The beat of her blood threatened to deafen her. "Do you want to?"

Another grunt of amusement. "What do you think?"

Imogen thought that he was avid for her, which she liked. She reminded herself that she'd been brave enough to seek him out. She'd even been brave enough to take off her clothes before she did. Surely she could be brave enough to occupy this new world of overwhelming sensual power.

She ran one hand along the hot skin of his shoulder and gave the soft curls at his nape a gentle tug. Speaking was difficult. His touch stole her breath. "I'm being silly."

When Caleb kissed her, she closed her eyes and sank into radiant darkness. By the time he drew away, she shook and her fingers tangled in his hair.

"No, all this is new to you. We should expect a few collywobbles. If you like, we can wait until we get married."

"We've spent months waiting," she said almost in a wail. "I don't want to wait anymore."

"Perhaps I'm going too fast."

Imogen shook her head against the pillows. "No, I'm just letting fear of the unknown rule me. Do it, Caleb. Make me yours. I know you want to."

While she couldn't see his face, she heard conflict in his voice. "I want you to want this, too."

"I do." To convince him, she drew him down for more kisses. She widened her legs in wordless encouragement for him to touch her again.

On a groan that sounded like surrender, he began to stroke her cleft. Soon she was gasping and quaking and bowing up until her breasts squashed against his chest. Soft dark hair grew across his pectorals, and the friction on her tight nipples added to the storm of sensations assailing her.

Soon Caleb found a place that made her shiver and cry out. Heat washed through her in such a powerful wave that she took a moment to realize that he'd slid a finger inside her. When her body stretched to accommodate him, she moaned with surprise.

"Does this hurt?" he asked, his voice rasping. Under her hands, his shoulders were tense.

"No," she said, although like so much else tonight, the invasion felt...odd.

"I fear I'm going to hurt you when the time comes."

She hardly heard him as a troubling thought struck her. "Does it hurt your hands? I know my father's men did terrible things to them."

His laugh was rueful. "I'm not feeling any pain."

With a slowness that set off fresh quivers, he withdrew his finger. Then before she could suck in enough air to feed her starving lungs, he pushed inside again. She guessed that he used two fingers, because the fit was even snugger. This time, the incursion didn't feel so peculiar. In fact, as she became accustomed to what he did, it broached on pleasant.

All this time without Caleb, she'd felt painfully empty. She didn't feel empty anymore.

"I wish I'd talked to Stella about this," she muttered. Her observations of the natural world weren't helping quite as much as she'd hoped they would when she came here tonight.

Caleb gave another of those brief laughs and flexed his fingers. "You'll just have to trust me to bring you through."

"I do." Her nails dug into the sinews of his shoulders. "Do that again."

"You like it?"

"Yes," she said on a long exhalation. She pressed up into his hand.

As his hips shifted, Imogen dragged him down for a blazing kiss. The pressure between her thighs became harder and hotter.

Jittery excitement crashed through her. The time had come. She wanted this. She wanted it more than she could say. But it still felt peculiar, now that his flesh joined with hers.

When he pushed forward, her discomfort increased. Her earlier giddy pleasure receded, as all the nerves in her body concentrated where Caleb edged into her.

She'd always loved his touch and his kisses. She loved *him*, for pity's sake.

So far, she wasn't loving this.

Still kissing her, Caleb hitched her hips up to allow him to inch a little further. A muffled complaint escaped her, and he raised his head.

"I promise it will get better." His voice sounded raw, as if it hurt to talk. She felt him staring down at her through the gloom.

"It's not too bad," she said in a tight whisper, which made him laugh.

His amusement vibrated through her. It really was as if they melded into one. Despite the awkwardness and discomfort, the overwhelming intimacy pleased her. Physical pleasure might have ebbed, but there was something extraordinary about the way her body accepted Caleb.

"That's what I told you when you asked about my injuries."

"You were lying."

"So are you." He paused. "It might be easier if you breathe. You're as stiff as a board."

Imogen was braced for more pain. He was right. Holding her breath didn't help.

She bit her lip until she tasted blood and stared up at him. Part of her wanted to see his eyes – they were always alight with so much love for her. But another part of her was grateful for the darkness. She feared that if he could read her expression, he might stop. They'd come so far, she refused to give up now.

He kissed her, while his weight inside her made her feel as if he split her apart. "Breathe, my love."

Imogen realized that she hadn't yet followed his suggestion. She curled her fingers into his shoulders and opened her mouth to snatch a gulp of air. It helped, so she did it again. The frantic clutch of her intimate muscles eased a fraction.

Caleb made an incoherent sound of approval and caught her legs to bend her knees higher. She bit back a moan, although at last her body adjusted to his size. As the fraught seconds continued, she went back to holding her breath, afraid he'd hear her distress.

His muscles tautened, until they felt like granite under her hands. His hips surged forward. Pain sliced through her like lightning.

She cried out, even as he seated himself fully within her on a great exhalation. He buried his head in the curve between her neck and shoulder. In an attempt to find some anchor in a whirling world, she flung her arms around him. Her blood pounded in great thumps, and her whole body hurt.

Tears trickled down her temples, as she tilted her chin toward the ceiling. She had a sudden memory of Stella, sneaking back from her lover's bed at Prestwick Place. Her cousin had looked as though she'd dined on rainbows. She'd been as sleek with satisfaction as a cat after a good hunting expedition.

She couldn't doubt that Stella had enjoyed Lord Halston's attentions.

So why didn't Imogen feel like that?

"For heaven's sake, breathe, Imogen," Caleb muttered against her skin, after what felt like a century of lying motionless over her. He was heavy, and heat radiated from his body to hers.

By heaven, she had to get some air, or else she'd pass out. Already stars danced in front of her eyes. Not, to her regret, the kind of stars that she'd imagined she'd see when she made love to Caleb.

She gasped and as she'd feared, she heard a betraying sob in the sound. Caleb rose on his elbows, and this time she inhaled properly. Immediately the world's fuzzy edges sharpened.

"I hurt you."

There was no point trying to lie. He always caught her out. "You said it would hurt."

He sighed and settled deeper, when she'd thought that he was as deep inside her as he could go. "Is it so bad?"

It was. It was awful. It was like being torn in two. It was...

She opened her mouth to tell him the truth, and in the process wriggled down in the bed. And realized that while Caleb had held himself unmoving, the worst of the agony had retreated.

"I must be malformed," she said in a shamed mutter.

That surprised Caleb into another laugh. "Don't be a ninny, Imogen. You're perfect."

More tears sprang to her eyes. "I don't feel perfect. I feel like a failure."

"Sweetheart, nobody is a failure. We've only just started. We've got plenty of time to get this right."

"I admire your optimism," she said with a hint of irritation. "And don't you dare laugh at me again."

"I'm not."

"You are."

"Perhaps a little."

Before she could express further resentment, he kissed her with an unfettered carnality that turned her blood to honey. It seemed mad that his lips delivered such heavenly pleasure, when the other...didn't.

Except...

Perhaps it wasn't so bad anymore. Perhaps it was even...quite nice.

Perhaps it went beyond nice.

Another squirm sparked pleasure. With unthinking eagerness, she lifted her hips.

"Caleb, that was..." Words eluded her.

"Better?"

Her pain had faded to a distant ache, more memory than active nuisance. Caleb's invasion of her body now made her feel claimed rather than ripped apart. She wriggled again. Just to make sure. And also because the sensation improved, every time she did it.

"Yes." Imogen stretched up and kissed him again, while another thrill coursed through her.

He kissed her back, using his tongue and teeth to excite her. This time, that bizarre inner melting pleased instead of embarrassed her.

He made an encouraging sound and sucked her lower lip. She wriggled against the sheets. Those enjoyable sensations between her legs became such an extended experience that she couldn't tell where one response ended and the next started.

With a yielding sigh, she tightened her thighs around his hips. When he moved, powerful reaction shook her and her moan expressed nothing but cooperation.

It turned out that she wasn't deformed. What a relief. Her body now had no difficulty opening to Caleb's thrusts. In fact, she loved the way that he filled her. At the peak of each glide, she felt complete in a way that she'd never felt before.

Her deathly grip on his shoulders relaxed. She flexed her hands, sore with clinging onto him like a limpet to a rock. She started to stroke his skin, discovering the hard shoulders and the rhythmic contraction and release of his back as he moved inside her.

"I love you, Imogen." He rose above her, supporting his weight on his arms. Deep feeling turned his voice into a subterranean rumble. "I didn't know I could love anyone the way I love you."

When he plunged inside her, the new angle changed the stimulus in a most enjoyable way. "I love you, too, Caleb." Then daringly, "I love this."

He went still, before he spoke with such joy that she wanted to cry. "My darling..."

He increased the pace, and Imogen gasped in amazement as enjoyment spiraled into something much more profound. The pressure inside her coiled tighter. It was like racing toward the sun, faster and faster, until she couldn't breathe. As she whirled higher, sensation gripped her whole body.

"Caleb, what's happening to me?" she managed to stammer, while the entire world shrank to his body shifting over her and the hot waves of yearning washing through her.

"This is meant to happen, Imogen." His voice was raw and choppy, and he rocked faster, as though he strove to cross some ultimate threshold. "Give into it."

He penetrated so deep, surely he must touch her heart. Everything dissolved in a blast of searing white light. It was like stepping over the edge of a cliff and discovering that she'd grown wings.

"Oh!" she exclaimed, as she clenched around him. Her body ignited to dazzling flame. "That's wonderful."

He moved once more, then went still on a long guttural growl. A flood of heat inside her told her that he'd poured his seed into her.

Imogen quaked through to the limit of incandescent rapture, then drifted down from the outer reaches of the stars. As the peak of astounding experience ebbed, she wrapped her arms around him.

When he buried his head in the side of her neck, his lips moved in a phantom kiss. Tears prickled her eyes as tenderness flooded in to follow that earth-shattering climax. When she was so ecstatically happy, it was insane to want to blubber her heart out.

Caleb rose on his elbows, and she sucked in a huge gust of air. His eyes glittered through the darkness. When she'd first come to this room, she'd been grateful that he couldn't see her blushes. Not to mention that she wasn't sure, despite her boldness, that she was ready to go to his bed in a blaze of light.

Now she was sorry that she couldn't see his expression. Not that she doubted his pleasure in what they'd just done. Or that she'd satisfied him. When he'd pumped into her, his groan had held a note of triumph.

"You're marvelous." When he kissed her, she tasted weariness and pleasure and love on his lips.

"Is it always like that?" she asked in wonder. "I can't describe what just happened, but it was like listening to a choir of angels singing."

"I'm not sure angels were involved." Tiredness weighted his laugh, like his kiss. "I was feeling rather devilish when you came to my bed."

"It was definitely angels. There was too much heaven in what we did for it to be anything else."

"To answer your question, it's never been like that for me before."

That answer pleased her so much that she kissed him again. Silence reigned for a delightful interval.

"I'm sorry I hurt you," he said, after what felt like a long time.

"I've almost forgotten that. Anyway it was worth it for what came afterward." She tightened her embrace. He was still inside her. The intimacy of the joining inspired more of the poignant emotion that made her feel stupidly tearful. "Let's do it again."

He kissed her. "I love you, Imogen. You're all spirit and pluck."

"I'm all yours, that's what I am."

"Yes, you are."

She basked in his masculine contentment. Her hands stroked down the damp skin of his back to clutch his firm buttocks. "I love you, too."

Caleb rolled to the side. His weight had been wonderful, but breathing now became easier. The air was thick with earthy scents. He drew her into his arms, and she rested her head on his shoulder.

Despite asking him to do all that again, she was weary. As pleasant little flutters stirred her blood, she bit back a huge yawn.

"I tired you out," he said with the fond teasing that always turned her bones to syrup. "I didn't think I'd see the day."

Imogen gave a soft huff of laughter. "You – and a long day of traveling."

"Well, that, too."

An unwelcome thought struck her. Leaning one arm on his chest, she rose and struggled to see his face through the darkness. The candle had long ago guttered out. "Did this hurt you?"

"It's not the same for a man."

She made an impatient sound. "No, not that. But you're still getting over a beating, and what we did took a lot of energy."

He caught a hank of hair and guided her down for a brief kiss. Tiredness strengthened his American drawl. "Believe me, I wasn't thinking about anything, except how much I wanted you."

That was a nice answer, but it didn't ease her worry. "What about now?"

"Maybe the odd ache here and there, but any pain was worth it to make you mine at last. The reality was so much better than my most vivid fantasies. I might have heard the angels, too."

Gratification flooded her. "I'm so glad. I didn't know things would get quite so strenuous." She frowned. "Actually I'm not sure what I imagined. Not what happened."

The hand holding her hair loosened into a caress. "I'm sure I can still rustle up a surprise or two."

She knew that he was smiling. "Oh?"

"I want to save something for our wedding night."

She wanted to ask him more, but another yawn took over. And while he made light of his aches and pains, he must need some rest, too. "I can't wait."

"Nothing to be nervous about now."

"No. Only love to look forward to."

"Only love from now on." Exhaustion roughened his voice.

Imogen kissed him once more, letting her lips convey what marvelous changes he'd wrought in her tonight. She closed her eyes on a sigh and slept safe in her beloved's arms.

CHAPTER NINETEEN

Imogen married Caleb in Barrowford's pretty little stone church two days later. After the dramas and complications of their courtship, the simple morning ceremony passed with a smoothness that she could barely credit.

They'd arrived at Barrowford late the evening before the wedding, after making an early start. Imogen barely had a chance to enjoy her role as a fallen woman before she was in the curricle and on her way north again. Before leaving the inn, they'd only had time for a wash and breakfast and a few kisses.

Caleb had arranged for her to stay with the vicar and his family the night before the ceremony. She appreciated his care for her good name – to a point. The bed had felt very empty without him beside her.

The vicar and his wife gave her a warm welcome and didn't seem to mind that Imogen had already journeyed over half of England alone in her betrothed's company. The stark truth was that Imogen's reputation had been in ruins from the moment she left Hamble Park without even a maid to accompany her.

In eloping with Caleb, she abandoned her old life forever. Her family would disown her. Her friends would be forbidden to speak her name. Her fall from grace would be subject to cruel gossip, once the ton discovered that she'd followed her heart and thrown away a glittering future.

Much as she loved Caleb, she'd sometimes wondered whether her choice would spark some small pang of regret.

But speaking her vows, she hadn't suffered any nerves. From the moment she saw Caleb waiting at the altar, standing tall and straight without the aid of his stick, she'd known that she was the luckiest girl in England. And she was luckier than any girl in America, too.

When he slid the familiar gold band onto her finger, her heart filled with such happiness, that she feared she might float up to the timber vaulting on the church ceiling. From the moment that she'd met Caleb, she'd known he was the man for her. Their wedding today only placed the final seal on a decision that she'd taken months ago and never wavered from.

She'd chosen love. She'd never look back.

Caleb studied his bride of three hours across the remains of the fine meal that the Star and Garter had put together for the wedding breakfast. The vicar and his wife joined them in a private parlor overlooking the garden at the back of the building, as did the two genteel spinsters with whom he'd struck up a friendship. The Misses Webb were sweet and unworldly and had been more than happy to serve as witnesses for the wedding service.

Imogen charmed everyone, which didn't surprise him at all. He found the bride as charming as everybody else did.

As she accepted heartfelt good wishes from the guests at this small gathering, she looked gorgeous. To his relief, nobody seemed to guess quite how elevated his lady's station was. Although he'd noticed the vicar's wife scrutinizing Imogen's wedding dress. Caleb was no expert on fashion, but even he could see that the ice-blue silk gown screamed expensive London tailoring. He doubted that Barrowford had ever seen its like.

What a wedding day it had been. Imogen glowed with happiness. The church had been bright with flowers. And over the last few weeks, he'd become fond of the locals who had filled the congregation. In a village this size, his arrival had caused a flurry of interest. Now his marriage to a woman of obvious quality deepened the mystery. But however curious they were, the villagers hadn't pried. Although they must guess that this was a runaway marriage.

"What are you thinking about?" Imogen murmured from where she sat beside him.

He lifted the hand he held and placed a kiss on the gold band that proclaimed her his at last. "You."

A smug smile quirked her lips. "Well, naturally."

Caleb's laugh received approving nods from his four guests. They all knew he was besotted. The Webb sisters had wept sentimental tears all through the service. He'd made his vows to the sound of discreet sniffling. "And my family."

Sympathy softened Imogen's gaze. "You wish they were here?"

"Yes. And no. It's wonderful that today is just for us. *En masse,* my kin are a rowdy lot."

"But you love them."

"I do indeed. When we get back to Saratoga, we'll have a party to celebrate the wedding."

Her grip tightened on his fingers. "I hope they like me."

"They'll love you because I do. They'll also love you because you're lovable."

She sent him a melting look. "You're biased."

"True."

The vicar rose to his feet. He clutched a glass of the champagne that Caleb had ordered in to celebrate his nuptials. "Thank you to Mr. and Mrs. Black for including us in this blessed gathering. I was honored to join these two young people together in holy matrimony. Now on behalf of Mrs. Faraday and myself, and I'm sure I speak for the Misses Webb as well, I'd like to congratulate you both on your marriage and wish you a long and happy life together." He waved his glass in Caleb and Imogen's direction. Caleb hid a smile, as he realized that the respectable clergyman had overindulged in the expensive wine laid on for the meal. "To Mr. and Mrs. Caleb Black."

The other three guests raised their glasses and repeated the toast with unconstrained sincerity. Moved, Caleb rose, keeping hold of Imogen's hand. After so many months of touching her in stolen moments, he couldn't bear to relinquish the physical link.

"Thank you, my friends. My beautiful bride and I couldn't have received a better welcome anywhere, and we'll always remember your generosity and kindness. I've wanted to marry my lovely Imogen since I fell in love with her at first sight. This is the happiest day of my life. I'm grateful to share it with you."

"Oh, Caleb, that was perfect," Imogen said in a husky voice. "Thank you."

He glanced around the table and saw that all four women blinked away tears. By Harry, he felt rather choked up himself.

Mr. Faraday turned to his wife. "Now I fear I must return to my study to work on this week's sermon. Are you ready to go, my dear?"

"You mean you're ready for a snooze where nobody will disturb you, my love." His wife smiled at him with tolerant fondness. When everyone laughed, the vicar looked sheepish.

"Such a pretty bride. Such a handsome couple. Such a lovely wedding," the younger Miss Webb twittered on her way out.

"You've had too much champagne, Elsie," her older sister said in disapproval, then hiccuped, which made Imogen stifle a giggle.

"Shall we retire, darling?" Caleb murmured in her ear, drawing in her fresh, floral scent.

The dark blue eyes that met his sparkled with an eagerness that reminded him that his honeymoon was about to start. Not that his craving for his bride was ever far from his mind. "That's an excellent idea."

He could still hardly believe that she'd been bold and brave enough to come to him two nights ago. Those hours with Imogen had been the most profound experience of his life. When he'd lost himself inside her, he felt that they became one. All the next day, he'd struggled to concentrate on driving. He'd been too inclined to drift off into distracting reveries featuring that glorious encounter.

Now they had sanction to close the door on the world and stoke the sensual fire that had already flared between them. For a man impatient to have his bride to himself, the farewells from his wedding breakfast took far too long.

At last, he and Imogen were alone and climbing the stairs to the inn's best suite of rooms. "What a lovely, lovely day," Imogen said, her fingers curled around his elbow.

He glanced down at her, as he turned left at the landing. "You've been indulging in the champagne, my darling."

"Maybe." Her smile was soft at the edges. "But I'm also tipsy with happiness. I can hardly believe that we're here and together and married."

Caleb couldn't help smiling back. He'd been smiling like a lunatic all day. Tipsy with happiness proved an excellent state to be in. "Nobody can ever separate us again."

Her gaze turned misty. "Oh, Caleb..."

He couldn't resist kissing her. Her lips tasted of champagne and desire. A heady combination. When he came up for air, she was still misty-eyed.

"I hope that you always look at me the way you're looking at me now," he whispered.

Around them, the corridor was empty, although there was no guarantee that it would stay that way. He'd had his fill of people interrupting, when he wanted to concentrate on Imogen. Another quick kiss before he pushed the door open.

He edged her inside, still kissing her. He loved her broken moans of pleasure. While one hand tangled in her thick black hair, pinned up in an elaborate arrangement of curls, the other reached back to pull the door shut and push the bolt across.

As the kiss exploded into urgency, Caleb turned and pressed her against the door. She linked her hands behind his neck and arched breathtakingly close. Her scent, sharp with arousal, was a more powerful intoxicant than champagne, however good.

He began to lift her skirts. The heavy blue silk gave a most satisfactory rustle as he crushed it in his hand.

Panting, she rested her head against the worn oak door. "Caleb, it's daytime."

She sounded enchantingly flustered. Her cheeks were pink with excitement, and her eyes were heavy with burgeoning hunger.

His laugh was a low rumble. "I know."

"Don't they talk about a wedding *night*?"

"We'll need the night, too."

Her eyes rounded with amazement – and anticipation. "I feel rather wicked."

He laughed again. "Fie, Mrs. Black, we're wed now. You've left all your wickedness behind to become a respectable married woman."

He watched shock recede and interest blossom. "I don't feel respectable."

"Nor do I." He paused. "I feel happy."

"So should we go to bed?" A large four-poster occupied a corner of the generous room.

Caleb's lips twitched. "Later."

"Ooh." Thick lashes veiled her eyes, and the color in her cheeks deepened. "I'm feeling less respectable by the minute."

"Good." He stepped back long enough to tear off his neckcloth and tug his navy blue coat from his shoulders. He flung both to the floor.

Imogen sagged against the door, as if her knees threatened to buckle. During those dazzling kisses, he'd felt a bit wobbly himself. He'd spent all day in a lather to have her. At the first touch of her lips, he'd gone as erect as a flagpole. He'd thought that he couldn't want her more than he had in London. But now that he'd sampled the magic of her body, he starved for her.

He unbuttoned his waistcoat and hauled it and his shirt over his head in one movement. He pitched the garments after the coat.

Imogen regarded him with unwavering fascination. When she licked her full pink lips in feminine appreciation, longing stopped his breath. "Should I take anything off?"

He recalled all the lonely nights without her and how he'd occupied the restless hours. "I've long cherished a fantasy of undressing you."

Her lips turned down in self-mockery. "That's good. Because you'll have to unlace me anyway. Mrs. Faraday got me into this gown. I couldn't have managed on my own."

"I'll play your maid. Later." His smile turned wolfish. "Although you should take off your drawers."

"I can manage that."

"If you can't, I'll tear them off."

"Heavens above," she said with no trace of censure.

She lifted her skirts and fumbled with the ties. She had lovely legs, shapely and firm. Stockings in a paler blue than her gown covered her to the knees where pretty cream silk garters fluttered.

Caleb loved what he'd done to her two nights ago, but he was desperate to see her. In the dark, she'd been all voluptuous warmth and tempting woman, and his senses had fed on her. Every sense except sight. This afternoon, he intended to indulge his eyes with a feast of Imogen.

"Tear them, or I will."

For a searing second, her flashing glance dwelled on where his cock pressed against his trousers. "You do it."

He crossed the gap between them so quickly that he swore his feet didn't touch the ground. Just as he reached her, she gave a satisfied little growl and flimsy linen pooled around her ankles.

His shaking hands went to the fastenings of his trousers, although in his urgency, he wasn't much more adept than Imogen had been with her drawers. His dick sprang free, large and hard and throbbing with need.

When her eyes fixed on his rampant arousal, he read wonder in her expression. "My stars." She licked her lips again. "Perhaps it's a good thing that it was dark last time. I might have swooned with maidenly dismay."

He laughed. "You're not the swooning kind."

As if to prove it, she stepped out of her drawers and kicked them to the side. "I nearly swooned two nights ago. I had no idea that I could feel like that."

He stepped closer and caught her face between his hands. "I can't wait to show you more."

Wanton curiosity lit her gaze. "I may end up swooning, after all."

He kissed her and found the familiar welcome. Imogen always kissed him as if the whole world stopped the instant their lips met. It was devilish powerful.

"I have to have you," he gasped.

"I'm yours," she said in a raw voice. "I've always been yours."

He kissed her again, then took her hand and drew her across to the sturdy armchair. He sank into the seat, his gaze unwavering on hers. "Kneel over me. This way, you can control how much of me you accept. It might make the act less painful."

Her flush heightened. "I wasn't uncomfortable for long."

By Jericho, it had felt like an eon at the time. He'd come close to giving up the whole idea, no matter how hungry he was for her. "I'm delighted to hear it."

She frowned. "You know that I loved what you did, don't you?"

"Yes. But I didn't like hurting you first."

Secret knowledge curved her lips. Suddenly his lovely, not-far-off-innocent Imogen looked like a practiced seductress, a woman who understood sensual satisfaction. More, she looked ready to share that expertise with the lucky man who took her fancy. "It was worth it."

He stared at her. "You really don't mind?"

Her laugh conveyed fondness and impatience. "It wasn't very nice at the start, but I love you and I want you, and I imagine that it won't hurt again."

He hoped to hell not. "Try this."

For a moment, she regarded him with a trace of uncharacteristic uncertainty. Then she straightened her shoulders and called on her courage. With a purposeful manner that made his loving heart leap with anticipation, she hitched up her skirts and petticoats. He caught another enthralling glimpse of pale, slender legs.

With some delightful squirming, she arranged herself over his lap. The seat was generous enough to leave room for her knees to frame his hips.

As she wriggled, her sex brushed his penis and he bit back a groan. She was so hot and ready, and he hadn't even touched her cleft yet.

With unfettered passion, they kissed. On a stifled sound of excitement, she rose to her knees. To save her from overbalancing, he caught her waist.

She hooked her hands over his shoulders and stared down into his face. "I've never kissed you from this angle," she said with a hint of surprise. The heavy silk skirt draped across his lap, lending an air of propriety to an act that wasn't proper at all. "I like it."

Appreciation lengthened his lips. "I thought you might."

Her delighted laugh ended on a sigh, as she pressed her mouth to his in a kiss that made the blood roar in his ears. When he bumped his hips upward, she smiled against his lips.

"Can I touch you?" she asked.

"I'd love that."

She shifted back and curled shaking fingers around him. "Oh!"

Almost as soon as she made contact, she let go. He met eyes wide with astonishment. Even that fleeting touch made him quake. He hoped to hell that she didn't mean to toy with him for long, or he'd lose all control.

She reached down again. This time, her grip was more confident. All the air squeezed out of his lungs. He groaned and tilted his hips to encourage her. She tightened her hold, as he tipped his head back against the chair. "Yes..."

"You feel so hard and powerful." The hesitant glide of her hand nearly blew off the top of his head. "It's like I'm holding the secret of life."

When she moved, his grip on her waist firmed. Then the world transformed to red-hot darkness, as she took the tip of his cock into her body. It was her turn to gasp. Her sleekness beckoned, but he'd promised to leave her in charge. Even if it killed him – and right now, it felt like it very well might – he intended to stand by that promise.

"It's easier than I thought." She sank an inch or so, bathing him in wet heat. With a sharp inhalation, she took all of him in one spectacular movement. "That's..."

He waited for some hint of complaint, but the blue eyes that met his were brilliant with excitement. She gave an experimental wiggle. He set his jaw until it hurt and fought the urge to lose himself.

"...glorious."

With a strangled laugh, he bumped higher. Her eyes went glassy, and her lips parted on a stuttering breath. "Do that again."

When he obeyed, she clenched around him.

"Move, Imogen. You'll like it."

She kissed him with open-mouthed enthusiasm. Each time she shifted, a volley of sensation blasted him. He'd chosen this position because he hoped that it would wipe away any lingering memory of their awkward first encounter. It turned out that having his wife take him like this tantalized and tortured and pleasured him to the edge of madness.

Eager hands stroked his bare chest. Under her caresses, his heart leaped and flipped and stumbled. He throbbed inside her, part of her at last. Part of her forever. From the first, he'd shared an uncanny affinity with Imogen. But this union on their wedding day sealed a bond that nothing could break.

With heart-stopping languor, she rose, then lowered again. Her sigh expressed unalloyed delight. "That's wonderful."

He couldn't doubt how she relished what they did. "It is."

She braced herself on the arms of the chair and moved with more assurance, finding her rhythm with gratifying ease. His vague worries that the physical side of love might prove a problem evaporated between one shuddering breath and the next. This was the brazen, irresistible creature who had kissed him to lunacy at Prestwick Place.

Caleb's hands cupped her breasts through the slippery silk of her dress. His thumbs discovered the impudent jut of pert nipples. Imogen moaned her approval, then to his astonishment, circled her hips until he saw shooting stars.

"How did you..." He couldn't find the breath to finish the question.

A cracked laugh escaped. Shivers of delight made her clench and release around him. "I don't know. It just seemed natural."

He squeezed her breasts. "I love it."

"I love you." She kissed him, and the shift of her body on his thundered like a cannonade.

He groaned against her lips. She lifted her head and stared down, her eyes almost black with desire. "Am I hurting you?"

His lips turned down. "I'm dying." He stopped to snatch a breath. "Of love for you."

A little gurgle of amusement with an intriguing hint of self-satisfaction. "What a lovely way to go."

"I so agree." With an unsteady hand, he reached under her skirts to stroke her just above where they joined. The damp curls were silky under his exploring fingers. When he rubbed the stiff little protuberance, she tautened with growing excitement.

"Caleb, that's—"

"Good?"

"Better than good."

Her eyes lost focus, and her movements became wilder. His balls were so tight, he feared that they must burst. For an eternity of excruciating rapture, he struggled to hold back. He wanted her to climax first, but maintaining that intention became more difficult by the second.

Just as he reached a point where he feared that he couldn't last, she cried out. The muscles gripping him so snugly spasmed into ecstasy. She surged forward to throw her arms around him, as she clung to a gasping pinnacle of sensation.

Caleb groaned and lifted his hips to fill her. The juddering, overwhelming orgasm took him beyond earthly bounds and into a new universe of heat and joy and love.

By the time he drifted back to reality, Imogen was slumped on his chest, panting for air. He flattened shaking hands along the sides of her head and tilted her up for a ferocious kiss that expressed everything that words couldn't encompass.

While his adoring heart performed cartwheels, he realized that he did have the words. The most profound words he knew. "I love you, Imogen, my perfect, beautiful wife."

Imogen opened her eyes to darkness. She had no idea what time it was. The inn around them was quiet, so it must be late. Or perhaps somewhere near dawn.

Her murmur expressed satisfaction. She stirred to place a glancing kiss on Caleb's bare chest. He lay on his back, and she snuggled into his side. His arms cradled her, as if he never intended to let her go.

That suited her fine.

"Don't stop," he said drowsily.

She leaned on her elbow to gaze down at him. Not that she could see anything. "You're awake."

"I am." She heard the smile in his voice.

Despite the darkness, she found his lips with unerring skill. His embrace tightened and for a long moment, she was lost in bliss.

It had been a night overflowing with bliss. Bliss that surpassed all her expectations, despite her shocking forwardness in anticipating her marriage vows.

"I love you, Caleb," she said. "It's been the most wonderful wedding night. Beyond my wildest dreams."

"My darling…"

More kissing, so she couldn't stifle a murmur of disappointment when he rolled out of the bed. In his laugh, she heard a weary happiness to match her own. "I'd like some light."

After a few scrapes, candlelight bloomed. She pushed up against the pillows and watched Caleb move about the room, lighting more candles. He was naked, and while she'd become familiar with her husband's body during the previous hours, she was still struck with admiration.

He turned and caught Imogen's avid gaze. As his body reacted to her amorous inspection, she smiled with greedy anticipation. He was so long and lean and powerful. And even better, he was all hers.

Inevitably, her gaze dropped to the column of flesh rising between his thighs. He had hair there, too. She now knew how his virility felt in her hand. She also knew the heavenly sensation when he pushed inside her body, until she wasn't sure where she ended and he began.

After that volcanic encounter in the armchair, they'd finally managed to undress and tumble into the bed. They'd made love again, until time spun out around them like a web of endless golden threads. Every time they came together, the experience was different yet equally splendid.

"What a handsome fellow you are."

His response was a self-derisive grunt. "I'm glad you think so. But I'm nowhere near as beautiful as you are."

His gaze on her bare breasts made familiar heat well inside her. Restless with arousal, she shifted against the sheets. She couldn't help recalling the way that his lips had tormented her breasts, driving her insane with desire.

"Caleb, aren't we lucky?"

"Aren't we?" A smile curled his lips. "You make me so happy."

For a long while, they stared entranced at each other, before Caleb gestured toward the chest in the corner. Wine, bread, cheese, cold meats, and dishes of nuts and fruit had been set out. They'd had a sumptuous dinner delivered to the room in the early evening, but that was hours ago. "I thought you might be hungry."

She was, but not for food. Or not as her most immediate requirement. Given Caleb's visible excitement, she guessed that he felt the same.

Under her husband's adoring gaze, she stretched out like a cat. She'd abandoned modesty, once it became clear that Caleb relished her unconstrained pleasure in what they did together. "Food can wait."

His smile expressed heartfelt agreement. "You're right, food can wait."

She shrieked with excitement as in two strides, he reached the bed and leaped in to join her.

CHAPTER TWENTY

Imogen was folding one of her new gowns into a trunk when a knock came on the door. Caleb looked up from the desk, where he was writing to the Tierneys to explain his sudden disappearance. At last, he could hold a pen.

"Did you request anything?" he asked.

"No." She paused, and thought. "Well, I arranged for them to bring us supper before we go, but that's not until around ten."

They'd been staying in Liverpool's best hotel for the last week, enjoying a rapturous honeymoon and preparing for their voyage to America. Their ship sailed with the tide at midnight.

Caleb glanced toward the heavy gold pocket watch that he'd set out on the desk. "It's not even seven yet."

The knock came again, sharper this time. Caleb and Imogen shared a worried look. "Papa could have found us."

Was it likely? They were booked into the hotel as Mr. and Mrs. Richard Rose, and they'd chosen to leave from Liverpool's docks. Not just because of the wider choice of ship, but also because nobody here was likely to recognize Imogen.

Caleb rose and crossed to the door. Despite sparking fear, Imogen couldn't help admiring the easy grace of his movements now that he'd regained his fitness. She often caught herself staring lovestruck at her new husband. Ten days of marriage had deepened her love for Caleb to a point where she felt that she couldn't live without him.

"Who is it?" Caleb asked.

"Jake from downstairs, Mr. Rose. There's a message about the boat."

Imogen sucked in a relieved breath. Jake was the young lad who worked at the hotel as a general runabout.

The tense line of Caleb's broad shoulders relaxed, too. He unlocked the door and opened it. "I hope there's no word of a delay."

Imogen caught a glimpse of Jake in the doorway. Then large, brawny men shoved the boy aside and filled the space.

Large, brawny, *familiar* men.

"Lady Imogen is here, my lord," Gibbs said to someone further up the corridor.

"Jake, run and get help," Caleb said. "These men mean harm."

Imogen had a second to note Jake's tear-filled eyes. "I'm sorry, Mr. Rose, but they said they'd break my arms, if I didn't show them up to your room by the back stairs."

"It's all right, Jake," Caleb said, kind even at this sickening moment.

"Hold onto the lad," Gibbs said, his eyes roaming over the luxurious room and its stacked luggage. Jake disappeared from sight. "We don't want no interruptions."

"I mean no injury to my daughter, Mr. Black," an even more familiar voice said. Terror rose to choke Imogen, as the bully boys in the doorway parted to allow her father to stroll into the room as if he owned it. "In fact, I'm sure that she'll come to thank me for saving her from the consequences of her abysmal judgment."

Imogen stepped away from the trunk on legs that felt like wet string. Churning fear made her queasy. She'd noted the omission of Caleb from her father's oily assurances. "Papa, what are you doing here?"

It was a stupid question. He was here to force her to resume a life that she'd grown out of. A life that in many ways had never fitted her.

These days with Caleb had offered so many marvelous revelations. Sensual delight. Growing emotional intimacy. The hope of a new start in America. But one of the most profound was that with Caleb, Imogen felt as if she became the woman she was born to be.

That freedom was heady. The prospect of losing it made her heart cramp.

"Don't act more of a fool than you already are, Imogen," her father said in the imperious drawl that always made her skin crawl. "I'm here to take you back to where you belong."

He sounded calm, but she knew him well enough to recognize his rage. She didn't miss the tight jaw, or the way his hand clenched on his cane until the knuckles shone white.

"This is where I belong." She tilted her chin and struggled to sound strong and determined, even as dread knotted her stomach. "You have no rights over me anymore, Papa. I'm of age and I'm married. Let us go. The law demands it."

Her father's eyebrows arched in contemptuous dismissal. "Bugger the law. You're my daughter. You belong to me."

"She belongs to herself," Caleb growled, moving closer to Imogen with unmistakable protectiveness.

Papa's snort was scornful. "She certainly doesn't belong to you. Or at least she soon won't."

Imogen reached out to curl a shaking hand around Caleb's arm. He appeared calm and in control, but the muscles beneath her fingers were rock hard. He was ready to fight for her, she knew, but what chance did he have against her father's henchmen? She couldn't forget the horrific damage that they'd already wreaked on him.

"Leave this room, and take your thugs with you." Caleb's voice was steady and confident. "You can't stop Imogen coming to America with me."

A sneer twisted her father's lips. "Of course I can stop you. You forget who I am."

"No, I don't. But it's too late to separate us. We've been man and wife for over a week."

The sneer deepened. "Brave words, but futile. The question isn't whether Imogen returns to the life she was meant to lead. The question is how much unpleasantness is required to achieve that outcome." He gestured to Gibbs. "Wait in the corridor. I wish to have a private word with my daughter."

Gibbs bowed. "As you wish, my lord."

After Gibbs closed the door, Imogen pressed into Caleb's side, making a silent proclamation of allegiance.

"Won't you ask me to sit down?" Papa said.

"I didn't invite you in," Caleb said coldly, watching her father the way he'd watch a snake. "Be damned if I'll pretend this is anything more than an illegal invasion."

"No, you didn't invite me, did you?" Without waiting for permission, he occupied the wooden chair near the unlit fireplace.

Her father's anger seemed to have receded, but she knew that it still simmered beneath his sudden unpleasant amiability. He was convinced that he'd won. That always improved his temper.

"Papa, I love Caleb."

"Don't speak like a henwitted looby, Imogen. You're a great heiress from a powerful family. You owe a duty to your name and position. This ridiculous fancy for a lowborn ruffian needn't destroy your life."

"Caleb *is* my life," she stated, even as icy apprehension trickled down her spine. Her father was so sure that he'd prevail. The grim truth was that he usually did.

"I'm not interested in any money your daughter might once have inherited from you, Lord Deerforth," Caleb said. "I'd take Imogen in her petticoat."

The sneer reappeared. "Very gallant, Mr. Black. And so easy to say, when you know my daughter comes into a fortune once she turns twenty-five, no matter whether I disinherit her or not. Her late godmother was fond of the girl. She'd be appalled to know that her generosity ended in Imogen falling prey to a ruthless fortune hunter."

Caleb looked away from her father to gape at her in shock. "A fortune?"

"I'm sorry I didn't tell you." Imogen met his eyes and shifted from one foot to another. "It never seemed relevant. We always had...other things to talk about."

Other things to talk about, and other things to do. Like touch. And kiss. And since they'd been married, explore a world of breathtaking passion.

Papa looked annoyed. "Don't pretend you didn't know."

"Caleb doesn't lie." Imogen glowered at him. "Whereas you lie all the time."

Her father's cheeks reddened at the accusation. "If a judicious bending of the truth works to one's advantage, I doubt it's such a sin."

Her lips tightened. "But it's always to your advantage, never anyone else's."

Tutting, he shook his head. "I'm appalled at such disrespect. It's another sign that I overindulged you as a child. I always thought you loved me, daughter."

She regarded this self-satisfied, manipulative old man, who had done such wrong to Eliot and Stella. And Caleb. And wondered how the ghost of any affection lingered.

Despite everything, it did.

"You're my father," she said flatly. "Something in me will always love you. But I'll never forgive you for hurting Caleb."

Aristocratic surprise lifted Papa's eyebrows. "I have no idea what you're talking about."

Once, in her innocence, she might have believed him. Now she knew better. "Yes, you do. You set Gibbs and his cronies on Caleb, because he dared to dance with me at the Tierney ball. Don't bother to deny it."

As was his wont when caught out in a misdeed, her father didn't apologize. Nor did he keep up a pretense of ignorance that he couldn't sustain. "I wish I'd killed the lout. If I'd realized things had reached this pass, I would have. For your sake."

"Am I meant to be grateful?" Caleb said dryly.

Papa ignored him as if he didn't exist. The fear oozing along Imogen's backbone turned even colder.

Her father spoke of murder the way he'd speak of the weather.

"I'm now to understand that you were sneaking around and deceiving me well before that night. Even you wouldn't run off with a pretty ne'er-do-well after one waltz."

She hid a wince at her father's disdainful tone. Yet again, she recognized that she'd never rated much higher in her father's estimation than his favorite hound. "I met Caleb not long after I came to London."

Her father pursed his already small mouth in disgust. "I'm disappointed in you, Imogen. I thought I'd brought you up with more of a moral compass."

Despite her growing unease, a bleak laugh escaped Imogen. "Why on earth would you think that? It's not as if you possess any ethical framework."

Her father's eyes narrowed. She waited for him to deny her assertion. But instead, a superior smile curved his lips, and all her impulse to amusement fled, leaving queasy dread behind. "I'm glad you're aware of that. Don't forget it, while we try to work out this mess that you've got yourself entangled in."

"There's no working out to be done. Imogen is my wife and we're sailing tonight." Caleb still sounded self-assured. She might wonder whether he realized their danger, except that he'd had enough dealings with her father to understand what was at stake.

"On the contrary, sirrah," her father responded with unhidden derision. "This marriage will not stand. There's no question of that. The issue is what steps we take to end it. There's an easier way and a hard way. I may occasionally lie, but I'm absolutely sincere when I say that you won't enjoy the hard way at all."

"Papa, I'm of age. You have no say in who I marry," Imogen said, knowing that she wasted her time. He'd never listened to her. Why would he listen to her now? "That's why we waited until I turned twenty-one, so you couldn't part us with legal quibbles."

Her father ignored her and kept his attention on Caleb. "You can come out of this pretty well, young man. You've played a clever game, and I can see you're bright enough to make sure that your efforts aren't wasted. As a fellow who's played a few clever games himself, I'm almost impressed that you managed to woo my brainless flibbertigibbet of a daughter without stirring a whisper of suspicion. But your strategy has reached its end, and it's time to cash in your markers."

Caleb straightened to his full impressive height and glared at Imogen's father. "I've already told you that I'm not interested in your money. In fact, I'm not interested in you. It's time you said goodbye to Imogen and let us go on our way."

Papa studied Caleb as if he were a slug on a marigold. "You should listen to me."

"And if I don't?"

"I'll revert to the plan I made when I discovered that you'd kidnapped my daughter and forced her into this travesty of a marriage. The thought of a Ridley mingling her blood with a mongrel American who's little better than a laborer makes me want to vomit."

"Caleb is the best man I know." Imogen raised her chin. "He didn't force me into anything."

Again, Imogen's father went on as if she hadn't spoken. "The easiest way to end this disgraceful union is to arrange a fatal accident for you, Mr. Black. The docks are dangerous. If your body washes up in a week or so, nobody will question that you lost your footing and ended up in the Mersey." He paused. "Because you have lost your footing, you presumptuous bastard. You had no right to lure my daughter away from her family."

Caleb put his arm around Imogen. He'd know now how she shivered. "Your threats don't frighten me."

"They should."

"He means it, Caleb," Imogen said, before she faced down her father. "If you harm one hair on his head, I'll never forgive you."

Her father shrugged. "You'll understand when you're older."

"I will never agree to marry anyone else."

"Of course you will. In fact, your secret courtship works to my advantage. If you'd run away from London, I wouldn't have had a hope of scotching the gossip. Once you're a widow, even if word gets out that you eloped, there are no impediments to a second marriage. Believe me, Mr. Black's demise is by far the simplest way to solve my problems."

"I won't let you kill him," Imogen said, knowing that they were just useless words. Her father and his men could overpower her with little difficulty.

"It's in your hands, my dear."

She flinched at the "my dear." Her father didn't love her. If he did, he couldn't threaten her husband's life. "You can't blackmail me."

Her father shrugged. "I'm just giving you a choice. You know what I'd rather do, but in recognition of your infatuation with the cove, I'll allow him to take ship tonight for his barbaric country, on the proviso that he never comes back."

"You can't wipe out all trace of our marriage." Imogen fought the urge to cry and rage. Hysterics would only lead her father to dismiss her as a weak and emotional woman. "What about Reverend Faraday? He conducted the ceremony."

"I have a paper prepared that I'd like Mr. Black to sign. It says that he married you under false pretenses and that he already has a wife in America. He will acknowledge that he's a bigamist and that the vows he made to you have no legal standing. You'll come back to Hamble Park, where you'll accept Lord Chippenham's proposal."

As she contemplated the trap that her father had laid, nausea soured her stomach. "What if I'm with child?"

Revulsion contorted her father's expression. "Pray God you're not. If you are, I'm sure Chippenham is prepared to wait. You can have the baby in secret, and I'll make arrangements for its adoption."

Horror piled upon horror. For a split second, darkness clouded her vision before she sucked in a breath and came back to awareness. Her father was lying. She'd lay good coin that he'd never allow any baby of hers and Caleb's to live. "You can't steal my child from me."

Her continued defiance only incited more of that weary contempt, as if her wishes were of no consequence. "I think you'll find that I can do as I want. If there's no child, you'll wed Lord Chippenham within the month. Then you become his problem instead of mine."

"Does he know that I'm no longer a virgin?"

"I won't tell him, just as I won't tell him about this ill-advised attachment. But I called on him in London when I was there, searching for you. He's still most eager to make you his wife."

"So you lied to him, too?"

Her father shrugged. "He'll get an heiress and an alliance with the Ridley family. If he discovers the bride isn't quite as…intact as he might prefer, I'm sure he'll come to terms with the situation."

"He'll blame Imogen. You're condemning her to a life of misery," Caleb bit out, his arm firming around her shoulders. "She's your daughter. Don't you have any consideration for her?"

"She's made her bed. Let her lie in it." Papa's eyes were frosty as they dwelled on her, and she realized that his show of composure was just that – a show. He was seething. While she'd never forgive him, he'd never forgive her either. He couldn't countenance that she'd gone against his will.

The last of her childhood illusions shattered. Her father was an evil man with no care for anything but himself. Nothing – not parental love, not the claims of the law, not even right and wrong – would persuade him against taking his revenge.

"I won't marry Chippenham." She pressed closer against Caleb's side, struggling to draw strength from his warmth. But the creeping chill had taken over her whole body. She felt like she was made of ice. "I won't marry anyone. I already have a husband."

Disappointment weighted Papa's sigh. "You'd rather see your lover dead than safe and on his way to America? I hadn't thought you so selfish."

She raised her chin and glared at her father. "Not selfish, just too familiar with you and your ways."

"You have my word."

"Your word isn't worth a groat."

"You're saying that you're prepared to consign Mr. Black to a watery grave?"

"I'm saying that I'm not going anywhere with you. I'm staying with my husband."

"Don't be a fool, Imogen."

Caleb remained silent, but she felt the vibrating tension in his body. She squared her shoulders, still refusing to give up.

"I'd be a fool to believe that you'd risk Caleb coming back and claiming me as his wife. You mean to kill him, whether I obey you or not. I'm enough of your daughter to see that you wouldn't leave such a loophole open."

"If he goes back to America—"

"You won't let him. And I won't let you hurt him." She paused and tried one last time to appeal to her father's better nature. "Let us go, Papa. For the sake of Mamma, who I know you loved. For the sake of the affection that you once had for me. Please, I beg of you, have an ounce of pity."

There was no hint of softening. She didn't think that there would be. Caleb clearly reached the same conclusion, that they battled for their lives and that nobody was going to offer them any quarter. "You're wasting your breath, Imogen."

Papa lumbered to his feet. "Gibbs!"

The door slammed open to reveal the ex-prizefighter. "Aye, my lord?"

"Restrain Mr. Black, while I take Lady Imogen out of the way."

"No!" Imogen arrayed herself in front of Caleb.

"Step aside, my love," he murmured in her ear. "I can't fight with you so close."

"You can't fight anyway." She gazed up into his beloved face, and the tears she'd fought for what felt like hours stung her eyes. He was so dear, she couldn't bear the thought of losing him. "There's half a dozen of them."

Despite their dire situation, the courage in his smile cheered her heart. "I'm ready for trouble this time, and there's only so much room. We're not defeated yet, my darling."

"Brave words," her father said. "But it will be better for you if you come peacefully. Imogen may be injured in a scuffle."

Imogen cast her father a glare burning with hatred. "Don't pretend you care for me beyond my use as a political pawn."

She was aware of Caleb backing away. Out of the corner of her eye, she saw him grab the poker from beside the cold hearth.

"Get behind me, Imogen," he growled, as her father's men crowded in behind Gibbs.

Through the fraught silence, she heard a few dull thumps and a shout from the hallway. What on earth...

There was a triumphant cry. Jake must have managed to escape. Perhaps all wasn't as lost as she'd imagined. She prayed that he brought help. Then she glanced at her father, and her fragile hopes dissolved to nothing.

"Caleb, he's got a gun."

To her surprise, Caleb didn't lower the poker. "You won't risk bringing everyone in this hotel down upon us."

"I'm sure you intend to act the gallant knight and try and fight your way out of this," her father said with such odious condescension that bile rose in Imogen's throat. "But that would be most unwise. I'll have no hesitation in shooting you. In such a confined space, who knows where a bullet might end up? What a pity if my daughter falls victim to the mayhem."

Imogen couldn't take her eyes from the elegant pistol in her father's pudgy hand. "If you kill Caleb, I'll swear it's murder, Papa." Her voice shook. "I won't care about family bonds or scandal. I'll see that you face the full force of the law."

"Gibbs will swear this cur attacked me."

"And I'll swear you shot an unarmed man."

For the first time since he'd come in, Papa looked at her properly. She read surprise in his expression. "There's steel in you, Imogen. You're more my daughter then I realized. Even more of a tragedy that you fell into a tradesman's filthy clutches. You could have made something of yourself."

"Whatever I make of myself, it won't be in your image," she snapped.

"If you persist in this idiocy, you won't be making anything of yourself. I'm not letting you go to America. Under *any* circumstances."

"Papa..." Even after today's vile revelations, she struggled to accept that her father had just threatened to kill her. Yet what else could he mean? Despite the grudging respect in his eyes, she couldn't doubt that if it came to saving his reputation, he'd sacrifice her without a qualm.

Caleb must see that, too. "Get behind me, Imogen," he repeated in a grim tone.

She was trapped in a horrendous nightmare. "He'll kill you if I do."

Her father leveled the gun at Caleb. "Yes, get behind him, Imogen."

CHAPTER TWENTY-ONE

Caleb met Lord Deerforth's flinty gaze and saw death waiting there. For him. And also, God damn it, for Imogen.

Deerforth had intended to cart her away, back to her life as a fine lady. But she'd shown too much mettle. He now knew that he'd never bully her into concealing her husband's murder.

Caleb grabbed hold of his wife. While she was here, he couldn't risk attacking Deerforth with the poker. He wished to heaven that he could send her out of the room. But her loyal heart wouldn't let her desert him. He prayed that her devotion didn't lead to her destruction. "Get out of the way."

"He won't shoot if I'm in front of you."

Neither of them believed that.

Lord Deerforth cocked the pistol, the click loud in the sudden silence.

Rage and an absurd feeling of unreality held Caleb motionless. For pity's sake, it couldn't all end like this. Not after he'd finally discovered the meaning of love and hope and happiness.

With sudden force, he shoved Imogen away. On a broken cry, she staggered to the side.

Caleb braced for the impact of a bullet.

But a sudden noise from the hallway made Deerforth pause. Caleb glanced toward the doorway, surprised to see that Gibbs and the others no longer occupied the space. Deerforth turned, too fast for a man of his bulk, and stumbled as he lost his balance. A sharp crack rang out, and the pungent stink of gunpowder filled the room.

Caleb waited for the pain. From that distance, it would be impossible to miss him.

Nothing.

Then an unendurable thought struck him. A thought so cruel that it carved a rift as deep as an abyss across his heart. "Imogen?" he croaked.

"I'm here," she said from behind him, her voice quavering.

He whirled to look at her. "Are you unharmed?"

"I am." He didn't believe it, until he felt her trembling hand encircle his arm. Her voice sounded unnaturally calm, as she glanced at the wall behind her. "I can't say the same for that rather banal landscape over there."

A rush of overwhelming relief made him stagger. "Thank God."

"Yes, thank God." With a muffled sob, Imogen flung herself into his arms.

Still unable to believe that he was alive and even more important, so was she, he hugged her for all he was worth. She shook as though she had a fever. Caleb was no steadier. He closed his eyes and struggled to understand what had just happened.

When he looked up, Lord Deerforth stared at the door, as if the devil himself was due to come through it. The discharged pistol dangled useless from one hand, and his lordship looked pale and unwell. Sweat lined his jowly cheeks, and his eyes were sunk into his skull.

It wasn't the devil who prowled into the room. To Caleb's astonishment, it was Lord Halston, and just behind him, Imogen's former governess.

"What in heaven's name is going on here?" Halston snapped, taking in the scene with one blazing glance. "The proprietor has called the authorities."

"Stella!" Imogen said in shock, releasing Caleb and stumbling forward to hug her cousin. "What are you doing here?"

"Do you have another weapon?" Caleb snapped, although everything about the older man's posture shouted defeat.

"No," he muttered, without looking away from Halston.

"Imogen, are you all right?" Stella's arms closed around her, and the question held a wealth of love and concern.

"Of course I'm all right."

"Mr. Black?" Lord Halston asked.

"In fine fettle, thank you." Although he'd come a little too close to getting a bullet in his gut to carry off the light response with any conviction. It might break every rule of etiquette, but he was so pleased to see Halston and Stella that he walked up and offered his hand.

To his surprise, Halston responded with a firm handshake.

In the corner, Deerforth slumped into the chair with a groan. His complexion looked pastier by the second. It was clear that with the accidental firing of his pistol, all the fight had gone out of him. Thank the Lord. It was hard to believe that this feeble old man had been on the verge of obliterating Caleb's every hope of happiness.

"Lady Imogen, we thought you'd been kidnapped," Halston said.

Imogen drew away from Stella and stepped back to take Caleb's hand in a silent gesture of devotion that Caleb knew wasn't wasted on their audience. "I left a note."

"Not a very informative one," Halston said shortly.

"I didn't want anyone to stop me from marrying Caleb."

"It took us forever to work out that Mr. Black was involved," Stella said. "Once we realized that Richard Rose and Mr. Black are the same person, it became easier to track you."

"I wish you'd found us before Papa did," Imogen said. "He's been making the most awful threats."

"We meant to get to you first, but my uncle trumped us."

"You arrived just in time," Caleb said, still having trouble coming to terms with this last-minute rescue.

"What have you done with my men?" Lord Deerforth asked in a wavering voice.

"The hotel staff have them confined downstairs. A young lad came running to warn us all that murder was being done," Halston said, his tone flat. It was clear that there was no love lost between Halston and his wife's uncle.

Good for Jake. Caleb would make sure to leave the lad a substantial tip.

"Papa tried to kill Caleb." Horror and incredulity frayed Imogen's tone. "He threatened to kill me."

Caleb lashed one arm around her and tugged her against his side. He'd come so close to losing her, he basked in the knowledge that she was safe.

Stella made a sound of distress. "Imogen, I'm so sorry. I was sure you were the only person he felt any genuine affection for."

"He was fond of me while I was of use," she said sourly, and Caleb saw Stella's dawning recognition that Imogen was no longer the innocent that she'd once been.

The proprietor, Mr. Mills, appeared in the doorway, wringing his hands. "My lords and ladies, Sir John Tilley, the magistrate, is downstairs and insists upon an explanation for these disturbances. This is a respectable hotel." His eyes darted about the room, dwelling for a long moment on the bullet-hole marring the undistinguished picture. "I've had numerous complaints from my other guests about the noise. I hope you can offer some reason for this unprecedented behavior. We're not used to the aristocracy and their hijinks here at Paston's, although we attract a very good quality of patron."

Halston and Caleb shared a glance that spoke volumes before Caleb answered the man. "My wife and I are due to sail in a couple of hours."

"That's all very well," Mills said. "But damage has been done."

Halston turned to him. "I'll speak to the magistrate. I'm sure I can set out everything to his satisfaction, and naturally I'll cover the cost of any repairs."

His well-bred confidence visibly smoothed the proprietor's ruffled feathers. The man even managed a bow. "As you wish, my lord."

"Thank you," Halston said with noticeable graciousness. "If you'll excuse us for a moment and inform Sir John that Lord Halston will be with him presently, I'd appreciate it."

"Very good, my lord." Mills bowed again and left as gentle as a lamb.

Caleb would never cease to be amazed at the automatic respect that the British paid to a fancy title. With a shock, he realized that through his marriage to Imogen, he was now related to a bunch of these hoity-toity wastrels. It wasn't a welcome revelation, even if right now, he couldn't help admiring Halston's swagger.

Once they were alone behind a closed door, Halston turned to Imogen and Caleb. "How do you want to proceed? Do you wish to lay charges against Deerforth?"

"By God, you've got a nerve, you bastard." Deerforth stood up. He'd recovered enough of his self-assurance to bluster. "You have no right to interfere. A father has a duty to keep his daughter from a fatal misstep."

It almost had been fatal, curse this puffed-up polecat.

Caleb cast the man a contemptuous glare. "Not when the daughter is of age and acting within the law. Not when you threatened to kill her as well as her husband."

"Well said," Stella said.

Halston's attention remained on Caleb and Imogen. "He deserves to hang for attempted murder."

"Steady on, old man." Deerforth turned sallow again and backed away, as though attempting to distance himself from the consequences of his recklessness. He only managed two steps before he bumped into the wall.

The swine was boxed in. Caleb couldn't help seeing that as symbolic.

Halston continued as if Deerforth hadn't interrupted. "I personally won't turn a hair at seeing his lordship pay for his crimes, but you'll miss your sailing. You'd have to stay to testify at any trial."

Imogen glanced at Caleb. "It would ignite the most dreadful scandal, too. Eliot and Stella don't deserve that."

"Nor do you," he said.

Imogen's gesture was dismissive. "I'll be in America. The gossip can't touch me there."

Stella studied her cousin. "You don't have to run away, you know. You could come to us, until you decide what you want to do. I'd love to hear how you managed to deceive your sharp-eyed governess."

Caleb was relieved to see Imogen smile at Stella's small joke. Her father's betrayal had left her looking so stricken that he'd wanted to smash something. Preferably Lord Deerforth's toad-like face. "I want to go with Caleb and see his home and meet his family, although I appreciate the offer. I've had enough of England just now."

"I haven't done anything to be ashamed of," Deerforth insisted, but his words lacked force.

"Horseshit," Caleb snarled.

While the profanity still echoed, Imogen regarded her father with a hard light in her eyes. "You made Stella's life a misery, going out of your way to humiliate her. You tried to bully Eliot into becoming another version of you. Thank heaven, he had too much strength of character to succumb. You've run the estate into the ground to pay for your ridiculous political ambitions. You set your bullies on Caleb, because he had the effrontery to dance with me at a ball where he was an honored guest. You were quite prepared to kill him to force me back under your control. When I defied you, you even had plans to kill me." She paused for a shaky breath. "You deserve to rot."

"Imogen, I'm your father," he spluttered. "You owe me some respect."

"You don't deserve anyone's respect," Caleb snapped. "Least of all Imogen's."

Renewed fear entered Deerforth's eyes. Perhaps at last, he realized that his habit of riding roughshod over anyone who stood up to him threatened to destroy him. Even cost him his life.

"I couldn't agree more," Halston said. "But if you and Imogen are abroad, a trial will be unlikely."

Caleb set aside unworthy thoughts of seeing this egotistical mountain of lard swing at the end of a rope. By Harry, it would have to be a stout one. Imogen might no longer love her father, but she'd regret watching him meet such an ignominious end, no matter how much he'd earned it. "I don't see why Lord Deerforth's sins should be visited on his children, any more than they already are."

His wife bestowed a smile of unalloyed approval upon him. "Thank you, Caleb."

Deerforth's massive shoulders relaxed. "That's the ticket. No point in making a public spectacle."

"No, there's not." The stern line of Halston's lips didn't relax. "But I cannot permit a man who's half-mad on his lust for power to continue to play a part in government and society."

"*You* cannot permit?" Deerforth said in rising outrage. "Who in Hades are you, sirrah, to make ultimatums to me?"

A superior smile lengthened Halston's lips and for once, Caleb appreciated all that aristocratic bombast. "Who am I? I, sir, am the Earl of Halston, and I have influence that you've only dreamed of. I have evidence of your wrongdoing. I'll have more when Imogen and Mr. Black provide me with a signed statement, once they see a lawyer in America. I can squash your pretensions with less effort than it takes to snap my fingers."

Deerforth looked sulky. "It's my duty to serve my country."

"You've only ever served yourself," Imogen said with justified bitterness.

Halston still eyed Deerforth. "You will resign from all your public roles, including justice of the peace. You will retire to your estates in Gloucestershire, and you will stay there. If I hear of you attempting to extend your influence beyond the borders of your property, I'll ensure that you face the full consequences of today's violence."

"You have my full support, my lord," Caleb said. "Society isn't safe as long as this brute is on the loose."

Deerforth had gone even paler, until the red veins across his nose and cheeks stood out like webbing. "That's house arrest."

Halston shrugged. "I can arrange for a more stringent captivity, if you prefer. Imprisonment in Newgate is an option, should you find the prospect of the rest of your life at Hamble Park too confining."

Deerforth's frantic gaze skittered over every person in the room, but there was no escape. "Damn you, Halston. And damn that trull you married. And damn you, Imogen. I rue the day your mother bore you. And damn that clodhopping oaf you threw yourself away on. I look forward to the day you come crawling back, begging my forgiveness."

The malicious rancor in his voice made Caleb's blood run cold. His grip on Imogen tightened, to keep her safe from her father's spite.

"My husband is a thousand times the man you are." Imogen lifted her chin with a defiance that made Caleb proud. "We're going to be happy, Papa. Even more, we're going to be free of you. That will needle you until the day you die. Stella escaped you. Eliot escaped you. Now I've escaped you. We've all married the people we love, and the future belongs to us. Whereas you'll stew alone and lonely and unloved at Hamble Park, while you repent your sins."

"Never," her father spat. "You can all go to hell, for all I care."

Halston arched his eyebrows. "You're the one consigned to Satan's realm, Deerforth. Now come with me while I arrange for your toadies to leave with you – and thank your lucky stars that Mr. Black and your daughter aren't seeking the retribution that's theirs by right."

Caleb saw Deerforth consider further complaints, before he must have thought better of it. He straightened and spoke with heavy irony. "I'm at your disposal, my lord."

As he gestured Deerforth out of the room ahead of him, Halston looked unimpressed at the dramatics. The moment Deerforth was gone, the atmosphere eased.

Caleb drew his first full breath in what felt like hours. It gradually dawned on him that he and Imogen had won. Deerforth and his ambitions were no longer a threat to their happiness.

"We have supper coming, Lady Halston," Caleb said. "Our ship sails at midnight, so we have to leave the hotel once we've eaten, but you and his lordship are most welcome to join us if you'd like to."

Stella took off her black leather gloves and dark blue pelisse and dropped them onto a chair. Beneath the coat was a fashionable traveling dress in a brighter blue. Now that the danger passed, Caleb couldn't help noticing that Imogen's cousin had left the dowdy governess far behind.

"I'd love that. And all jokes aside, I'm desperate to find out how you and Imogen came together. Gray and I have managed to piece some of it together, but I'm agog to learn the full story."

Imogen regarded her cousin with an uncertain expression. "You aren't angry?"

Stella laughed, as she waved away the question. "Dear me, no. I'm rather impressed. Eliot, you and I managed to conduct love affairs under society's eye. Yet somehow the gossips didn't find out until we were well past the point of no return."

Imogen stepped away from Caleb to hug her cousin once more. By the time the two women separated, Imogen's eyes were bright with tears. "I'm so going to miss you."

Stella looked rather emotional, too. "And I'll miss you. Gray and I must visit you in America soon." She glanced across at Caleb. "Unless you can revive your commercial projects here in England, Mr. Black?"

Caleb smiled at this woman who clearly loved Imogen. That was all he needed to know to approve of her. "Given we're now family, you should call me Caleb."

Stella dug a lace handkerchief out of her pocket and wiped her eyes. "Caleb it shall be. And you must call me Stella."

"Thank you," he said, and his voice held little regret when he answered her question. "I doubt that the scandal of our elopement will promote my prospects. Black & Sons can try again, once the talk has died down. Or stay in New York and continue to prosper there." He smiled at his lovely Imogen. "I came to England in search of fame and fortune, and I'm taking home the most wonderful girl in the world. I'd count that a success, whatever the wider world makes of my adventures in the Old Country." He caught Imogen's hand once more, reveling in the warmth of her touch.

He saw her blink to shift another rush of moisture to her eyes. "Caleb, I do love you."

Then she blushed as he leaned in and kissed her in wholehearted endorsement of that statement.

The shore lights were mere pinpricks in the distance, as the *Candida* sailed for Ireland, its last stop before braving the wild Atlantic. The breeze and the tide combined to speed the vessel toward America.

Imogen leaned on the wooden rail and sucked in a deep breath of salty air. It smelled like the ocean. It smelled like freedom.

"Can't you sleep?" Caleb said softly from the shadowy deck behind her.

She turned her head. "I'm too excited to sleep. We're on our way to a new life."

He came up behind her and twined his arms around her. She straightened and rested against him, glorying in his strength and the evocative scent of his skin. That scent had become part of the framework of her life. It spoke of trust and safety and love. Always love.

"Any regrets? After all, you're leaving your home."

"You're my home." She nestled closer. "You've been my home since the day we met."

"I feel exactly the same way." He tightened his embrace, as she basked in his protection. It wasn't long past midsummer, yet the brisk wind held a chill edge.

For a long moment, they stared across the waves as England receded. She hadn't quite banished the remnants of the terror that she'd felt when her father produced a gun and tried to kill

Caleb. But here on this empty deck, she felt that she broke free of the old, painful ties at last. When she faced the future, her heart overflowed with hope. She and Caleb were young and strong and ready to meet any challenges that life threw at them.

After a long silence, Caleb dropped a kiss on her cheek. "Come down to our cabin, beloved. You're getting cold, and I know just how to warm you up."

A husky chuckle escaped Imogen. "I have a feeling it's going to be an interesting voyage."

His low laugh vibrated against her back. "My beautiful darling, I promise you that it's going to be an interesting life."

EPILOGUE

Buckinghamshire, May 1826

"Do you think the children have destroyed Maddox House yet?" Imogen asked idly from where she sat beside her husband in the luxurious coach.

With a grunt of amusement, Caleb turned away from watching the lush spring countryside through the window. "I doubt that there was a stone left standing an hour after we left."

As she laughed, he lifted the hand that he held to place a quick kiss across her knuckles.

After nearly a decade of marriage, Imogen remained susceptible to a tender gesture from the man she loved. "Oh, Caleb," she said in a melting tone and leaned forward to press her lips to his.

A satisfying interval later, they drew apart and she stared into smiling brown eyes. "Why do we have to be so close to Prestwick Place already? It's been heaven having you to myself all the way from London. At home, it's always such pandemonium."

He kissed her again. "You'll start missing the little monsters before we get back to them in a week."

"How dare you call our delightful offspring little monsters?" she asked without heat.

Humor lit his eyes. "*Big* monsters, then?"

She giggled. "Much more accurate." Her sigh contained no genuine regret. "It was easier when there was only one."

"So why did we go ahead and have another three?"

"Because I can't keep my hands off you?"

Humor set attractive creases in his beloved face. "That's a factor."

"And because you kept telling me how wonderful it was to grow up in a large, happy family."

He tilted an inquiring eyebrow. "Was I mistaken?"

"No. But I must say it's a relief to know that for the moment, the children are your parents' problem."

"They'll manage them without turning a hair, although Gray might live to be sorry that he offered his London house to my family for their visit. In fact, he and Stella are to blame. If they hadn't decided to hold a ball to celebrate their tenth anniversary, the children would be terrorizing us instead of laying waste to his town house."

"Our children can be good."

Caleb looked unimpressed. "When they're asleep perhaps."

"At least they've got plenty of spirit. If I'd been too afraid to break the rules, I'd never have met you."

His groan was heartfelt. "Now all I can think of are the problems ahead of us when they're all old enough to fall in love."

"Oh, dear." Imogen had no difficulty imagining the merry chase that their sons and daughters would lead them over the coming years.

"Exactly. We might look back on their childhood as a golden era."

"Phoebe's only nine. That gives us at least ten years' reprieve, surely. Richard is two years below that, and Magnus another year younger again. We hardly need to worry about little Stella at all. She's only four. We've got time to prepare."

"Batten down the hatches, don't you mean?"

She squeezed Caleb's hand, so used to the scars that she barely noticed them anymore. After the beating, it had taken months for him to regain full use of it, but these days he could draw with all his old facility. "At least we won't be bored."

"I still think my parents are saints to take on our four, as well as Stella and Gray's three and Eliot and Verena's two."

"There's an army of nursemaids and governesses to help. Not to mention that Eliot and Verena's children are little angels."

"Wait until those little angels have spent a week with their cousins. It mightn't be only Stella and Gray who want our guts for garters after all this."

Imogen's laugh was rueful. "Then we should make sure we have a lovely time while we're at Prestwick Place. We mightn't be asked back."

His expression softened as he curled his arm around her. "We always have a lovely time at Prestwick Place."

"Yes, ever since our first visit."

"At least these days, I don't have to get out of bed in the dark, so that I can work my seductive wiles on you."

"No, now you can work those seductive wiles in comfort." She rested her head on his shoulder, as she contemplated all the wonderful changes that ten years of happy marriage had wrought in her life. What an eventful time it had been, packed with love and work and incident.

Imogen had loved Caleb's family from the day she met them. They'd accepted her straightaway, and she'd soon settled into a productive, satisfying life in beautiful Saratoga as Caleb's partner in life and work. Caleb had told her that the business was a thriving enterprise, but even so, she'd been surprised to see the wealth that Black & Sons generated.

When she discovered not long after her arrival that she was pregnant, it had seemed yet another blessing. And so it had proven. She'd had an easy confinement, and she'd adored her oldest daughter Phoebe from the day she was born. Three other children had followed, all equally adored, all little hellions. As Caleb pointed out, with a hellion for a mother, how could they be anything else?

During those first years in America, Imogen had kept up with the news from England through Stella's letters. Harriet and Lady Lumsden had written, too, despite Imogen's elopement with a gardener making her *persona non grata* in society.

So it was at second hand that she learned of her father's travails, all self-inflicted. The scandals that engulfed the Ridley family during the 1816 season were only the start of his troubles. Over the following months, his unwise investments collapsed about him and his political cronies deserted him. He ended up like a captive animal at Hamble Park, raging against everyone he blamed for his downfall. Anger and spite ate away at his health and vigor, until he verged on becoming an invalid.

When Phoebe was born, Imogen had grit her teeth and written to tell him that he had a grandchild. There had been no response. She hadn't expected one. Or even wanted one, in truth. She couldn't forget or forgive his willingness to kill Caleb in Liverpool. Not to mention his threats to her.

As she'd always feared, Lord Deerforth's explosive temper brought about his demise. Two years after Imogen left England, Stella wrote to say that her uncle had become impatient with his agreement to stay at Hamble Park. Determined to regain his old influence and status, he'd set out in a rage for London, riding a half-trained stallion.

The next day, his body had been found on the side of the road ten miles from home. The horse was only caught a day later, its sides marked with whipping. The official verdict was that a broken neck had finished Lord Deerforth, although Imogen knew the real causes were overweening pride and spleen and arrogance.

Despite everything, she'd shed a tear or two. More because of lost opportunities than genuine grief. She now knew what a happy family life was like, and her father had caused so much unnecessary misery from the first. What a lot he'd missed out on. What a lot he'd made other people miss out on.

By that stage, Caleb had revived his plans to expand the landscaping business to England. Lord Tierney had sulked for a couple of months over losing his designer, then approached Caleb to come back and take over the Cumbria project.

Once the gardens at Sander Hall were finished at last, they were such a sensation that Black & Sons had been inundated with offers of work. Enough time had passed by then for his runaway marriage to Lady Imogen Ridley to seem romantic rather than disgraceful. Especially as Lady Imogen had proven herself a brilliant garden designer, too.

Her masterpiece – at least to date – was the grounds at Hamble Park.

Eliot and Verena had lived there since he'd inherited the title. He'd been appalled at the chaos that his father had left behind. Everything from the manor house to the lowliest tenants' dwelling had been in disrepair. Eliot had immediately set out to restore the estate to its former prosperity, and part of that had involved inviting Imogen to fulfill her original plans for the gardens.

Except that now she had the budget and the manpower to do justice to her concepts. Imogen's work at her childhood home had created a fashion for employing the former debutante to update aristocratic estates all over the kingdom.

These days Black & Sons were as well known in Britain as they were in America. Imogen and Caleb and their family spent most of the year in England, returning to Saratoga for Christmas when they could. They'd settled on a beautiful little estate near the sea in Kent, where the children reveled in a freedom that had been denied to her as a girl.

Life was good. Glorious in fact. She said a silent prayer of thanks, as she nestled closer to her husband's long, lean body.

When the carriage turned through the elaborate wrought-iron gates and followed the winding drive to the house, Imogen couldn't help remembering her first visit to Prestwick Place. She'd just met Caleb, and she'd been in a lather to see him again. Stella had been her downtrodden governess, *en route* to her own encounter with love.

"You're still thinking about our first time here," Caleb said softly.

She sat up and smiled at him, suspecting that she looked rather dreamy-eyed. Their frequent visits to Prestwick Place always made her feel sentimental.

"We were so afraid that everything would come to disaster."

He smiled back, his eyes glowing with the love that turned every day to gold. "We beat the odds, my darling."

"We did. You make me so happy. I thought I loved you then, but I've only come to love you more each day since."

"And I love you more than I can say." He leaned forward to kiss her again. The tender pressure of his lips conveyed gratitude for the powerful bond that linked them and for this extraordinary life that they'd created together.

When he at last raised his head, she sighed with contentment. She was almost sorry that the carriage pulled up in front of the house, ending their privacy.

Then she glanced out the window to see Stella and Gray strolling out to greet them. And just behind her hosts, Eliot and Verena, holding hands and looking like April and May. Seven days with some of her favorite people in the world beckoned. Like Caleb and Imogen, all of them had defied convention to claim their place in the world and to wed the person they loved.

"We've all been so lucky," she murmured, as a footman bowed and opened the door to the coach.

"We have. Love has blessed us."

She sent Caleb a laughing glance. "Love, and a bit of self-help."

He grinned back, as dashing and handsome as the man she'd fallen in love with in a dark gazebo all those years ago. "You sound like an independent American, sweetheart. I like it."

"Well, my heart belongs to an American, so I'm not surprised."

Ignoring the footman – although the servants at Prestwick Place were used to turning a blind eye to romantic moments – Imogen kissed Caleb, then descended from the carriage to join the people she loved so very dearly.

ABOUT THE AUTHOR

Australian Anna Campbell has written 11 multi award-winning historical romances for Avon HarperCollins and Grand Central Publishing. As an independently published author, she's released more than 30 bestselling stories. Right now, she is working on a new series called Scoundrels of Mayfair, set amidst the glamour and sensuality of Regency London. Anna has won numerous awards for her stories, including RT Book Reviews Reviewers Choice, the Booksellers Best, the Golden Quill (three times), the Heart of Excellence (twice), the Write Touch, the Aspen Gold (twice), and the Australian Romance Readers' favorite historical romance (five times).

Anna loves to hear from her readers. You can find her at:

Website: www.annacampbell.com

facebook.com/AnnaCampbellFans

twitter.comAnnaCampbellOz

bookbub.com/authors/anna-campbell

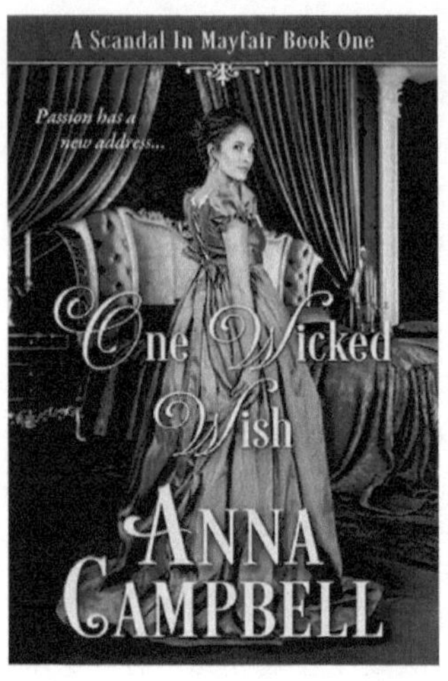

Her secret lover...

Stella Faulkner has been a despised poor relation in her odious uncle's house since she was forced to flee Italy ahead of Napoleon's invasion. In return for a roof over her head, she acts as her cousin's unpaid governess and companion. Stella knows that if she shows the slightest trace of her disgraced mother's wildness, she'll be cast out to face destitution. But after ten years of thankless servitude, Stella encounters a dashing libertine who turns her world to flame. Handsome Lord Halston is irresistible, but every kiss, every caress carries the risk of discovery, and with discovery, disaster.

The rake beguiled...

Grayson Maddox, Earl of Halston, glories in his reputation for charm, seduction, and ruthlessness. His mistresses know that the profligate lord offers them pleasure and luxury, but when he says goodbye, the affair is over. To Halston, love is a sentimental myth and fidelity a trap. One night at a glittering ball, he sees a beautiful woman trying to fade into the crowd of dowdy chaperones and every instinct clamors to make this mysterious lady his. But all bets are off when Stella Faulkner promises to become the lover he'll never forget.

Forbidden passion.

Halston and Stella start a sizzling affair under the cover of a respectable house party at his country estate. But once this interval of heady delight comes to an end, what will become of the humble governess and the wicked earl? Must they return to being strangers as they originally arranged, or will five days of intoxicating sin turn into forever?

Two Secret Sins:
A Scandal in Mayfair Book 2

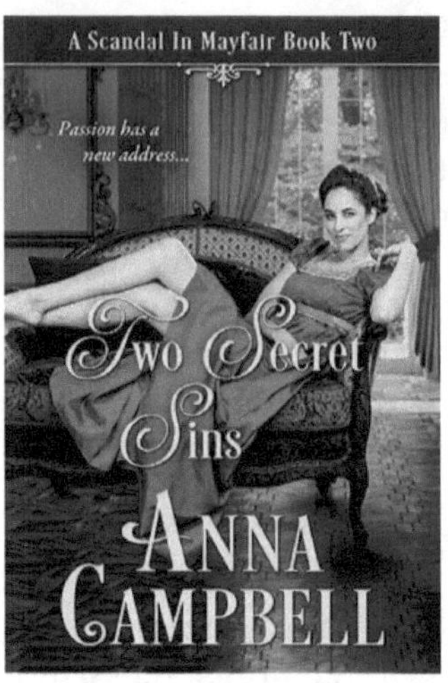

The Saint and the Sinner!

Eliot Ridley, Viscount Colville, is a man of immaculate character with lifelong ambitions to make his mark in parliament. Lady Verena Gerard is a headstrong, independent widow with a string of lovers in her scandalous past. Two people with absolutely nothing in common, apart from the irresistible desire that draws them into an explosive, secret affair.

Now Eliot is so determined to claim the reckless beauty as his own that he's ready to throw away his stainless reputation and his political hopes. What choice does Verena have when he proposes but to end the liaison? Taking a notorious woman as his wife will taint Eliot and his family, not to mention that after the brutal misery of her first marriage, she's vowed never to wed again.

Never say never.

In the glamorous, sophisticated world Eliot and Verena inhabit, wickedness thrives behind closed doors and the only unforgivable sin is falling in love. Will the handsome viscount defy society and Verena's fears to win the bride he wants? Or will Eliot and his wild lady part to follow their separate destinies and forever spurn the forbidden longing in their hearts?

Three Times Tempted:
A Scandal in Mayfair Book 3

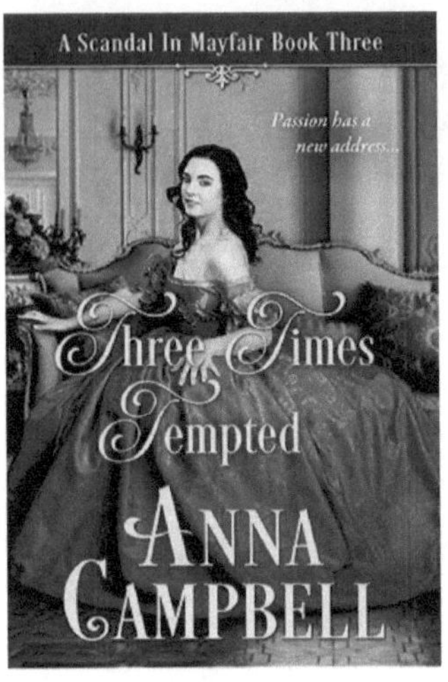

A secret rebel...

Beautiful, spirited Lady Imogen Ridley is the toast of London's glamorous season. Her blue-blooded admirers would be shocked to know that beneath her glittering veneer, she loathes society's shallow snobberies. All she wants is to return to her gardening projects in the country.

Her reckless attempt to spark a scandal that will result in a quick trip home goes awry when she meets a handsome stranger in a dark gazebo. A string of forbidden trysts follow that fateful encounter, as immediate attraction soon turns to blazing passion. But Imogen has been promised to another, and her father is powerful and ruthless. He won't tolerate any challenge to his ambitions for his daughter.

A man from a different world…

American Caleb Black finds himself at odds with
England's hidebound rules. Despite his wealth and
brilliance as a landscape designer, he's considered
little better than a servant in status-obsessed
Mayfair. So when he sets his sights on marrying the
Earl of Deerforth's lovely daughter, he knows he's
asking for trouble.

And trouble is exactly what he gets. Caleb needs to
call on all his cleverness and determination to court
his exquisite lady, let alone engineer a chance to
make her his. With every secret meeting, every
stolen caress, desire burns hotter, while danger and
disgrace loom ever closer. Will this impossible love
affair shatter the towering barriers of class and
pedigree? Or will noble lineage, family duty, and
centuries of tradition forever separate this man of
the people from his aristocratic beloved?

Four Christmas Kisses:
A Scandal in Mayfair Book 4

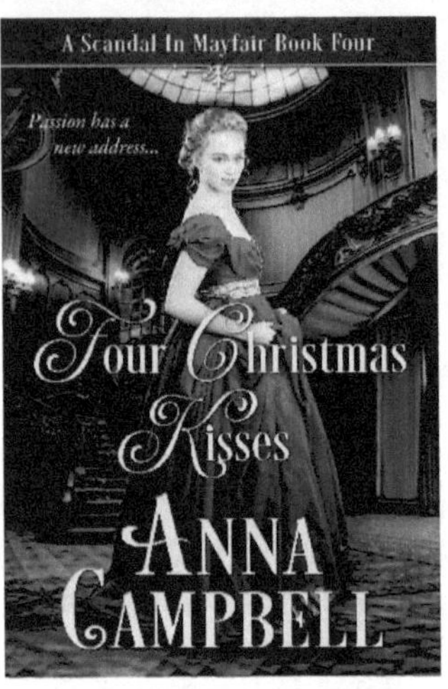

A mysterious guest at Christmas.

Spirited Anthea Bryars already has enough
problems to deal with when a few days before
Christmas, she stumbles across an unconscious
stranger in the woods. She and her half-sisters will
be homeless after New Year, now that Lord Denton
has inherited Yardley Hall and given the family
their marching orders. The last thing Anthea needs
is a handsome, smart-mouthed distraction who
makes her long for forbidden pleasures.

Secrets and passion...

After rakish Christopher Trant, Earl of Denton,
tumbles from his horse in a snowstorm, his rescuer
is the loveliest woman he's ever seen. But waking
up the next morning, he's horrified to discover that
at Yardley Hall, he's universally hated as Wicked

Cousin Christopher. He'd left London assuming the remote manor house was empty, but it turns out it's occupied by three unknown cousins and an alluring lady called Anthea. To play for time, he pretends that his injuries have stolen his memory. But one small lie leads to others, until he's so tangled in desire and deception, he doesn't know where to turn.

A season of goodwill?

Will the revelation of Christopher's identity destroy all his chances to win Anthea? Or might the magic of Christmas unite these two unlikely lovers and conjure up a bright new future for the whole family? Could four Christmas kisses mean goodbye or happy forever after?